Reciprocity

Copyright © K.I. Lynn

Cover image licensed by shutterstock.com/ ©Valua Vitaly, 123rf.com/ ©Frugo
Cover design by L.J. Anderson

Editors
Marti Lynch
Chanse Lowell
N Isabelle Blanco

Publication Date: June 9, 2014
Genre: FICTION/Romance/Erotica
ISBN-13: 978-0692235447
ISBN-10: 0692235442
Copyright © 2014 K.I. Lynn
All rights reserved

RECIPROCITY

by
K. I. Lynn

ACKNOWLEDGEMENTS

Special thanks to:

My husband, David, for putting up with me and the madness of writing.

To Massy, the voice of clarity in my chaotic mind and one who understands it all. Forever my twifey and BFF.

To Crystal, my pervy twin, for everything.

To Nyddi, for her support, friendship, and big heart.

To all the fans. Thank you for loving Nathan and Lila, and for joining them on their journey. Your support, pimping, and love for the series keeps me going. Words can never express my gratitude and love to you all.

CHAPTER 1

Lila

"Lila!" Nathan called from the closet, a frantic edge to his voice. "Have you seen my black silk tie? The one with the cream-colored stripes?"

I looked around the room and smiled when my gaze hit the headboard. Oh, I'd seen it—and felt it the night before when he'd wrapped it around my wrists. He was an animal and fucked me until I came three times.

I grabbed one end and slipped the tie from between the wooden slats, then pulled it around my neck. My body heated from the simple feel of the silk and all the reminders of what this tie meant last night. I smiled and looped one end over the other, tying it as I walked to the closet where he was rummaging around. He bumped his head into hangers, jostling the clothes and knocking a suit jacket loose. I'd never hit my head like that, but then again, he

1

was almost eight inches taller than me. The mop of brown hair on his head was still wet from his shower and was sticking out everywhere.

I stifled a laugh from seeing him so disoriented. He was a hot mess—emphasis on *hot*.

He looked so good in only his slacks, his muscles rippling as he picked things up. His blue eyes were wild in their search for the article of clothing resting around my neck. I leaned against the door with the tie resting between my bare breasts and waited.

"Is this the one you're looking for?" His head snapped in my direction, and I watched as all thought stopped. "It was still attached to the headboard."

He stood up straight and stalked toward me, licking his lips. "Miss Palmer, you're going to make me late, and I can't afford to be late to this interview."

I already knew there was no way he could leave in the state I'd created.

He reached me and pulled me close, his hands grabbing my ass and lifting me slightly from the ground. I let out a squeak and a small moan when his hard length pushed against my stomach. His lips crashed to mine, and I wrapped my arms around his neck while he picked me up, my legs tangling around his waist.

"Fuck, baby. Such a little minx, getting me all riled up. My fucking cock wants to pound that sweet pussy of yours so badly," he said with a groan, his fingers digging deeper into my ass.

"You have time," I said, pushing my hips down and rubbing against his length as I took his bottom lip between my teeth. His eyes moved around, searching for something.

Finding what he was looking for, he took a few steps forward, and I found myself sitting on the counter in the bathroom. He moved his hand between us and pulled my panties to the side. The clicking of the metal teeth of his zipper echoed off the tile walls before he pulled his cock out and slapped it against my clit.

"Such a fucking naughty girl, running around in only your panties and my tie?" A ripple ran through his body, causing me to draw in a shuddered breath of excitement. "Acting like a little slut, begging me to fuck you. That's what you are, isn't it?"

I bit my bottom lip and moved my hips, rubbing his cock against my aching pussy.

"Isn't it, Delilah?" he whispered in my ear, nipping at my neck along the way.

"Fuck, yes!"

He pushed his hips against mine. "What do you want, my little slut?"

"Fuck me! Baby, please fuck me!" I was rewarded when he lined his cock up with my pussy and slammed it all the way in, sending fire racing through my veins.

"Oh, fuck!" he hissed, then pulled out and slammed back in.

I cried out each time he entered me, the friction satisfying the need I always had for him. He was the euphoria-inducing injection I needed daily—better than any of my medications. I needed him every morning to chase away the monsters in my dreams, and I wasn't going to let him shirk it off because of an interview.

What kind of asshole scheduled one so early, anyway?

3

All thought left me, white blanketing my mind and making it fuzzy as he pulled my hips to him and thrust in hard and deep. He set up a furious pace, wiping everything from me and replacing it with nothing but him—his love, his need, his desires.

I pulled him close, loving the feeling of his skin against mine. His teeth nipped at my lip, then moved down my jaw. I clenched around him when his teeth scraped down the length of my neck and bit down.

"Baby…baby, oh fuck! Feels so fucking good when you clamp down on me like that."

My muscles coiled tight, tensing, making me arch against his body. I couldn't breathe—everything in my body stopped as I teetered on the edge of shattering in his arms.

"That's it—come for me," he groaned in my ear. "Come all over my cock. I fucking love watching you come."

His dirty words were enough, and I let go, screaming his name as he continued to pound into me. I shook, my body convulsing as wave after wave moved through me.

As I was coming down from my high, his grip tightened and he tensed. Unintelligible moans and groans slipped past his lips as he spilled inside me.

He slumped against me, placing light kisses on my neck. "You're a bad influence."

"*Me?*" My voice went up in pitch.

"Yes, you." He nipped at my neck. "Way too sexy, fucking insatiable, and you walk around with nothing but your fucking panties on. That's the international symbol for 'bend me over and fuck me.'"

I kissed his cheek. "Will you?"

One brow hitched up. "Will I what?"

"Bend me over and fuck me if I wear no panties?" I whispered in his ear. His cock twitched inside me, making me smile.

He would.

"Ung! Woman, you drive me crazy." He pulled away, kissing me hard on the lips before letting go.

He helped me clean up and pulled me down from the counter before resuming the task I'd interrupted. I stretched out on the bed, sleepy from our morning fun, but was startled when Nathan's hand slapped across my ass, making me look up with wide eyes.

"No sleeping. You have to get ready for work," he said, chastising me while he buttoned up his shirt and pulled the tie from around my neck.

I groaned and snuggled back into my pillow. "Five more minutes."

"Baby, it's seven already."

"Shit!" I jumped out of my comfortable position on the bed and ran into the closet, pulling a skirt and dress shirt down from the rack. My fingers fumbled with the buttons as I tried to dress at top speed, all the while Nathan chuckled at me from the bedroom.

I looked through the doorway and scowled at him. "Meanie."

"*Me*? Who was it seducing me not half an hour ago? My interview is before you start today." Nathan shook his head as he tied his shoes.

5

It'd been just over a month since Nathan left Holloway and Holloway, and he was heading out for his fourth interview. I gazed down at my left hand and the large diamond that adorned my ring finger. It had also been that long since Nathan and I had been engaged.

Engaged.

The word still seemed foreign to me. Engaged. Betrothed. Fiancé.

Nathan was my fiancé. Nathan and I were getting married. I was marrying Nathan Thorne.

I was loved and getting married.

I staggered a bit at that realization, as I always did. Never did I think I would get married, because I never thought I was good enough, or that anyone would want me. That was how my family had conditioned me, after all.

Yet, I was the one engaged to the office god. Though that didn't mean I wasn't still getting shit from the Boob Squad.

Nathan's public proposal had really thrown them for a loop. Jennifer, the one who outed us, thought she could get her claws in him. In her mind, we were just a fling, and I was some chick he was screwing with.

Oh, how I loved the look on her face when she found out we'd been living together, and even more so when he got down on one knee in front of everyone.

Still, they were on me, telling me that it wasn't going to last or informing me of the divorce rates. They even went so far as to say they'd seen him when they were out to lunch with another woman and that he was doomed to cheat on me. I had to laugh at that one, because the woman was Erin, his cousin.

Life without Nathan in the office took some getting used to. The day after Nathan left, Owen moved to Nathan's desk and became my new partner. It was nice not to have the Boob Squad interrupting the day except when they really needed help. Owen was a cutie and really sweet, but he was of no interest to them—it was a shame they couldn't see it, because he really was a catch. Lucky for Amy, his girlfriend, the bitches were blind.

I ached for Nathan as I watched the hours tick by until I was able to leave and return home to him.

"Quit daydreaming, future Mrs. Thorne. It's fifteen after," he called, pulling me from my thoughts.

"Shit!" I rushed to the back of the closet and pulled out some heels, slipped them on, then raced into the bathroom for a little bit of makeup. "Will I be seeing some random dirty texts from you today?"

"You miss my ass, don't you? Admit it."

I sighed and rolled my eyes. "Yes, Nathan—just like I told you yesterday and the day before that." I used a higher-pitched girlie voice as I continued on, my hand resting on my chest as I over-acted. "I ache for you all day long. I watch the hours tick by until I can return home to you. My life just isn't the same without you ramming me against the office wall and threatening me with your manhood when our office peers have their backs turned. " I fluttered my lashes at him for a second and smirked.

He laughed out loud, kissing my forehead. "Smart ass." He slapped my ass.

He knew I missed him like crazy. He just liked to rub it in and get me to tell him over and over how much I needed and wanted him all the time. Bastard.

7

I loved it, too. It was one of my favorite games we played.

"You know you can't get enough of my cock. That's why I send you those dirty texts. When you get home, you're so wet, and it's all for me. All I have to do is shove your panties to the side and I'm in."

"Charming, as always." I rolled my eyes, but he caught me biting my lip and smirked. "But you're all talk." I waved my hand at him. "You send some sweet ones, too. So, it turns out there's a heart attached to that dick somewhere."

"Fuck, yeah, I do. Those make you even wetter than the dirty ones. I'm no fool—chicks love a guy who's sentimental." He laughed and wrapped his arms around my waist, placing a kiss on my neck. "And you eat it up when I tell you how beautiful you are and how much I love you."

I nodded as I finished brushing my hair and tossing it up into a bun. "Yeah, yeah. You're the man."

He caressed my ass. "Hopefully I'll get this job so I can quit spending the majority of my days searching for openings that are nowhere close to where you are. That shit just pisses me off. The idea of you so far away…"

"At least you're able to make good use of old contacts from when you were a prosecutor." I angled my head around and kissed the tip of his nose.

He smiled. "True, but how many fucking interviews does one man have to go to before someone gets a clue and hires me?"

"Things are looking good. You'll find the perfect position soon. I'm sure of it."

He nuzzled my hair and kissed the top of my head. "I have to go."

I turned in his arms and wrapped mine around his neck. "Good luck. I know you'll do great."

"Yes, I have a feeling it's going to be a good day." He chuckled and leaned down to kiss me.

"I love you," I said as we pulled away.

"I love you, too." He gave me a smile and another quick kiss before heading out the door.

I spent the next ten minutes frantically getting ready before I also headed out the door, into the cold Indiana January, and to the office.

When I pulled into the parking lot, I held my breath as my stomach clenched and my heart dropped over seeing his usual spot empty. He wasn't going to be here today. He wasn't going to be here any more days at all. I wouldn't have him here, watching over me, brightening my day with his gorgeous smile and his intense blue gaze.

I made my way up to my empty office and sat at my desk, sighing and counting down the minutes until I saw Nathan again. God, I really was pathetic, and hopelessly in love with him. No matter how much I joked about missing him during my days, it was all true. Every bit of it. Nothing was the same without him.

Time was moving backward, or maybe just inching by, to torture me.

CHAPTER 2

It was mid morning when an event popped up in my email. I opened it up to find an all-hands meeting scheduled in thirty minutes. My gaze moved over the piles and piles of work we had, and I sighed. I'd been doing that a lot lately—sighing my way through the day. It was never a good time for a meeting, and it was the usual meet and greet of some new employee to the firm.

Begrudgingly, Owen and I moved toward the conference room where everyone was milling around, waiting for the meeting to start. After a few minutes, Jack Holloway—boss and ruler almighty—walked in the back door to the room and asked for everyone to settle down.

"Good morning, everyone! I know it's a busy day, but what day isn't? I'll try to make this short," he began.

I felt a buzzing in my pocket and discreetly pulled my phone out, looking down at the message from Nathan.

Things went well. Tell you all about it soon. We can celebrate tonight. Oh, yeah, and you're beautiful as

fuck. Can't stop thinking about my cock wrapped in your pussy.

I smiled and slipped my phone back into my pocket, focusing my attention back on Jack.

"Today we have a new employee I'd like to introduce. He's getting back into the courtroom for the first time in a few years and may need all of our help getting reacquainted with the process. He'll be taking over for Frank Kettle, who retired last year."

I leaned against the wall in preparation from the bound-to-be-longwinded greeting from whatever pompous ass Jack hired. Frank Kettle was the biggest one I'd ever met, and he needed to be for the position, but he didn't have to extend that to his coworkers. I hoped this new guy wasn't the same, but chances were that he was.

"Without further ado," Jack said as the back door opened, "I'd like to introduce you all to…"

"Nathan?" Owen whispered next to me.

My head snapped up and, sure enough, in he walked, wearing his black and cream-stripped tie, his eyes the brightest shade of blue.

He was too delicious for words, though my mouth was dry due to shock and hanging open as I gaped at him.

"… Nathan Thorne," Jack finished with a smile, and the whole room exploded with chatter.

I, on the other hand, was staring at Nathan in surprise. His gaze found mine, a sheepish grin forming as he shrugged his shoulders.

"Surprise," he said. I barely heard it over all of the commotion.

Out of the corner of my eye, I spied the Boob Squad's illustrious members performing a synchronized fluff, puff, and tuff for his benefit. Their actions garnered a few strange looks from their peers who were not a part of their elite club.

I was lucky bile wasn't crawling up the back of my throat—they were so nauseating.

Jack continued the meeting, and fifteen or so minutes later, the room began to clear out. I stayed behind to talk to Nathan, and of course that earned some piercing glares from the Boob Squad.

Once the room was emptied of most people, Nathan approached me, and I swatted at his arm as I scowled up at him.

He held his hands up in front of him. "Don't be mad."

My eyes narrowed at him, and my arms crossed over my chest. "Why did you keep this from me? Why didn't you tell me?"

"I wanted to surprise you," he admitted, his hand reaching forward and brushing through my hair. "It was tough, too. I've missed you so much during the day, Honeybear. I hoped that you missed me just as much and would be excited about it."

"I am, but I'm also pissed that you kept it from me. How long have you known?" I asked, then immediately wished I hadn't when his eyes grew wide. "Nathan?"

"Jack and I were working on this for a few months before I quit."

I slumped back against the wall. "I don't…I don't like being in the dark like that. We're in this together."

He pouted, looking all sad and trying to get into my good graces again. "I know. I'm sorry. I just... I wanted to make you really happy to see me, I guess. And it wasn't solidified until last week, anyway."

I snorted at his comment. "I'm always really happy to see you. I just wish I'd been given some warning. We don't keep things from each other."

"I know. I won't do it again. Are you happy to see me?" he asked, his body almost flush with mine.

"I am so happy to see you." I reached up and wrapped my arms around him, pulling him tight. "I'm so happy you're back. I'm so happy I'll get to see you every day at work. God—you have no idea..."

He smiled against my neck, then placed a light kiss there. "Me too."

"You're just happy for the chance to have sex in the office again."

He smirked. "That's part of it." His hands squeezed my hips and pulled me tighter to him. "I've really missed that, but I've also missed seeing you all day."

I let out a sigh. "You know you're not in the clear yet, right?"

"I'll make it up to you."

I pursed my lips. "I'm not sure I believe you."

He leaned in closer, his lips ghosting across mine. "I'll make sure you do tonight."

His lips met mine with a soft kiss that quickly grew in intensity. I moaned into his mouth, his tongue lapping at mine as his body pushed me into the wall.

We were both panting when he broke away.

"Better be careful before I bend you over that table. It's my first day—I want to make a good impression."

"Well, that would make a good impression with me, if that counts for anything," I said under my breath, giggling a little at myself and my uncontrollable urges when he was around.

He snorted. Yeah, he heard me. "Minx."

I rolled my eyes and slipped my hand into his as we walked toward the door. "Like that would stop you anyway. Never has before."

"It might. You never know. I could grow some self-control."

I snorted at that. "Yeah, right. You're only good at growing one thing, and it doesn't take long before you're showing it to me and shoving it in my mouth."

He smirked. "I have priorities, baby."

We walked down the hall, earning stares as we passed. They were used to seeing us together, just not holding hands and smiling at each other.

"What do you think?" he asked when we stopped at what used to be Frank's office.

"I think it's too far away."

His hand slipped around my waist. "Me too, but at least we're on the same floor."

I let out a sigh, then pressed my lips to his. "I have to get back to work, you infuriatingly tempting man."

"I know. My baby's such a hard worker." He grinned, then grimaced and held on to my hand as I walked away, my fingers slipping from his grip as I separated us.

The day was going pretty well, and I smiled as I walked, happy to have my Nathan so close by. I felt lighter

14

with him near. If he couldn't be in the same office as me anymore, at least he was just down the hall.

———————— ⸺•••◉◐◉•••⸺ ————————

Later that night, I moved about the kitchen, dinner in the works, and jumped when the door slammed, startling me. Nathan walked into the kitchen, a bottle of wine in his hand.

"Hello, beautiful," he said with a smile. He gave me a quick kiss, then moved to set the bottle on the counter as he shrugged out of his suit jacket.

My gaze followed him. "That took a while."

"We needed the perfect wine to celebrate."

"I thought we were celebrating with a couple of orgasms."

He grinned. "Oh, we'll be doing that later, once we have fuel in our systems. It's going to be an all-nighter, I think."

"Think you can keep it up that long?"

His hand slapped down against my ass, making me jump. "Are you challenging me? Because I'd rethink that, if I were you. Don't make me break out the handcuffs and rope."

My eyes widened and I smiled. "Ooh, what do I have to do to make that happen?"

"Fuck, stop talking." His hand slapped my ass again, then grabbed my hair, pulling my head back. "Does my little slut need punishing?"

I hissed as his grip tightened. "Yes."

He froze behind me. "Why? What did you do?"

15

The change in his demeanor had me shuddering in anticipation. Fear of his reaction kept my lips sealed tight, while my body was begging for him to know.

His hand slipped under my skirt and between my thighs. "Tell me."

My heart was hammering in my chest as I drew it out longer. Nathan unleashed was the best, and I'd learned tricks. The more I denied him something, the more the dominant side of his personality took control.

So, I baited him.

"I played with myself."

His grip tightened, and he growled in my ear. "When?"

It only took two seconds of silence for his hands to become heavier on my flesh. His cock was digging into my back, rocking against me in small thrusts of his hips. The hand that was so close to my pussy left and slapped my ass before returning.

"When did you touch what's mine?"

I couldn't see his face, but by the low, gravelly tone of his voice, I imagined he was snarling at me. He would snap any moment, and a fire burst through me at the thought.

"Today. In the bathroom at the office."

He spun me around to face him, and I gasped at the anger on his face. A shiver ran through me when his hand gripped my chin.

"Did I just hear you correctly?" One side of his lip twitched up, and his eyes turned to slits. "You touched my pussy when I was only feet away?"

My gaze flickered from his lips to his eyes. I needed him to take me. He was so close. After all, he did say he'd make it up to me, and there was no better way than unleashing the beast.

"And I didn't wear panties for the rest of the day because they were soaked."

He pulled my jaw closer and crashed his lips to mine.

He could barely breathe as his fury mingled with his cravings for me and for what was his.

It fueled me on as well.

I clawed at him as his teeth scraped down my neck before sinking against my skin, tingling and sending jolts through my body. His hands grabbed at me, pulling my skirt up as he picked me up and walked into the living room.

He set me down and began to unbutton his shirt. "Undress. Now. And I expect you to be sopping for me."

That wasn't going to be difficult—I already was. Now I just needed to get rid of my clothes as fast as possible. I bit my lip as I grabbed the hem of my sweater and pulled it over my head. When I popped free, Nathan was already down to his boxer briefs.

He snarled up at me and stepped forward, reaching out and yanking my bra off the same way I had my sweater. "Too fucking slow, Delilah." He pinched and pulled at my nipples, making me cry out. I was having a hard time remembering which side the zipper to my skirt was on. When I found it, I tried to get it down, but it was stuck on something.

"I'm going to fucking rip it off if you don't get it now."

Fuck. If I didn't like the skirt so much, I'd let him.

I gave the zipper another try, and it finally came free. The skirt slipped from my hips to the ground and I stepped out. He stood in front of me, completely naked and very hard.

His blue eyes were stormy as he stepped forward, grabbing onto my hair and bending my head back, then smashed his lips to mine. I moaned, lips parting as his tongue touched mine like he was trying to devour me. I gripped onto his shoulder and arched into him.

We were both out of breath when we parted, but his eyes were still dark and heavy.

My hand was wrapped around his shaft, lightly moving up and down before I squeezed with more pressure. I licked my lips and looked from his menacing, lust-filled eyes to the bead at the tip of his hard cock. A whimper crawled out of me—I was dying to be fucked by him and the monster in my hand.

His jaw clenched while his head dropped back. The cords in his neck stood out, and so did his Adam's apple.

"Jesus, my slut likes to tease me twenty-four-seven. It's no wonder I have to send her dirty texts—to remind her what she does to me, and what she's going to get in return."

I chuckled. "It's a tiring job, but someone's gotta do it, and I can't allow anyone else to since they won't do it right." I grabbed his hand and placed it between my thighs.

"Goddamn…you're soaking wet. Such a fucking good girl. Makes me proud." He growled low in his throat, his jaw clicking closed and clenching again.

I shuddered when his middle finger slid over my clit and dipped inside my pussy.

"Fuck."

Two of his fingers began pumping into me. "Oh, I will, but first I need to teach you a lesson before I fuck you into the floor, listening to you begging me to stop."

The intensity of his mood directly transferred to me through his hand rocking into me and against my clit. His teeth dug in, biting his way down my neck with a harsh edge. I cried out when he bit down and pulled at my nipple. It was all so much, driving me with force to the edge. I was shaking, muscles tensing, but it wasn't enough.

"Please." I needed his cock in me, not his fingers—his body on top of mine, weighing me down, doing just as he described.

Wrapping his other arm around me, he lifted me off the ground, hand still fucking my pussy, and guided us over to the kitchen table. The back of my thighs dug into the edge.

"You're going to fucking come all over my fingers, and then I might think about giving you my cock."

A tearless sob shook me and his hand moved faster as his hips rocked his cock against my thigh. The heat and friction was driving me crazy with want. His fingers curled inside, and my eyes flew open, back arching against him again and again until I snapped, screaming out.

His fingers left me, and he lined up and slammed his cock in my pussy before the first waves were done. My orgasm hiccuped, or at least that was what it felt like when he filled me. I wasn't even through my first when his cock forced me to my second.

I could barely breathe, and my body was shaking. That was two almost right in a row.

He kept pushing me for more, thrusting harder and faster. My pussy was twitching, still coming down from the last high. His hips angled up, hitting my sweet spot while his fingers pinched my clit. Three was the most I'd ever come in one session. I was done, but it seemed he was determined to force one more out of me.

My nails dug into his forearm as my body tensed, coiled so tight I thought I would burst. It felt like I was about to pee, and I was desperate to keep it in but too tired to care. Something exploded from me, and it was more than just my orgasm. I screamed out, crying as wave after wave coursed through me.

I couldn't hear, couldn't speak; I could only feel the light, boneless weightlessness. My mind was clear, my body tired, and I collapsed, unable to hold myself up any longer.

"Holy... Damn... Shit." Nathan's curses were followed by him tensing as well, his body jerking as he spilled inside me.

Once he was done, he fell down on me, both of us breathing heavily. Neither of us moved, both spent.

"What the fuck was that?" I asked once I could breathe again.

Nathan sat back and looked down at where we were joined and now thoroughly soaked.

"I think you just squirted." He beamed at me, proud of himself. "Damn, I'm good."

"If my arms had any strength in them, I'd swat at you." I chuckled with a tired, drained sound. I *was* drained. My entire body empty of all energy to move.

"If my legs had any strength, I'd be back inside you right now, making you do that again." He chuckled and sighed, sounding more than high. He sounded like he'd died and gone to a sinner's heaven.

It couldn't be more true—Nathan was the war God of sex.

CHAPTER 3

It took a while to recoup from our activities and to resume cooking dinner. A nap followed by a shower killed a few hours. The sun had set long ago, and there wasn't much left of the day.

My leg muscles quivered as I stood at the counter. They were weak from all the things Nathan did to me, and threatened to give out. As I pulled the pasta out of the pantry, I looked at the trash can. I had to throw everything out, and even considered pitching the burned pot. Nathan boasted about his ability to clean it, and I was giving him the opportunity to prove it before throwing it away.

He also promised to clean up the…mess by the kitchen table.

The cracking noise of the pasta breaking as I put it in the pot covered up all other sound, so I didn't hear Nathan as he stepped up behind me and wrapped his arms around my waist.

"Trying again? I thought we'd just order in."

I shrugged. "Pasta is quick and easy, and I'm hungry."

His lips pressed against my neck. "Me too. I worked up an appetite."

He let go and backed away, heading over to the now warm bottle of wine and placing it in the fridge.

I grabbed a slotted spoon from the drawer and stirred, breaking up the pasta so it didn't clump. "Guess that will have to wait until tomorrow."

"It's not going to go bad." He pulled out the butter and pasta sauce and placed them on the counter. "So, now that I have income again, let's talk about the wedding." I stopped stirring the pasta and turned to look at him. He arched his brow at me. "What?"

"I… Well, what kind of wedding do you want?"

He shook his head. "This is your thing. Plus, I've already done it. Isn't it what women dream about and begin planning in the womb?"

I pursed my lips. He'd already had a big wedding when he married Grace, but did he want another one? "Maybe normal women, but I'm not exactly normal."

"You are normal, but the way you grew up makes you unique." His eyes softened the way they always did when I talked about my upbringing.

Hopefully that would change soon, and my abusive past would fade away. Adam's trial date was set, and we were all ready to give our depositions in a few weeks.

"Oh, you're a smooth talker tonight."

He chuckled and ran his hand up and down my arms. "Honeybear, I just want to marry you. I don't care how it happens. I'm sure you've thought at some point about getting married."

I shook my head and returned to cooking. "I was pretty sure it wasn't in the cards for me, so why waste my time dreaming about something that was never going to happen? There was no Prince Charming in my fantasies."

"Well, there's one in your life now."

I quirked my brow at him. "You, charming?"

"I am very charming." His lip twitched as a smile grew on his face. "In fact, I bet I can charm you right out of your clothes."

"Hasn't happened yet," I said and stirred the pot.

His eyes went wide, and he stepped back. "Ouch! You're feisty tonight."

I sighed and looked up at him. "Can we just go to the courthouse?"

His lips formed a straight line and his brow crinkled, the light in his eyes dimming. "Is that really what you want?"

There was a pain in my chest from the expression on his face. "What else would I want besides you?"

He shrugged. "Flowers, friends and family—a beautiful dress?"

My mind whirled with that information. Was that what I wanted? Or was the quick and simple trip down the street the way to do it?

The more I thought about it, he was right—at one point in my life, I did think about a wedding. Long ago, back when I believed in Disney fairy tales, before the monsters of Grimm-like creations took away my childhood innocence, replacing it with fear-induced obedience and solitude. The days when my mom was still alive.

I sniffed and brushed a tear from my eye. "Maybe we could do something small."

He smiled and leaned forward, kissing my forehead. "Small sounds perfect. With small, we could even do a destination wedding."

I blinked at him, and images of blue skies and turquoise waters filled my mind. Our Florida vacation had been the best time I'd ever had.

I stepped toward him without even thinking about it. "The beach?"

He smiled down at me and brushed his fingers against my cheek. "I love that idea."

I grinned and wrapped my arms around him.

"Any beach in particular?"

I stared at him and whimpered. "You're overloading my brain with girly things."

He laughed out loud and kissed me. "Do I need to get my mother and Teresa to help?"

I nodded furiously. "Otherwise I might have a panic attack even thinking about all the stuff I don't know that has to be done."

"First things first—where?"

Reaching up into the cabinets, I pulled down two plates. There was only one beach I'd ever been to. Was one beach better than another?

"All I've got is beach." I gave a half-hearted smile.

"Okay, we've got time. We'll look this weekend. How's that?"

"Sounds perfect."

He smirked at me. "By the way...where are your panties?"

"The ones from today?" He nodded. I bit my lip. "They're in your pillowcase."

"Fucking hell, baby." He licked his lips. "Are you trying to make sure I fuck you while you're sleeping tonight?"

"Maybe." I shrugged.

"Next time, bring your wet pussy to me. You know I'm always up for taking care of you and your needs."

"Oh, I know. I just wanted to see your reaction." I winked at him and returned to finishing up dinner.

⋙•••◗◖•••⋘

Owen slammed his hand on his desk, startling me. "Do you know what time it is?"

I glanced at the clock. "Five." My lip curled up as I also noticed that I was only halfway through the file I was working on. It was going to be another late night.

"You know what five means, right?"

I quirked a brow at him. "Isn't that the time normal people get to leave work?"

"Yes!" He pulled his suit jacket off and threw it over his desk and onto the floor. "You know what I'm doing today?"

A small laugh slipped through my lips. "Pretending you have a normal job with a steady schedule?"

He frowned and threw his hands in the air. "Lila, it's Friday! I want to take Amy out on a date. Maybe have a nice long roll in the hay." He slammed his file shut...or

26

slammed it as well as file folders did. "I like you, but I spend more time with you than I do with anyone else. Let's run away and spend more time with those we love."

"That's a nice dream." I stretched my shoulders and neck for a moment, feeling stiffer with each second we imagined leaving the place we'd been stuck in all day long. I settled back into my seat and tried to get as comfortable as possible.

"It doesn't have to be a dream. All you have to do is hit the save button, bookmark your place in the file, sign out of your computer, and walk out the door. Simple."

"I don't know—that sounds like anarchy in the making." I glanced at the clock on my computer.

A couple of keystrokes later, Owen's monitor went black.

"Fine, stay here. I tried to save you. Always remember that."

I waved my hand at him as he walked around his desk and picked up his jacket off the floor. "Have a good weekend."

He saluted, then disappeared down the hall. I shook my head, chuckling at his antics, then returned my focus to the file in front of me in hopes that I would also be able to leave. I fully expected to see Nathan pop in my office any minute, and wanted to get as much done as possible before that happened.

I finished another page before my phone whistled at me, signaling a text message. I picked up my phone and opened up the mailbox.

Congratulations on your engagement.

27

My brow scrunched as I looked at the number. It wasn't someone from my contacts, and it wasn't from an area code I was familiar with.

I set the phone down, my bottom lip trapped between my teeth. Part of me wanted to text back to find out who it was. The other part of me was washed with dread, knowing who it might be.

———————•••••●•••••———————

Nathan and I spent the weekend surfing the Internet, looking for resorts and beaches to hold our nuptials and reception. We decided on the island of Aruba. From the pictures, it looked like the oasis I'd formed in my mind. Being such a tourist destination, there were lots of beautiful places to contact. Most were booked up.

"Divi Aruba Pheonix emailed." I stared at the screen, rereading the beginning of the message on my laptop to make sure it wasn't just an automatic notification or something.

Nathan scooted up behind me, his chin resting on my shoulder. "Yeah? What did they say?"

My eyes scanned over the lines of print. "They're booked until September, and they sent us more information."

His frown reflected in the screen. "That's so long."

I arched my neck back and quirked a brow at him. "In a hurry, Mr. Thorne?"

He nodded. "Yes. You're mine, and I want you to be mine in every way right fucking now. Problem with that?"

Warmth blossomed in my chest, spreading throughout my body. "No. I like it."

"Makes you feel special, doesn't it?" he asked, leaning in. I nodded. "Good, because you *are* special. You're my everything."

"There you go being all sweet and mushy again." I pressed my lips against his neck.

"You love it, because you know when I'm done, I'm going to show your body who you belong to. I'll bring out my dirty slut that begs to please me with her body. And if she's a good girl, I'll make her come over and over, giving her the pleasure she gives me."

I squirmed against him, his words affecting me as always. His hand slipped around my waist to between my thighs, the heel of his hand digging in and rubbing against my clit.

My cheeks warmed, and I fought back a moan. "You're distracting me. I'm trying to read."

His teeth scraped against my neck. "Read later. I'm going to fuck you now." His other hand pulled down my tank top and pinched my nipple, sending tingles through me.

"Insatiable much?" I asked, smiling as I teased him, trying to resist as long as possible. It always made him more aggressive when I put him off.

His hand was rough, grabbing at my pussy. "I haven't had you today."

"And you're aggravated at having to wait so long."

"Yes."

"But if you let me read, I'd be able to tell you they have a last minute cancellation, creating an opening in three weeks."

All movement stopped as he froze, reading the screen over my shoulder. "That's just after Valentine's. Fuck. Tell her we'll take it!"

"But that's so soon."

"We're fucking taking it." His voice was firm.

"Are you sure?"

"Are you getting cold feet or something?" He arched an eyebrow at me and pursed his lips.

I shook my head. "No, it's just…"

"What?"

I rubbed my knuckle against my lower lip. "Freaks me out."

He slumped against me, groaning. "Why does it freak you out, baby?"

I was silent, unsure how to say what I felt—how my chest bubbled, my hands tingled, and the urge to run away from the conversation grew. "I'm still getting used to the idea that we're engaged."

His mouth rested against my shoulder. "Do you love me?"

"Yes." What kind of question was that?

"Do you want to be with me forever?" He angled his head a little so he had a better view of my entire facial expression.

"Yes." I blinked and swallowed, though I wasn't nervous. I just… Well, I didn't know what.

"Do you ever want to be apart from me?"

My head shook once more. "Never."

He smiled at me. "Neither do I. So what does it matter when we do it? The sooner we get married, the sooner we can move on with our lives."

Somehow, his words calmed me. "You have a point."

He nodded and stared at me with a serious look in his gaze. "And I have a pointer I'd like to poke you with, so fucking tell her we'll take it so we can celebrate with my cock shoved up your cunt."

"Ass." My lip quirked up, and I turned back to the computer.

"Not right now. I need to get off, and it's going to be in your pussy first. Maybe I can hit your ass up later."

He was pissy, which meant a quickie. Not that I had any problem with that—the man knew how to get me off in a short period of time.

As soon as I was done and my laptop was on the coffee table, he was leaning over and lowering me down to the floor. His lips found mine, almost bruising with the force of his kiss. One hand was pushing my pants down while the other pinned my arm beside my head. I was already wet from his groping, and even more so when he restricted me, even in the slightest ways.

My free hand reached between us, sliding against his abs until I reached his waistband. I pulled the front down just enough for his cock to join the party. It was more than enough room, because he swatted my hand away and pushed himself into me.

We both groaned as he entered, my hips angling up to get him deeper.

31

"Damn! It's fucking Sunday. I should have wrecked this pussy this morning, but you wanted to go out for breakfast."

I bit my lip.

"You planned for this, didn't you? You wanted me to attack you like a fucking animal." He pulled back, then slammed his cock back inside, making the breath leave my lungs and my back arch. "Throw you down like a slut and pound you until you can't walk. Bruise your skin with my hands and teeth." Another hard thrust of his hips, accentuated almost every other word. "That's what you want, isn't it?"

"Yes."

"Then take it. Take *me*." He sped up, driving his cock into me at an unrelenting pace.

Talk was replaced with grunts and groans—chants to deities above. Each stroke was delicious torture, pushing me, dragging me.

My eyes and mouth were open as I screamed out, clamping down on him, milking the come from him with each pulse.

"Fuck!" He grabbed hold of my chin as I came down so we were face to face. The man before me was menacing and powerful, and I bowed to him. "Look me in the eyes when I fill you with my seed."

I shuddered, the sexy words making me clench around him. I loved watching his come-face—the way he screamed out, face scrunched up, the tendons in his neck taut. It was followed by euphoria taking over, filling his eyes, and a lazy smile as the last drops seeped from him.

He collapsed down, trying to catch his breath. "I need a nap now."

"Ditto."

My limbs seemed boneless, unwilling to respond to my commands.

Job well done.

———— ••••◍•••• ————

I let out a yawn as the elevator doors opened, blinking back the drowsiness fighting to send me back to dreamland. Fingers tangled with mine and tugged, forcing my feet forward.

"Come on, sleepyhead. I'll walk you to your office," Nathan said, smirking at me.

We rounded the corner and headed down the hall. I wasn't paying much attention. I only knew someone was headed toward us, so I leaned into Nathan, making space. Despite my efforts, my shoulder grazed someone.

"Excuse you," Tiffany said, sneering at me.

"Sorry," I said. When I realized who it was, I knew she had run into me, not the other way around. I stopped and turned toward her, my body jerking as Nathan was still pulling my arm. "I didn't realize you were blind. I mean, we moved over for you, but you still felt the need to run into me."

She threw me her bitch brow. "What are you talking about, crazy town?"

My eye twitched at the name she called me. I was getting so close to laying one of the bitches out, and I wasn't a violent person. How much more was I expected to stand?

"Why did you run into me? Is the need to feel superior to me, to bully me, that great? What do you get out of it?"

She gaped at me like a flustered fish. "You... I..."

"What? You do know your actions are hostile, and I can file a complaint against you, right? I mean, you would know this if you read the handbook." She stared at me, unresponsive. "Oh, or was I wrong in thinking you could understand the legal language or read at all?"

Tiffany sputtered but failed to produce any words, her face growing red. I rolled my eyes and faced forward.

"Forget her," Nathan said as we continued on our way.

I leaned against him, a new pep in my step. "Already have. She's just a jealous bitch anyway."

"Has their shit gotten better or worse since I came back?"

I shrugged. "It's a toss-up. The good thing is they don't interrupt my work anymore." I looked up at him. "Do they come to your office?"

He shook his head. "No. I can't help them with anything, and we're not in the same department. They tried the first few days, but I shot that shit down immediately. No more bugging the crap out of me and trying to seduce me."

"Only I get to do that." I stood a little taller.

He smiled down at me and pulled me close. "I love it when you seduce me." His lips pressed against my

34

forehead. "Too bad we have an appointment tonight. I'd let you do it right after work."

I'd forgotten about Dr. Morgenson. Due to the holidays, we hadn't seen him much over the past few weeks.

"What do you think Darren will say? Do you think he'll approve of the fast timeline?"

"He's the one who encouraged us to go forward with our relationship. I'm sure as hell not asking our therapist when I can marry you."

I patted his chest. "He's not going to tell you what to do. He never does. It's his job to tap his pen, look concerned, and sigh a lot. You know… like a parent would do to his son when he knows he's whoring around with some little slut."

"My little slut." He pulled me in tighter.

"Tell that to him and then throw in a 'By the way—I've nailed her repeatedly, so now it's time to marry the little slut.' See how he reacts to that."

I giggled, and he pinched my ass. "You and that dirty mouth."

I smiled and pushed off his chest, then sauntered away.

Seduction was for wimpy Boob Squad members. I knew what he wanted.

He wanted to tussle—to pull, yank, grab, and demand I be his.

Even though I already was.

CHAPTER 4

——••••◦●◦••••——

"You two look like the cat that ate the canary. What's going on?" Dr. Morgenson asked, looking between us.

"We're getting married in two weeks." Nathan smiled, but his eyes hardened as he stared at the good doctor, almost as if warning him.

Darren blinked, his gaze shifting between us, studying. Then a chuckle slipped from the smile forming on his face. He shook his head and continued to laugh.

"What?" Nathan asked. It was obvious he was as confused at Dr. Morgenson's reaction as I was.

"I'm beginning to wonder if you even need me anymore. The rate at which you're improving is astonishing and has very little to do with me," he said as he lifted his glasses and wiped away the tears in his eyes.

I leaned forward and shook my head. "But we owe you so much."

His eyebrows shot up and he chuckled. "I mediate at best. I get you to open up to each other and communicate. But it's been months since you've needed me in that capacity. I am in no way saying you're both fine, but I believe you're no longer in need of couples therapy."

"Why? You were so insistent we needed it, and now?" Nathan's brow furrowed.

Dr. Morgenson turned to Nathan and leaned toward him a little. "Seven months ago, you two had just gone through the equivalent of an atom bomb in your relationship. I was there, helping you pick up the pieces and put everything back together. Four months ago, I had a strong feeling that you were finally headed in the right direction after some very hard months and encouraged you to move forward. You were strong and united together. Lila has blossomed and stands up for herself and her wants, whereas you've relinquished a lot of fear of the Marconi and guilt over Grace."

"The Marconi will always be watching and waiting."

"But you're better prepared this time. They will always be there, so why would you let them hold you back from being happy?"

"So, you don't think we're moving too fast?" Nathan took my hand and squeezed it.

"No, not at all. Especially for you two." He leaned forward a little more and smiled. "I do, however, expect an invitation to the blessed event."

"Wouldn't be a party without you," Nathan said, smiling, but it wasn't at Dr. Morgenson—it was at his friend, Darren.

⋙•◗◗●◖◖•⋘

I chewed at my nail—a bad habit I seemed to be picking up. Granted, said nail had broken earlier in the day, so I was really just trimming it with my teeth.

My stomach was in knots because of the anticipation—the next morning, I'd be giving my deposition.

My eyes scanned over the document, but my mind was too distracted to focus on anything. I needed to talk to Nathan about what I was feeling, but it was so hard to put it into words. I was drowning in worry, but there was also another issue clawing at me.

Knowing it was sometimes easier for me to communicate via email, I opened up my Outlook and composed a short message.

To: Nathan Thorne
From: Delilah Palmer
Date: 2/4/2014 9:47 am
Subject: Are you sure?
Why don't we just go to the courthouse?

I returned to biting my nail, telling myself I was just trying to make it straight again when I knew it was really because I was nervous. Not only that, I was scared of the deposition and the wedding.

To: Delilah Palmer
From: Nathan Thorne
Date: 2/4/2014 9:49 am
Subject: RE: Are you sure?
No. You want a wedding. Stop stressing. Plus, I want you walking down the aisle to me. Or are you saying you don't want to marry me?

I blew out a breath as I read. I never meant to imply that.

To: Nathan Thorne
From: Delilah Palmer
Date: 2/4/2014 9:53 am
Subject: RE: Are you sure?
I want to marry you. Very much so.

I was just scared out of my wits and trying to find the easy way out.

To: Delilah Palmer
From: Nathan Thorne
Date: 2/4/2014 9:54 am
Subject: RE: Are you sure?
Good. Now stop stressing or I'm going to force you to relax.

I gasped as I read over a seemingly innocent sentence. It was anything but. Since Nathan and I no longer shared an office, our romps in and around the office had slowed to an almost halt. The thought of him finding me and taking me away was enough to wash away my panic and replace it with a need for him.

Time to flirt.

To: Nathan Thorne
From: Delilah Palmer
Date: 2/4/2014 9:56 am
Subject: RE: Are you sure?
And how would you force me to relax?

To: Delilah Palmer
From: Nathan Thorne

Date: 2/4/2014 10:01 am
Subject: RE: Are you sure?
Are you asking me to spell out in detail and dirty words the ways I would make you come over and over again until your body feels like Jell-O and you can't walk?

Fuck!

To: Nathan Thorne
From: Delilah Palmer
Date: 2/4/2014 10:02 am
Subject: RE: Are you sure?
Promises, promises. Where's the proof?

I bit my lip and sat back in my seat, staring at the screen, waiting for his response. Nathan was the exact distraction I needed. Only he could make it all go away.

To: Delilah Palmer
From: Nathan Thorne
Date: 2/4/2014 10:04 am
Subject: RE: Are you sure?
Conference room, 6th floor. NOW!

I sat up straight and quickly locked my computer. "Hey, Owen, I'm going to go get some coffee."

He looked at me, then down at my desk and back up. "Uh-huh. Have fun. If anyone comes looking for you, I'll tell them you're in the bathroom." I gaped at him. He shook his head and gave a little smile. "I'm not stupid. You've been distracted the last hour, and you have a full cup of coffee sitting on your desk."

I looked down and cursed under my breath at the untouched mug. Heat flooded my face, and I tried to find some response.

"Go on. Don't want him to wait, do you?"

I shook my head and stood to walk out the door. The cubes were bustling with chatter as I made my way past. Each step drew me closer to my goal, making my pussy twitch in anticipation.

I was in desperate need for him to take it all away.

My foot tapped as I waited for the elevator, half expecting Nathan to be waiting with me, but he wasn't. When I got off on the sixth floor, I meandered through the mostly empty cubes. The sixth floor was a recent addition to Holloway and Holloway, and not many employees were currently working on it. All that made it perfect for a midday romp.

I turned the handle and stepped in, closing the door behind me. I wasn't able to turn around when he grabbed me by the waist, his hand clamping down over my mouth.

"Shhh," he whispered in my ear. His hips rocked against me, pushing his cock against my ass as I leaned into him. My desperation rose.

He let go of me and I turned around, latching my arms around his neck and bringing him down for a kiss. It took him a second to respond—the surprise was evident in his eyes. He was grabbing and groping, drawing up the hem of my dress with his fingers.

I reached between us, popped the button on his pants, and lowered the zipper, then reached in the opening and pulled his hard cock out. He drew in a shuddered

41

breath, his eyes fluttering as I pumped up and down his length.

"Fuck, baby." He gritted his teeth and picked me up, setting me down on the conference table a few feet away. He pushed my panties aside and slapped the head of his cock against my clit. "Something you want?"

"Please!" I was needy, desperate for our connection. He ran the length of his cock against my pussy, pushing the tip in, then out, torturing me. "Nate, please." I was a whimpering mess.

He pulled on the back of my neck and smashed his lips to mine, then lined up and thrust in. My eyes rolled back in my head, shivers running through my skin as flames licked the inside. I groaned against him.

"I'll take care of you, baby," he whispered.

His hips rocked, pulling out and pushing back in until he was all the way in. For a minute he sat like that, as close as we could be. The tension started to leave me—the world was coming back into focus. One hand still held my neck while the other gripped tight on my ass as he moved in a slow, steady rhythm.

My hips moved against him, a plea for more. Harder. Faster. *Everything.*

His hand on my neck moved away, sliding down my back, and I grabbed tight on his shoulders. When he reached my other ass cheek, I knew the message was received. His eyes met mine, desire and lust clouding them and sending another shiver through me.

He kissed down my jaw to my neck as he pulled out, then slammed back in. I drew in a hard breath of surprise and bit back a moan. My nails dug into his shirt, wishing it was skin to pierce, driving him as the pounding picked up.

He leaned back and used the leverage on my body to pull and push me like a ragdoll with each of his thrusts. It was what I asked for, what I needed. Each thrust fanned the fire, whiting out everything around me. I was gasping for breath, muscles coiled tight, on the edge of falling.

It wasn't enough.

I let out a strangled, muffled sob. He leaned forward, pressing his lips to mine.

"Come for me, baby." He trailed kisses down to my neck, then turned them into tiny bites.

His teeth sunk into my shoulder right as his cock slammed in. I crumbled, shaking in his arms as I came, his body rocking with mine. He was still latched onto my neck, marking me, as he tensed and shuddered.

I stayed curled in his arms, my legs holding him securely to me. Once we were breathing steadier, he leaned back and looked me in the eyes.

He brushed away a strand of my hair with his fingers. "What was this really about, Honeybear?"

My brow scrunched, and I looked at his chest. "It was about the wedding, but it was also about the—"

"Deposition?" I nodded and snuggled into his neck. He ran soothing strokes up and down my back. "I won't lie to you—tomorrow is going to suck, and in the worst way possible. The wedding is going to be easy compared to the trial and all the shit that goes along with it, but you know what?" I shook my head in the crook of his neck. His voice softened. "At the end of it all, you and I will be together, husband and wife, and that piece of shit will be locked up.

43

It's not going to be pretty, but it will be worth it in the end. I promise."

I wanted to believe him, and I hoped he was right. Could it really be my first step to ending my nightmares?

⸻ ❧ ⸻

I was drained. My mental state was affecting my physical state as I stumbled out of a conference room at the prosecutor's office. It felt like my limbs were filled with lead, all the while my brain was drifting in the waves of the ocean.

Giving my deposition had been harder than I thought, and I was wrecked. Nathan wasn't there to help as he was stuck at work until it was time for his. Not that he could have been in the room with me, but his presence outside might have helped.

All the trouble was in an effort to put my psychotic stepbrother, Adam, away for life.

"Hey, there," a familiar voice said, calling me from the depths of my mind.

I looked up to find Caroline smiling down at me.

"What are you doing here?"

She sat next to me. "I had a feeling you'd be beaten down and in need of a friend."

My bottom lip quivered and tears filled my eyes. Caroline wrapped her arms around me, drawing me close.

"Thank you."

She ran her hand up and down my back. "How was it?"

"Bad. Really bad." I sniffed and sat back. "I had to retell the whole thing—answer questions." I let out a hard breath, trying to settle myself.

She ran her hand up and down my back. "Soon you'll never have to talk about it again. You can push it all away and live your life."

I nodded. "I know, but I'm still not looking forward to telling it all again at the trial and all the time in between then and now."

"You should be."

I looked at her, questioning her sanity. "Why?"

She smiled at me, her hand brushing a strand of hair from my face. "Because in two weeks you're marrying the man you love and who loves you more than anything."

Her words washed away all the bad as I thought about all the good coming my way. It helped, more than words could say, to be reminded of where my future was going. Adam and his actions kept yanking me into the past, but soon that would be done, and he would be out of my life forever. Soon I would have a husband and be part of a family that loved me. All my wishes I once thought were an unrealistic goal for me were coming true.

"Come on." Caroline stood and held out her hand. "Let's go get some lunch."

"What about work?"

She rolled her eyes at me. "You forgot, didn't you?"

"Forgot what?"

"Jack told you to take the day off. We're meeting Sarah and Teresa at the dress shop at two."

"Oh, yeah." Only I would forget about shopping for my own wedding dress. My brow scrunched. "Were we meeting for lunch?"

"No."

"Then why did you come?"

She grabbed my hand and squeezed. "Because I knew my friend needed me."

I pulled her in for another hug. "I'm so happy you're my friend."

<hr/>

It would've been so much easier on me had I at least considered getting married any time in the last fifteen or twenty years. All that I didn't know—and had no idea I needed to know—was brought up by Sarah, Nathan's mom, and Teresa, my foster mother, and had my head spinning. At least we had a venue, and, with that, a helpful coordinator who worked to streamline the process.

Over the years I'd seen movies where the bride had a ton of people with her while picking out a dress. Somehow, that was how it ended up being for me, as well. Caroline, Sarah, Teresa, and Erin were scouring the racks, asking me questions that I had no answer to. What color did I want? What style? Plain or glitzy? Form-fitting or loose?

My impression that all dresses were white was squashed. Even though they all looked the same color to me, they were, in fact, not.

Caroline worked the dressing room, helping me bounce, slip, and slide into each dress. After each one, I couldn't help but think some gym could market the experience as a workout class, because it was. Some dresses weighed what felt like almost twenty pounds. By the third one of those, we whittled away the heavier fabrics. I finally knew something—I wanted a light dress for my beach wedding. A fabric that flowed in the ocean breeze.

"So, when do I get to repay this favor with you and Ian?" I asked Caroline as she yanked another dress off.

She grunted, and I popped free. "Whenever he gets off his damn ass and asks me."

My fingers moved through my hair, pulling it back from my face. "You've been together for almost three years."

She sighed. "Yeah, and I'm beginning to wonder if we're going anywhere. I mean, he never wants to talk about the future."

"Really? He always seems so glued to you."

"Yeah, but is it super glue?"

"You live together. Do you love him?" I asked. She nodded. "Then I'd wait to see if the glue dries."

She smiled at me. "Well, we do have an Aruban vacation coming up. Maybe we'll find out then. Until then, we have a quest."

I turned to the mirror so she could zip up the back of the next dress.

Caroline's eyes popped out before she caught mine in the mirror and smiled. "Yes."

I beamed at her.

It wasn't a strapless dress like most seemed to be— it was a lace-covered, v-neck cut, sleeveless top that ended at an empire waist. The skirt was light chiffon and moved with ease—ethereal almost. I turned to see the back. It was mostly sheer, with lace details around the edge.

It was conservative with a romantic elegance. It wasn't overly done up or covered in beads and fancy fabrics.

It was perfect. It was *me*.

There was no second-guessing, no "let's try on a few more." No, I'd found *the* dress. The one I'd walk across the sand in to join Nathan so we could finally become a family.

Family. I would be part of a real, loving family.

I deserved one, and so did Nathan.

CHAPTER 5

The countdown was on—three days. We still needed to finish up the workweek before boarding a plane, and my insides felt like a ticking time bomb.

That was probably why Drew, Caroline, Nathan, and I all went out to lunch—to relax. We'd decided on a sandwich shop not far from the office, specializing in grilled subs and fresh-cut fries. Drew drove Caroline and me, while Nathan was a few minutes behind due to a meeting with a client.

After ordering for Nathan and myself, I searched for a table for the four of us. The restaurant was pretty empty, being that it was mid-week, so there were lots of options. I found one and waited for the others to join me.

"So, are you changing your name, hyphenating, or keeping Palmer?" Drew asked as he took the seat across from me. He'd learned fast that the seat beside me was reserved for Nathan.

I shook my head like mad. "Hell, no... Am I keeping Palmer?" I scoffed. It wasn't hard to imagine where the anger stormed from for a name that'd been mine for thirty years. "As soon as we get back, Palmer is gone. I don't want to be associated with that man anymore." I smiled at him, pushing all the negativity away.

Drew nodded. "I figured. Can't call you DAP anymore. Maybe I'll just start DAT. Who DAT?"

I rolled my eyes and let out a small snicker. "That is the stupidest name. You haven't called me that in years, therefore *it* and all incarnations are void."

"I can always bring it back."

"No. Its statute of limitations is eighty years."

"I'd like to appeal."

"Appeal denied." I clasped my hands together and cocked my head at him.

"Why?"

"You don't have the appropriate paperwork."

"What the hell is going on over here? Lawyer porn?" Caroline asked as she sat next to Drew.

"We were discussing DAP."

Caroline paused, then shook her head. "That was the stupidest nickname."

"Oh, come on, it was different." The muscles in his forearm flexed, and he grinned.

"It made it sound like you were calling her some cleaning agent. 'DAP will get out all your stains!'"

"Lila works just fine," I said and took a bite of my sandwich.

"I've got some names for her, but they aren't for polite company." Nathan's arm wrapped around me as he sat down and pulled me close for a kiss.

I looked up at him. "What about Honeybear?"

"*Honeybear?*" Caroline and Drew asked in unison.

I could swear Nathan's cheeks pinked up. "Yeah, you're my Honeybear. Public or private, but I'd prefer private. I've got an image to keep up, after all."

"That's worse than DAP." Drew had a look of disgust on his face.

"I think it's cute. Very different and shows a different side of Nate." Caroline smiled across the table at us.

"Thank you, Caroline." Nathan smiled back at her, then took a bite of his sandwich, moaning as he chewed.

I let out a giggle. "Hungry?"

"Fuck, yes. I haven't eaten all day. Someone wanted to exercise this morning, and I missed breakfast." He elbowed me and grinned.

"Oh, God, I don't want to hear about the kinky, fucked up shit you two get into." Drew made a gagging sound, then set his sandwich down. "Great. Now all I can see is your fucking hairy balls."

"Hey, I said exercise—you're the one who twisted it into my ass being naked." Nathan chuckled. "And what the hell are you doing see my balls? I thought you'd be envisioning Lila, though I'm glad you weren't, but is there something you need to tell us?"

Drew glared at Nathan, then shot a fry in his direction. "Shut the fuck up."

Caroline rolled her eyes. "Yup, bunch of professional lawyers over here, not that anyone would guess."

Drew sat up straighter and held his head high. "Professional when we need to be."

Caroline quirked her brow at them. "Frat boys the rest of the time?"

Drew took a bite, then wiped his mouth. "You know I wasn't a frat boy."

"True, but I'm willing to bet Nate was." Caroline turned her blue eyes back to Nathan, and he held up his right hand.

"Guilty."

I gasped in shock and pulled back. "My God, what am I marrying?"

He eyed me sideways, his lip twitching up. "Prince Charming, remember?"

I scoffed. "This is one fucked up fairy tale."

Nathan nodded, then he turned toward me, his eyes softening as he pulled me closer. "Yes, it is, but it's ours."

"Oh, by the way, I ran into someone who knows you when we were at the bridal shop." I'd forgotten all about it.

His brow quirked. "Yeah? Who?"

I wracked my brain trying to remember his name. "Mack something. Said you met back when you were working on the Marconi case."

Nathan swallowed hard, and set his sandwich down as he turned away from me. His profile didn't stop me from seeing the color leave his skin. My stomach dropped, and a sickness washed over me. The air around him had become so thick that I was certain Drew and Caroline noticed his abrupt change in demeanor.

He only had that reaction when the Marconi were brought up.

"What else did he say?"

It'd been an innocent run-in, or so I thought. "Congratulations. That's it."

He turned back to me, his lips twitching into a forced smile, but his eyes couldn't hide the combination of anger and dread.

"So, did you hear about Blackwell?" Caroline asked. "Seems he's all the scandal with that intern Tara."

I turned to look at her, mouthing a "thank you" as Drew jumped in, steering the conversation away and saving our peaceful lunch as much as possible.

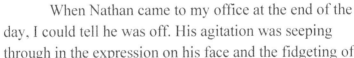

When Nathan came to my office at the end of the day, I could tell he was off. His agitation was seeping through in the expression on his face and the fidgeting of his hands. The silence as we climbed into the car and headed home was a dead giveaway that something was wrong.

I waited, knowing he'd spill when he was ready. It was better to wait and let his mood settle. About ten minutes into our drive, he opened up, but not on the subject I was anticipating.

"Adam's trying to get a plea bargain," Nathan said.

I turned in my seat to face him, stunned. "What?"

"I got a call this afternoon." Nathan's gaze never left the road, but his anger was evident by the grip he had on the wheel and the clenching of his jaw.

"He's trying to get out of it." Of course he would. His demented mind blamed me for all the hardships in his life. "How much will this push the trial out?"

"Depends on how long the prosecution lets it go until they put their foot down and say no."

"They *will* say no, *right?*" I asked, nervous that the prosecutor would deal. If they did, Adam could serve much less time.

Nathan nodded. "With his priors, they're not going to go easy on him."

I let out a relieved sigh. "Hopefully they won't let it go on too long. I want this over with."

Nathan reached over and squeezed my hand. "It'll be over soon. That fucker will be in jail, and we won't ever have to think of him or see him again."

"It's not soon enough."

"I know."

It was *not* the news I wanted to hear. We were leaving in a few days for our wedding, and it was souring the mood. The only reprieve was that there was more time for me to prepare for telling a courtroom of people the events of my life with Adam. At the same time, I was ready to get it over with.

My future awaited me, and I would live it, with Nathan, to the fullest.

<hr/>

My hand clamped onto Nathan's as the airplane engines geared up, and my eyes sealed shut as it rocketed down the runway. I was tense as the wheels left the ground, but I was able to relax after a few minutes.

"I don't know if I'll ever get used to that." My grip loosened, and I let out a long breath.

His thumb ran across my fingers. "At least we found a direct flight, so we don't have to do it again today."

"Yes, very happy about that."

"Just relax, Honeybear. In a few hours, we'll be on the beach."

I pursed my lips. "Good thing I brought my tablet so we can watch movies and take my mind off the fact we're over thirty thousand feet in the air."

He smiled and kissed my shoulder as he leaned over to pull out our earbuds while I let out a long breath.

Thankfully there was very little turbulence through our entire flight. However, finding all the baggage we brought along with the seven people we traveled with was a pain. Half an hour later, we found everything and everyone, and were off to the Divi resort where we were staying. It was a little cramped in the van that came to take us, but we managed.

George and Sarah, Caroline and Ian, Andrew, Teresa and Armando all accompanied us, whereas Jack Holloway and Darren Morgenson would arrive the next day with their wives. Unfortunately, Noah and his wife, Camilla, were unable to come.

"Do we need to call Erin and let her know we're here?" I asked to no one in particular. Erin and her family had gone down a few days in advance due to her vacation schedule.

Sarah turned around from the seat in front of me. "She said she'd meet up with us when we see the coordinator at three."

I nodded and looked out the window. The weather was much different than the cold winter in Indiana. The sun was shining and the palm trees were blowing in the sea breeze. Flickers of blue ocean appeared between buildings, and I could almost taste the salt in the air.

When we arrived at the resort, I couldn't help but smile. It was perfect—the exact image that appeared when I told Nathan I wanted the beach—sun, sea, and salty air. It reminded me of one of the happiest times of my life and would forever be a reminder of the happiest day of my life.

Nathan squeezed my hand and smiled down at me. I grinned back, then launched myself at him. He laughed, stumbling back a bit as he lifted me off the ground.

He kissed my neck. "Are you happy?"

"So happy."

"Me, too."

We checked in, and, by some luck, were able to get into our rooms right away. One of my bags went to the room I would share with Nathan, but for tradition's sake, I was spending the eve before the wedding with Caroline, and Nathan was sharing with Ian.

Nathan had insisted we do our honeymoon to the extreme and splurge on a suite. I wasn't about to complain.

We agreed to meet for lunch at the buffet after getting settled, and I headed in the opposite direction from

Nathan. Caroline took my hand and smiled, swinging our arms between us.

The first thing I did when we entered was unpack my dress and hang it up in the closet.

"Hmm, we may have to have it pressed," Caroline said as she looked it over. Her eyes scrutinized it as she pulled at the fabric and released it. "I'm sure the hotel can do it. We can ask Marie when we meet with her."

It did have a few wrinkles and was looking on the limp side. After all, it had been stuffed in a suitcase for the last eight hours.

I shut the closet and moved over to the sliding door that led to the balcony. The second I stepped out, I was hit with the warm sea breeze and the salty tang in the air. My hair blew around my face, and I sighed as I soaked in the warmth.

"Thank you for picking the beach." Caroline bumped my shoulder. "I needed a vacation."

"Thank you for coming."

"Wouldn't have missed it for all the tea in China."

"You don't even like tea."

She shrugged. "Okay, how about all the stars in the sky?"

My lip twitched. "The stars are in space." She huffed and pinched my side, making me cry out.

"I wouldn't have missed it for anything. How's that?"

I leaned my head on her shoulder. "Better than you could imagine."

CHAPTER 6

Meeting with the event coordinator, Marie, went smoothly. She was a petite brunette with a curvy figure, round face, and wide, bright green eyes that stood out against her tanned skin. Her bubbly and open personality set me at ease the moment we met.

She'd done a great job asking all the questions in the few short weeks before the wedding and rolling it all together in time. Granted, I wasn't a bridezilla. I let her fill in a lot of the blanks. In the end, I had a feeling she liked having the freedom to plan a wedding for a bride who wasn't so specific on every single detail. Especially with the short timeline.

Marie snapped her binder closed and stood after going over everything with us. "All right, I'll see all of you back here in two hours for the dress rehearsal. Hopefully you can round up the men by then." She snickered and waved as she headed back to her office.

I was so happy to have her. She'd made the whole process so much easier and kept me from having a panic attack.

"The boys will probably be at the pool bar," Erin said with a roll of her eyes. Her skin was pink from playing in the surf with her boys, and she had raccoon eyes.

Caroline snorted. "It's always five o'clock when you're on vacation."

"We should find them before they get trashed and sun-baked." Sarah sighed and smiled at me.

I wondered if Nathan was having a drink as well. After my accident, it was only some wine here and there or a margarita at Erin's—our Friday nights were a long gone thing of the past. Though, the reason we stopped was due in part to all the medications we were on, along with therapist directions. In the end, it was a good thing for both of us, but it was vacation, so I suspected we'd be partaking quite a bit more than normal.

Teresa slipped her arm in mine and smiled. "Come, mi niña, let's find them."

As we walked through the lobby, I couldn't help but take notice of how…different things were. Four women were paced with me, talking to me. I was involved and part of the group. In fact, I was the center of attention. It was surreal.

There'd already been so many "what do you want" or "what do you like" questions thrown around—people doing things for me and wanting to know what *I* wanted.

"There they are," Caroline said, pointing to exactly where we thought they were—the pool bar. Ian was sitting next to Nathan, his Cheshire grin aimed at Caroline. She beamed back at him. His blond hair was a mess, making it obvious he'd already been in the pool.

"Well, hello, beautiful ladies." Nathan grinned and pulled me between his open knees, wrapping his arms around my waist. "Extra special hello to my bride."

He pursed his lips, and I leaned down to meet them. They tasted like beer.

"Are you drunk already?"

He chuckled. "On half a beer? No."

"So, you're just being overly charming, laying it on thick." My eyes narrowed. "What are you up to?"

He quirked his brow at me. "What I am up to is cloud-fucking-nine, because I haven't felt this good or been this happy in years. If I seem drunk, it's because I'm drunk on happiness and…giddiness. I'm *giddy*."

I rolled my eyes at him. "You're being silly, but I have to admit, it's fun, and I kinda like it."

He gave me a quick peck. "Anything for you."

I drew a circle on his chest with my finger and looked at him from under my lashes. "Anything?"

Ian laughed next to us. "Uh oh, man. She's breaking out those feminine wiles."

Nathan backed up and looked me over. "Who is this temptress before me? Because my fiancée isn't like this."

"I guess I'm giving in to my inner harlot."

"Well, I like this inner harlot. Tell me more." He grabbed onto my ass and pulled me hard between his legs. "What was it you wanted again?"

I placed my arms on his shoulders and ran my fingers through his hair. "I want to go walk on the beach and play in the water."

"Now? What time is the rehearsal dinner?"

"In a few hours. So, we have about an hour or so before we need to get ready."

"All right. Let's go get changed." He stood up, taking a long last sip of his beer, then grabbed my hand as we walked off. "We'll be in the water."

Ian toasted us with his beer. "Have fun!"

We headed into the hotel toward Nathan's room, walking hand-in-hand. I couldn't keep the smile from my face.

"You look happy." He smiled down at me, his free hand brushing a strand of hair back. "It looks so good on you."

I grabbed hold of his arm and leaned against his shoulder. "I *am* happy."

He kissed the top of my head. "Good."

When we entered his room, I sat down on the bed next to his suitcase. It was a front row view to a strip show, and I'd left my singles back in the room. I licked my lips at the sight of one of my favorite parts of his anatomy swinging as he stepped out of his shorts. He noticed me staring at him and smirked.

"See something you want?" He thrust his hips, making his cock bounce up and down.

I nodded and gave him a pout. "But it's not hard yet."

"I'm trying fucking hard not to." He shook his head and picked through his suitcase, looking for his swim trunks.

"Why?" He was never one for holding back.

He slapped his trunks at me after he pulled them out. "Because we'll have all the time in the world for it after the wedding."

I sighed, enjoying my view, pouting at him as he got dressed. He chuckled and pulled his trunks on. Once they were up, hiding his cock again, we headed out the door and down to where I was staying.

As soon as we were in the room, I rid myself of my sundress. There was a groan behind me when I bent over to slide my panties down. I smiled, turned toward him and winked. He cursed under his breath, his hand rubbing at the back of his neck as he adjusted his stance.

Out of my suitcase came the small white bikini Caroline found for me in the fall. It was the only suit I owned, but I figured I'd buy another one while we were in Aruba.

I bent over to slip on the bottoms, and he groaned again.

Nathan's eyes darkened and he turned from me, his fingers rubbing against his lips. "Motherfucker." I also caught his hand on his cock. "You are a *very* bad girl."

"*What?*" I adjusted my breasts, fixing the top so it was just right.

"I fucking forgot about what you'd be wearing. You know how I feel about you in this sad excuse of a bathing suit, and you're teasing me with it." His muscles tensed and flexed, teeth mashing. "You're trying to push my buttons, and I'm not going to give it to you." His gaze narrowed on me. "I'm onto your games."

My jaw dropped open. "Are you denying me?"

He nodded. "For being a tease, you aren't getting any until tomorrow night."

"But…"

"Besides, we don't really have time for it."

I quirked my brow at him and shifted my weight as I crossed my arms, thus pushing my breasts out more. "Says the man who's perfected the office quickie."

He sighed and leaned back against the wall. "What have I turned you into?"

"Exactly what you wanted—a sexual deviant who can't live without your cock. I believe your official title for me when we're alone is 'my little cocksucking slut.'"

He grinned at me and shook his head. "I've created a monster."

"A cock monster."

"Yes, a cock monster. Now throw your dress back on, and let's go. You wanted to play in the ocean, remember?"

"You distracted me."

He rolled his eyes and shook his head. "Fuck, I love you."

We walked down to the beach, and I gave a happy sigh when my feet sank into the warm sand. Nathan was staring at me, and I turned to him. "What?"

"I need to make you insanely happy more often, because *you* are shining."

I beamed up at him, then took his hand and ran toward the crashing waves.

Waking up without Nathan beside me was strange. I didn't like it at all. Even though I wasn't alone—Caroline was beside me—I felt like something was missing. The worst part of it all was that I wouldn't see him until this afternoon at the wedding.

I stood, trying not to disturb my sleeping friend, and walked out onto the terrace. The sun was just over the horizon, and the humid warmth of the island increased with every passing minute. Waves crashed against the beach in a steady rhythm.

I wished Nathan was with me, standing behind me, his arms caging me against the banister as we took in the morning view. Then again, he'd probably only last about a minute before pulling down my panties and pushing his cock in me as we looked out.

The thought alone made my pussy twitch. No surprise that I was still wanting for him, especially after all the teasing yesterday and what he did under the table at dinner. His fingers not so innocently slipped up my skirt and brushed against my pussy more than once.

The sliding glass door opened behind me. "Morning." Caroline moved to the rail to stand next to me.

I looked over and choked out a laugh. Caroline's normally well-kept brunette hair looked like she'd been through a tornado. Some of her makeup was missed when taking it off the night before, giving her a black eye effect.

"You look…excellent this morning."

She pursed her lips and narrowed her eyes. "Shut it." She looked back out and sighed. "I love it here. Can I stay? Forever?"

"I don't know about that. You want to leave me? What would Ian say?"

"Pfft, he'd probably be up for it. I'm sure there are tons of IT jobs here." She leaned her head on my shoulder. "And I couldn't leave you all alone to deal with both Nate and Drew all the time."

"They *are* a handful."

"We need to find Drew a girl." She pulled at one of the tangles in her hair, trying to smooth it.

I nodded. "I want him to be happy, too. He's a great guy."

She pushed her arms out and stretched. "Maybe when we get back, we can convince him to go onto one of those online dating sites."

"We might be able to talk him into it."

"Especially now that you're off the market." She bumped me.

I shook my head. "We tried once. It didn't work."

She looked over the balcony down to the pool. "I know, and he does as well. Took his hardheaded ass long enough to see it, but he agrees with me."

I turned to her. "Agrees with what?"

She put her arm around me. "There is no better man for you than Nate, even with all the shit that surrounds him."

I sighed, smiling as I stared out. "I never knew I could feel like this. That I could love like this or be loved."

"You're a whole different person than you were six years ago when we met."

"He's everything to me. I can't live without him."

She was silent for a moment. "We'll make sure that never happens. Because guess what?" I looked at her. "I can't live without you."

I threw my arms around her. "I love you."

She chuckled. "I love you, too." She pulled back. "Come on, let's go get some breakfast."

I smirked at her and waved toward her head. "You are going to do something about *that*, right?"

She stuck her tongue out at me and headed inside. "I'll throw it up in a bun for now and get a shower when we get back."

I rifled through my bag for some shorts and a T-shirt. "Hey, I know I didn't go with the whole wedding party or anything, but you know you're my maid of honor, no matter what."

She snorted. "After all the heavy lifting I did when we were dress shopping, you bet your ass I better be!"

CHAPTER 7

I stood in front of a mirror, all alone, staring at a vision that wasn't the normal me. My hair was done in a low, loose bun with a white rose and some baby's breath. There was no more makeup than I usually had on, but combined with the dress and my hair, I looked foreign to myself.

Five minutes after Caroline ushered Teresa out, the anxiety was intensifying. My mind couldn't get over the fact that it was really happening. I had to be dreaming.

"They're ready for you," Marie said as she held out a bouquet of white roses.

I wrapped my fingers around the base, then took a deep breath, blowing it out slowly. She drew back the curtain, and I stepped out onto the sand. My arms shook out the tension that was building before I took another step. After all, what did I have to be nervous about? I was getting married, and I was happy.

We made it.

Against all odds and every obstacle we encountered, Nathan and I were going to be a family in a few short moments. There were more trials ahead of us, but we would face them—together. We were strongest that way, barely functioning apart. It was a lesson we learned all too well.

Everyone in the office knew I was Nathan's and he was mine, and today we sealed it. Out on a sandy beach in the Caribbean with the friends and family that could make the journey with us, we would say "I do." The belief still eluded me that at the end of the day I would no longer be Delilah Palmer. Instead, I would be Delilah Thorne—wife to the office god.

I made my way down the sand with butterflies in my stomach, the light fabric of my dress fluttering in the breeze. Every squashed Cinderella dream or princess fantasy I'd imagined as a child, about marrying a prince that would take me away from the evil, was steps away. He was waiting for me at the end of the aisle. He was damaged, but so was I, and together we were one soul, one heart.

My step faltered, and I was afraid I would fall, but I regained my balance. I turned the corner and moved my gaze up to where I knew he stood. My heart skipped a beat, and the warmth only he could give spread through me. Our eyes locked, and I could feel everything he felt in that moment. It was love. It was home.

With Nathan, I was finally home.

It felt like my chest was going to explode from everything I felt. I wanted to break down crying in joy, overwhelmed with a happiness I'd never experienced.

"Hi," he said, smiling at me when I reached him.

"Hi." I handed my bouquet to Caroline and took his hand.

The officiant began, but I hardly heard a word because my eyes were concentrating on Nathan's. Nothing could tear me away from his gaze—we were caught in our own little bubble.

I was lost in him as I recited the standard vows—in sickness and in health, for richer or poorer, till death do us part. He already knew all of that, as I'd long ago pledged all of that to him. When it was his turn, I caught the panic that flashed across his face when he spoke about death.

If I could help it, I would do everything in my power to make sure he died before me. The thought of him in despair as he watched another woman he loved die was gut-wrenching. I didn't want him to feel that pain again.

"I do," he said in closing, a waver of emotion in his voice.

I didn't wait for the officiant to pronounce us before launching myself at him, wrapping my arms around his neck and kissing him as hard as I could. Laughter was heard from the crowd behind us.

"Well, I guess I pronounce you man and wife. You may kiss the bride!" the officiant said, snickering with everyone else.

I pulled back, heat flooding my face as I looked at her. "Sorry."

Nathan chuckled and pulled me closer. "Can I kiss my bride?"

"Please."

His lips met mine, soft but with an intensity that zinged through me.

My *husband.*

<hr>

Following the ceremony was a whirlwind of photographs and congratulations that left my head spinning. I was happy when we all sat down to dinner in a secluded area of the resort. It was beachfront, but with bushes and trees on the sides for privacy.

Since our party was so small, we were all able to fit at one long banquet table. There were small tables set up around us for mingling.

As dinner was served, Teresa tapped her fork against her champagne glass to gain everyone's attention.

"I just wanted to say a few words about mi niña Lila. From the moment she stepped into our home, I knew it would take a strong, unrelenting man to gain her heart. I'm so happy to see her finally get the love she deserves." Teresa blew a kiss at Nathan. "And I'm incredibly happy that I could be here to see it."

I blew her a kiss and reached across the table to take her hand. "Thank you for showing me kindness and love."

A tear fell from her eye as she patted my hand. "You are so welcome. And thank you, Nathan, for making her happy."

Nathan smiled at her and looked at me. "She makes me happy. I'm the lucky one here."

Jack stood up and raised his glass. "And you owe everything to me. If it wasn't for me, we wouldn't be on this beautiful island."

Everyone laughed and took a sip.

Dinner was excellent, and afterward we sat around talking and drinking. I was happy I'd gone for the lighter dress, because the heat and humidity was stifling. Our only saving grace was the ocean breeze, which made it manageable.

Nathan had forgone the traditional tux, which I was more than okay with. He didn't even have on a suit jacket. All things considered, I understood. None of that mattered, though, because it was exactly what we wanted. His shirtsleeves were rolled up and he'd lost the tie. The top buttons were undone and inviting me to touch the skin that showed.

I licked my lips and leaned forward, placing an open-mouthed kiss on his neck, my tongue peeking out to taste his skin. A low rumble sounded in his chest, and he squirmed in his chair. It seemed he was still worked up from my teasing the day before.

Nathan took my hand and pulled me from my seat. "Come on, Mrs. Thorne, we need to have our first dance."

I blinked up at him. "I don't know how to dance."

"That's okay. All you have to do is move with me. You're good at that." He winked at me.

As we stepped onto the small dance area, he drew me to him as the music started up. We moved in slow steps.

"*With me*." He reminded me.

I took a deep breath and let him take over my senses.

It didn't matter what was playing. All I cared about was the man standing in front of me, holding me close as we moved around the dance floor. I'd never seen him so lit

71

up. His smile was blinding—happiness pouring out of him and infecting me.

He leaned his head down and rested his forehead against mine. "Be mine forever," he whispered.

"Yes." There was no other answer.

"Love me forever." His voice cracked as he spoke.

Tears swelled in my eyes. "Always."

<hr/>

A few hours later, we headed up to our suite where I expected him to tear me out of my dress. Instead, his fingers lightly caressed over my collarbone, drifting over the lace.

"I forgot to tell you how absolutely beautiful you looked today. You take my breath away. This dress…it's perfect."

My cheeks heated as I looked into his eyes that held nothing but love and warmth with a splash of growing desire.

"Thank you."

He looked back down at my body and sighed. "I almost don't want to take it off you." His fingers continued to roam around my body.

"There are photos."

His eyes flickered back to mine as he latched onto the zipper and began pulling it down. "I said *almost*."

I tingled with excitement as the teeth of the zipper slid down inch by inch. His lips met mine, soft and lingering as he slowly explored my mouth with his. I gasped when his hand slipped into the opening he'd made and our skin made contact. His lips ghosted mine as he moved up and swept over my nipple.

"I'm going to spend all night devouring you, inch by delicious inch."

I flicked my tongue out against his lips. "How about moving a little faster then?"

He shook his head and nipped at my lip. "Oh, no, Mrs. Thorne. I'm going to savor you."

I pouted at him, my thighs clenching. "You mean torture me."

He smirked at me. "That's one way of looking at it."

His fingers worked the buttons on my shoulder and the fabric flipped away, exposing skin that he immediately began kissing and licking. A small tug on my other shoulder and the dress slipped down, catching on my elbow. My nipples tightened as they rubbed against his shirt. He moaned as he kissed his way down, taking one into his mouth, sucking on it while he palmed and pinched the other.

I couldn't stop moving. My body was begging, searching for the friction it desired. Taking was his usual style, and I craved it. Loving was pure torture, but the reward was worth the frustration.

"Now, now. Patience." He licked his lips, groaning as he pushed the dress over the swell of my hips.

"You know I don't have that." I reached for the buttons on his shirt and flipped the top two before he swatted my hand away.

"Maybe I need to teach you a lesson."

His touch sent shivers through me as his hands moved around my body. Light caresses and loving tenderness—very different than normal. It was still very stimulating, especially considering they were coming from the man who was now my husband.

I whimpered when he stopped touching me, but was happy when it was only to pull his own clothing off. My fingers flitted across his chest, exploring his hard lines and soft flesh while he worked his pants down and off, taking my panties with him.

He was beautiful. His cock stood high and proud, almost waving at me with each breath he took in.

Hands on my hips guided me back to the bed, and he lowered me down, his body hovering over mine. His lips pressed against mine in a soft, slow kiss. Burning need simmered inside me, growing in intensity.

I drew in a shuddering breath when his fingers moved across my clit, pressing in. Before I could even reach between us, he grabbed my wrists, distracting me with a kiss, and pinned them over my head.

"I want to touch you." I whimpered, rocking against him.

He groaned, hips rocking, then crashed his lips to mine. No longer soft, we were full of want.

"You've had me worked up since yesterday. I want to ram my cock in you and fuck you until we're both unconscious."

"Then do it. We have the rest of our lives for lovemaking."

A growl ripped from him and he flipped us over. I was still in shock of the change when he lined up and pushed me down on his cock.

"Oh, fuck." My eyes rolled back, fingers flexing into his chest.

I cried out when his hips thrust up, hitting the spot that made my body sing for him.

"People are going to hear you."

I looked down at him. "So? Don't you want them to hear what you do to me?"

He gritted his teeth and flexed his hips up, his fingers digging into my hips. "Fuck. I want everyone to hear what I do to you. I want the whole damn island to know you're mine. Now get your ass moving and ride me like a good whore."

I couldn't help the moan that escaped my lips. He knew what his dirty mouth did to me.

I moved up and down his length, bouncing with each upward thrust and downward roll. He pushed on me, directing me where to go, cursing under his breath. My eyes fell closed, reveling in the feeling as my body took over, driving us both to the edge.

"Shit. That's it, baby."

My mouth dropped open and my muscles seized, coiled tight. He took over, holding me above him while he thrust up, drilling into me.

It was too much, and I screamed out as I came around him. Everything left me, and I fell forward onto his chest. He guided me up and down a few more times before grunting as he exploded.

"What happened to savoring?" I was breathing too hard to even lift my head.

"Overrated." He chuckled. "But it's a nice idea."

"Agreed." I turned my head to look at him and smiled. "I like our version better."

He caressed up and down my arm. "Me too." His thumb moved across my cheek as we stared into each other's eyes. "I just can't help myself with you. All my good ideas go out the window the second you touch me."

"Don't ever stop touching me."

"Never."

After I regained my breath, I peeled my body from his and moved to the bathroom. There was a chuckle from the bed as I walked.

"Best fucking sight ever—my come sliding down your thighs."

I rolled my eyes at him.

Once I was done cleaning up, I threw a wet washcloth at him.

I crawled back into bed, snuggling into his side. We lay there, tangled together, his hand gently stroking my hair. There was peace and happiness all around that I never wanted to end.

"I want to put something out there, and I want you to keep an open mind, please," he said, interrupting the waves crashing against the shore.

I looked up at him skeptically. "You already fuck my ass."

He blinked down at me before his lip curled up, and he let out a chuckle. His lips pressed against my forehead.

"Not that, my minx. Something a bit more life altering than anal sex."

I grinned at him. "I don't know, anal was pretty life altering."

He groaned. "You better start working that ass open, because when I'm done I'm going to shove my cock in."

"But you just…" I trailed off, the twitch of his cock against his stomach drawing my eyes down.

"Just the thought of fucking your sweet ass gets me hard at any time."

I looked up from the entrancing sight of his hardening cock. "All right, baby."

"And bringing me back to the subject."

"Life altering?"

"Yes." He paused, seeming unsure of how to proceed. "We haven't talked about it, but what do you think about kids?"

I was frozen in shock. "What?"

His eyes were locked on mine as he spoke. "I want us to have a baby."

I sat up and backed away slightly, swallowing hard. "Nate, I… I don't know anything about babies or being a mom."

He sat up as well, his hand brushing my hair behind my ear. "No, but we can learn. You are so loving, Honeybear. I know you'll love our children with all that you have. And, you already know how *not* to treat them."

My eyes were wild, looking around the room for anything to get away from the conversation. Once again, it was a subject I'd never broached. I didn't have a yearning for children, even with my biological clock ticking down. Maybe it was because a loving family was never in my reality scope before I met Nathan.

He changed everything, and now he was still changing me, making me face what I'd thought was an utter impossibility.

"You want a baby? Really?" Another fear popped up, almost like I was willing him to say I was right, but at the same time starting to dream about that future. "What about the Marconi?"

"They'll always be there, and Darren's right—I don't want them to stop me from living my life. I want you to have my baby more than anything. I want a family with you, Lila. So why wait?"

I was shaking slightly at the thought. Nathan, my husband, was asking me, *begging* me, to have a family. How could I deny him when I could feel how much he wanted it?

My mind drifted back to a long ago dream at one of the worst times in my life. In it, we had three children, and our lives seemed to be filled with nothing but happiness. A warmth spread through me at the romantic ideals my subconscious had come up with.

Yes, I did want the dream. I was afraid, very much so, but that warmth, the love, overpowered the doubt.

"Okay," I said in a low voice, then tried again. "Okay, let's make a family."

His face broke out into one of the most brilliant smiles I had ever seen. He took my face in his hands and brought my lips to his in a heated kiss.

"Thank you."

CHAPTER 8

Nathan

⚬ ━━━━━ ⟩⟩⦾⦿⦾⟨⟨ ━━━━━ ⚬

Waking up in paradise was bittersweet. It was the last day of our honeymoon, and we were heading back to Indianapolis in a few short hours. Lila was snuggled into my side, naked, as the sounds of the ocean filled my ears and the warmth of the sun coming through the windows heated my skin.

A part of me wanted to stay. If we were two thousand miles away, Marconi would never know what transpired a week ago. Going home meant the possibility, a very good one, of him finding out about Lila. No matter how much I tried to beat back the fear, it still sat in the back of my mind—the beast prowling in his iron cage. He knew and tore at my insides to remind me. My chest tightened at just the thought of it all.

I stroked my fingers up and down her arm, staring at the white gold band on my hand, still in awe that I'd done it.

"Fuck. Me," I whispered as I watched the ring on my finger while my hand drifted up her side.

She twitched, but otherwise she kept still and was completely relaxed as she continued to dream.

I smiled—even while she was out of it, she was still so damn beautiful.

I ran a fingertip down her arm and watched the flesh turn from pale to a light pink.

It took me back to the moment when I decided to ask Lila to marry me. The second morning she woke in my arms after officially moving in with me was when it hit—I wanted to be with her every day for the rest of my life.

Just like today, we had woken up together, but there was something surreal about that moment. It wasn't her place and my place. It was our place—*our* home. Lila's clothes took up residence in the master closet hanging opposite of mine. Her furniture and décor filled the rooms. The spare bedrooms were no longer empty.

I was no longer empty.

I sighed and looked at her face. She was still sleeping—my mild attempts to wake her didn't work, but I wasn't trying that hard.

She was mine, and I was hers.

And I wanted everyone to know it.

I blew across her skin, smiling as the goose bumps rose. Her face scrunched up in annoyance and she snuggled deeper against me.

I loved Lila, and I never wanted to be without her.

With her, I was reborn.

I lightly ran the tip of my nose across her temple and inhaled the scent of her hair.

"No more hiding for us. We were never very good at that anyway, but that doesn't matter now. None of it does. What matters is I'll always be here for you. Through the upcoming trial..." My gut twisted. Would it break her to live through all those fucked up memories of Adam she'd buried so deep? In some ways it was good that he came after her. It made me realize exactly how much I loved her and needed her in every way. "No one will ever hurt you again, and we won't ever be separated. I promise." I kissed her shoulder and released a soft breath across her skin. "I'll protect you with my dying breath. You'll always be safe from now on."

I stared out the open window, watching the palm fronds sway in the breeze and listening to the waves crash against the shore. Every day should have this kind of peace, but my memories wouldn't shut off, and neither would my fears that she might be a target now.

There was a smile on her lips as she slept, one I'd put there. I wanted to see her dreams, but I was content knowing she had peace and happiness.

Anything. I'd do anything to make her happy. My lips passed over her forehead. She was my missing half.

A high-pitched squeak accompanied her body stretching against mine, her mouth open in a long yawn. I chuckled to myself, looking over her well-sexed body. It was complete with multiple bite marks to let everyone know she was taken.

Her eyes fluttered open and she smiled up at me. "Good morning."

"Morning."

"What time is it?"

I peered over to the nightstand. "Just before eight."

"Were you talking to me a little bit ago? I was dreaming you were whispering in my ear, making me all sorts of promises." She hummed for a minute.

I simply grinned. "What kind of lawyer makes promises to someone who's unconscious?"

"One who's up to no good." She rubbed her eyes.

"Mmm… Good point." I chuckled. "I guess I was trying to take advantage of every moment we have here together."

She thought on that for a moment, probably doing the math of how much time we had left. Her lips moved to a pout. "We don't have time to take a last swim, do we?"

I shook my head. "But, if we hurry, we can take a last walk on the beach after breakfast. We're mostly packed."

She nodded. "It'll only take a few minutes to finish up."

I leaned down and nipped at her shoulder, earning a squeak and a smile. "And we can save time by showering together."

Her gaze narrowed on me. "I don't know about that."

"What do you mean?"

"You'll still fuck me in the shower."

I nodded. It was nothing new. "Exactly. This way, we can kill two birds with one stone."

She rolled her eyes and pushed on my chest. "Shower now or after breakfast?"

I looked her over and licked my lips. "After." She sighed. "What?"

"You just want everyone to see that I'm well fucked."

"And?"

She shook her head and sat up all the way. "Once a possessive perv, always a possessive perv."

"You should be used to it by now. It's not going to change anytime soon. I like marking what's mine so fuckers know."

She tried to give me a look of disapproval, but she couldn't pull it off. There was no denying it—she loved me claiming her. The world would know she was desired, wanted, and loved.

Her hand slithered under the light sheet, nails gently pressing into my thigh as she moved up. I hissed and bucked when her hand wrapped around my soft cock, stirring it awake.

"And how am I supposed to show the world you're mine?"

"I think the world knows my devotion to you."

"How?"

"The ring on my finger and my constant hard-on for you." She pursed her lips, the playfulness leaving her. "Or, I could eat you out, not wipe it off, and cover my body in your sweet juices."

She licked her lips as she thought it over, her eyes dark and her hips rotating. I knew how to get her wet. She was probably thinking about my tongue sucking on her clit, fingers pinching and pulling her nipples.

"I think that would work. Especially for the Boob Squad."

"Guess we'll have to save it for when they're around. Besides, I don't have time to do it properly today."

She smiled and let go of my now hard dick. "I'll hold you to it." She turned, slipping her legs off the edge of the bed to stand.

When she tried to get up, her legs shook, then gave out, sending her back down to the bed. I leaned back against the headboard, figuring I'd get a good view of the show from there. Another attempt left her standing, but bracing herself against the wall.

Nice, naked ass centered perfectly in my view. I groaned and squeezed my cock.

"Trouble?" I smirked, remembering the activities that left her muscles weak.

She turned her head, glaring at me, then pushed off the wall. It was a valiant attempt on her part to make it to the bathroom, and she did…barely. I tried not to laugh as I watched her walk around like a cowboy in a western who'd spent too much time on a horse.

Try as I might, the laugh came out, despite her constant glares in my direction.

"You, stop. This is your fault."

I licked my lips. "Oh, baby, I take pride knowing I fucked you so long and hard you can't walk straight."

"There goes our beach walk." She threw her hands up. "What am I going to tell everyone? I pulled a muscle…saving a baby…from a runaway moose?"

I stood up and walked to her, showing off my smooth and natural gait—even with my bad leg.

"A moose? In Aruba?" I was to the point of cracking out to full-blown, hysterical laughter.

She stuck her tongue out at me. "It could happen."

I wrapped my arms around her and kissed her neck, giving it a little nibble that made her sigh. "I don't think we need to tell them anything. It was our honeymoon—they understand."

She slumped against me, her hands slipping up and around my shoulders. "I hate that we have to go home."

"Me, too."

After freshening up, we had our last meal on our paradise. The ominous cloud that always surrounded us drew closer after its week-long exile. I could almost see it in the distance—its gray skies and turbulent winds whipping around.

Instead of walking on the beach, we stopped at the point where the waves licked at our feet. It was enough for Lila and her still shaky legs. Her smile tugged at my chest, and I squeezed her hand, savoring each moment, knowing we'd be gone in a few short hours.

When we got through the trial, I could take her away again, even if it was just for a long weekend.

Anything to see her smiling like she was at that moment.

━━━━━━━━━━◦•◦❂◦•◦━━━━━━━━━━

Ten hours later, the elevator doors opened to the fourteenth floor, dropping us feet from our door. We were both tired from travel, but happy to be home. Suitcases in tow, I pulled out my keys and unlocked the deadbolt.

I stood there for a moment, staring at it, then turned to Lila.

"What?"

I leaned down and swept her off her feet and into my arms.

"Nate!" Her eyes were wide in surprise as her fingers clawed up my shirt and around my neck. "What are you doing?"

"Tradition." I smiled at her and walked forward, over the threshold and into our home.

She shook her head. "This is utterly ridiculous."

"Yes, it is. That's why I'm doing it." I grinned at her.

She rolled her eyes, but I caught the smile she tried to hide from me.

"You can let me down now."

"I don't think so."

I set her on her feet but had no intention of letting her get far. Stepping back out into the hall, I grabbed our suitcases and pulled them inside, locking the door behind me. Once done, I picked her back up, making her squeal again. We walked into the bedroom and I laid her down, crawling on top of her.

"Was this part of tradition?"

I brushed a strand of hair behind her ear. "No. I just wasn't ready to let you go."

She smiled and sighed. "There you go again, being all sappy."

I shrugged. "It happens. Besides, we need to christen our bed as husband and wife." I nipped at her lower lip.

She smiled at me, running her hands across my shoulders and down my arms. "I don't know. I'm kind of worn out from last night's adventures, not to mention the traveling."

"Then we can start our evening with a rejuvenating nap, followed by some pizza and a movie, and top it off with eating whipped cream off each other."

"Maybe some chocolate sauce?"

I grinned down at her. "I think we have some cherries as well."

"Vanilla ice cream." She licked her lips and batted her eyelashes at me. "Can I have a Nate sundae?"

It was my turn to lick my lips. "Only if I get to eat a cherry from your pussy."

Her eyes widened, pupils dilating as her hips flexed up, pushing against my thigh.

Dessert was never going to be the same.

CHAPTER 9

The alarm went off, blaring in my ear, and I groaned as I slapped my hand down on it. I stared at the time, sighing as I registered it was Monday and we really did have to get up.

Going back to work was rough. Being on vacation had been a heaven of sorts, and reality was brutal, making me appreciate every moment away that much more.

Granted, it wasn't all bad—Lila was with me. My *wife*.

"Come on, get up," I said as I yawned, swinging my legs over the edge of the bed and stretching.

She whimpered, face down in her pillow. "Only if you promise Starbucks."

I snickered. "Trust me, baby, I don't want to leave this bed either. And I promise we'll stop."

Her head tilted up and she huffed, blowing the wild strands of hair from her face. She was pouty and grumpy, making her fucking adorable and my urge to hug her ferocious.

With a growl and a graceless stiffness, I jumped on top of her. She squeaked, trapped beneath me. I nibbled at her neck, biting like an animal, making her writhe and me stiffen in another way.

I smacked her ass and pushed off the bed before I got carried away. "Come on, before I shove my cock in you and we miss the chance to get coffee."

Her eyes popped open wide and she jumped from the bed. Apparently coffee won out over my dick—what the hell?

A few minutes later, we were out the door and on our way. The smile never left her face. I'd never seen her smile so much.

Sitting at a red light, it dawned on me. "You're thinking about the Boob Squad, aren't you?"

"Maybe." Her voice was light and playful.

"Ready to rub it in their jealous noses that *you* are Mrs. Nathan Thorne."

"Maybe." Her smile grew wider.

"You don't have to admit it. I know you are, and so am I. Those insipid bitches piss me off." My fingers flexed on the steering wheel. "I hate the way they think they can treat you, and for no reason except that you're with me."

She shrugged. "Before you came, they pretty much ignored me and were never friendly. Then again, I didn't make it easy—I didn't want to get to know them."

"They're shallow cunts anyway." I shivered in disgust when I remembered Jennifer grabbing my hand and putting it up her skirt. I'd been inches from her pussy and whatever disease it held.

She nodded. "Pack mentality, with Jennifer at the helm."

I snorted. "*She* is the worst of them, followed up by Tiffany."

Lila laughed. "Oh, yes, Tiffany trying to seduce you in the copy room. That was priceless."

I quirked my brow at her. "You saw that?"

She nodded. "Yeah, I stuck around, waiting to see if you needed rescuing."

I shook my head and brought her fingers up to my lips, placing a kiss. She never failed to surprise me. Or turn me on.

By the time we arrived, she was buzzing with energy, staring down at the rings on her fingers. I glanced at mine, still getting used to something being there after so long.

"I wonder if my new nameplate is up."

I wrapped my arm around her and pulled her close as we walked in the building. "Another way to stick it to them, huh?"

She nodded. "Oh, yeah. Plus, I love my new name. I want to scream it from the rooftops."

I laughed and kissed the side of her head. "You still need to get it changed legally."

"Yeah. I'm doing that tomorrow at lunch."

I quirked a brow as I held the door open for her. "I'm surprised you can wait that long."

She elbowed me in the ribs. "I figured there wouldn't be time today. I'm afraid to see what my desk looks like…and poor Owen. He hasn't been in the position long."

I pushed the call button for the elevator. "He can handle himself."

She pursed her lips, silent as the doors slid open and we stepped in. A loud sigh came out of her, and I looked down.

"What?"

"Yesterday we were on the beach. I want to go back."

The elevator slowed to a stop and the doors opened to our floor. I took a moment to lean into her. "Soon."

"Tomorrow?"

I chuckled as I grabbed her hand and started walking down the hall. "Not quite that soon."

Of course, turning the corner would put us right in front of the fucking BS bitches—some of their cubes were right in the hallway. I fucking hated seeing the lust light up their eyes, then turn to disdain when they noticed Lila. Then again, I'd rather have them not look at us at all.

"Another vacation? Jeez, Delilah, I'm surprised Mr. Holloway still has you on." The vile skank known as Jennifer rolled her eyes.

The other diseased one, Tiffany, held her hand up to her mouth, as if we wouldn't hear her. "You know she's only still here because Nathan was his son-in-law."

My eye twitched as my jaw tightened and flexed. When did my past start circulating? We were already water cooler gossip, but my relationship with Jack had been kept quiet.

"It's none of your business how I use my vacation time. I have a lot saved up over the years, and still plenty to go—I'll use it how I want to." Lila was cool and collected, and the venom in her voice turned me on.

My fingers flexed on her hip. I loved to see her fight back—it was so fucking sexy. She wasn't weak, no matter what that shithead or the bitches in front of us thought.

They rolled their eyes. "I'm surprised you have any left after all the time you took off last year."

Lila shook her head before narrowing her gaze on them. "You really are the stupidest bunch of rat-pack bitches, aren't you? I was hit by a car, unable to take care of myself, let alone work. That classifies as sick time and medical leave. Company policy allows a certain number of weeks to be taken with half pay in the event you are unable to work for medical reasons. Vacation time is not used for medical leave."

She glared at them as she explained in terms their collagen-filled brains might understand. I cringed and backed up when Jennifer puckered her lips at me. Fuck, if her lips got any bigger, they were going to explode. It was bad enough she put her hands on me and shoved her breasts in my face every fucking chance she got, but there was no way I'd want those monsters near me.

The BS bitches were tsking and getting riled up and yammering—pissing me off. It was too fucking early to listen to their squawking. I'd had enough.

I grabbed the back of Lila's head and turned her to me, fisting her hair. My other hand grabbed on to her jaw as I devoured her lips with mine. I turned, pressing her against the wall as I shoved my tongue in her mouth, claiming her as mine, hips thrusting as I practically fucked her in front of them.

It made me remember our honeymoon, just two days prior when I had to lay claim to her in front of a bunch of idiots who were trying to buy her a drink at the pool bar. I kissed her harder, deeper, fucking her mouth with my tongue. She was whimpering and moaning, her hands gripped tight on my lapels.

I pulled back, panting, happy at the complete desire and want on her face. I looked over to the bitches, their stunned expressions making me want to laugh.

"My *wife*." More than one of them gasped in shock, apparently unaware what had transpired the week before. "I don't want anyone but her, so stop trying to tear her down to make yourselves feel better or think you have a chance at getting to me. Women like you make me sick."

"You can't!" Jennifer screamed out, jumping up from her seat.

My spine straightened, and I turned to face them, glaring down at them. Tiffany's eyes widened and she scurried back behind the cube wall. Kelly, the least aggressive of the bunch, sat down in her seat when my head cocked in her direction, scooting it back to her desk.

"What can't I do?" My voice was even, smooth. From their shuddering, it also had the desired chilling effect. "I've been fairly tolerant of your advances, but your bleached brain doesn't seem to grasp that I am in a relationship and therefore unavailable. You have chosen not to respect that, and are no better than an insect, in my view."

Jennifer was defiant, yet to be broken. "She's an insect." Her lip curled up in insolence as she looked at Lila.

I stepped forward, looming over her and flashed my left hand so their leader could see. "I asked Lila to marry me, to be my wife. I wanted to marry her, to have her with me forever, to have her body on mine whenever and wherever I want. Not you. Never any of you. Only her."

Jennifer's jaw jutted forward and her arms crossed over her chest. "So, what you're saying is you married your whore."

My eyes widened and my body vibrated.

"Jenn, I think you should stop." Kelly's voice was low, reserved.

"Say that again, skank. Call my wife a whore again and I'll—"

"You'll what?" She stepped forward, her body so close I could feel the heat of her devil fire on my skin.

"Have you fired."

A hand clapped down on my shoulder and I turned to Jack. The BS bitches all gasped, and Jennifer's mouth was gaping open, stumbling over words as she stepped away from me. I relaxed back toward Lila, my muscles uncoiling at her touch.

"M-Mr. Holloway, welcome back." Jennifer blinked at him, a bead of sweat forming on her brow.

"Hmph. I don't see how getting accounts of you threatening another employee while I was away, witnessing the beautiful wedding of Nathan and Delilah on the beach, as much of a welcome."

She shook her head desperately. "No, sir, I didn't do anything like that."

Jack rocked back on his heels and stared at her. "I don't much like emails like that while I'm away on vacation. Especially when they are from your supervisor's supervisor with multiple accounts from different women in the office stating they'd been attacked by you." Jennifer's face paled and she sunk back. "Make sure your schedule is clear this afternoon, Miss Watson."

"Y-yes, sir."

"Now, I believe you all have work to do." He smiled at them with an almost eerie calm.

They all slunk back to their cubes, pretending to work—something I still wasn't convinced they ever accomplished.

Jack turned to us and beamed. "I'm missing that beach about now." He laughed as he patted my back and walked us down the hall.

"Thanks, Jack. I was about to lose it."

Jack nodded. "I noticed. You didn't even hear your wife calling your name and tugging on your arm."

I looked over to Lila, who nodded. "I was afraid you were going to punch her."

I sighed and pulled on my neck. "I almost did." I glanced at Jack. "Was that true?"

Jack smiled and leaned close, looking around to make certain no one overheard. "There have been whispered complaints going on from some of the senior staff for some time. While we were away, Owen took it upon himself to detail their actions. Some of it was on video. He emailed Stanley Wick, stating that her supervisor refused to take action and it was upsetting many of his coworkers."

Lila was right—Owen could hold his own. I laughed.

"Stanley looked into it. Seems Jennifer has been…coercing good progress reports from her supervisor, Daniel."

Lila scoffed at the news. "Doesn't surprise me in the least, especially after watching the way she went after Nate."

Jack looked around again. "David and I have taken an interest in the matter, especially seeing as a supervisor was involved and in a way that violates many company policies."

I looked at Jack when he referenced his brother—the other Holloway in the company name. "I thought David retired."

"He still pokes around from time to time, keeping tabs. Stanley contacted him first, since I was away." We stopped in front of Lila's door and Jack held out his hand, shaking mine before taking Lila's. "Have a good day, you two." He turned to leave, then looked back. "I'll keep you apprised of the situation, seeing as you both are involved and have had altercations. We'll probably need to meet with each of you later."

I nodded. "Sounds like a plan." I pulled Lila close as he walked away. She looked up at me as she leaned in, arching into me.

"Ahem."

We blinked at each other and peeked into the office. Owen was peering over his monitor, staring at us. "If you're going to make out, can you do it somewhere else?"

"Ha." I flipped him off and leaned down for one last succulent kiss to get me through the day.

It was hard to let her go, to be separated from her. She pushed away with a reluctant sigh and headed to her desk, a deep frown as she looked over all the files covering the top.

"Hey, thanks, Owen." I tipped my chin at him.

He looked up at me and smirked. "For what?

I nodded in agreement to his sneaky maneuvers and gave him a thumbs up. "You're all right, man." I looked back to Lila and kissed the air at her. "Have a good day, Mrs. Thorne."

She beamed at me. "You too, Mr. Thorne."

CHAPTER 10

Later that day, I worked my way through an easier case file, when my email pinged with a new message from Lawrence, the prosecutor in Adam's case. My eyes scanned over the message, and I cursed. Not news I needed to hear after such a wonderful week in paradise.

My knee bounced as I stared at the screen. The news was fucking up all of our hopes. It seemed that a dark cloud was now crashing down on us. I stood, throwing the door open and walking as fast as I could down the hall. I slammed my hand down on the open door, startling both the occupants of the large office.

Lila stared up at me. "Nate?"

"We need to take a break."

My agitation must have been obvious, because she nodded and locked her computer. She looked over to Owen as she grabbed her jacket and swung it on. "I'll be back."

My fingers tangled with hers as soon as she reached me, and I practically dragged her down the hall. I pressed the call button for the elevator over and over, but she didn't say a word. One finger slipped inside my wrist, followed by another, caressing the soft skin, and I settled down. It wasn't enough, but it helped.

By the time we arrived at the main floor lobby, I'd calmed down enough that I was no longer dragging her along behind me. I still kept a brisk pace, one she had a little trouble keeping up with for the few blocks down the street and around the corner to Starbucks.

I shuddered, a sickening feeling overcoming me every time I passed the intersection in front of the store. The memories always bombarded me—her totaled car, her blood, her lifeless body. There was no doubt I would never overcome the images—they were burned in my brain.

The door swung open as we approached, and I caught it, holding it open and guiding her in. We ordered our drinks and waited at the end of the counter.

She never said a word, never asked what was wrong. I looked down and caught her curious gaze. In the depth of her eyes, I swear I could see every question she wouldn't ask, and they were all laced in fear. I pulled her close and kissed her forehead, the action relaxing her a bit, and she blew out a long breath.

We found a small table and sat down. I didn't speak, taking a sip instead. As we sat there, the anger and agitation slowly slipped away. The email had gutted me, leaving me feeling helpless, unable to protect her from the devil that haunted her.

"I didn't know… I just found out, but they don't charge habitual anymore for anything other than drugs," I said, finally able to break the bad news.

Her face paled, and she dropped the cup from her lips. "Wha...what do we do now?"

I sighed and rubbed my face. "The prosecutor said he's going to throw everything he can at him. There are a couple of class D felonies and some lesser offenses."

"How much time is that?"

"Less than before." I shook my head. My body felt like it was weighed down by a lead ball on my chest. "Not for the rest of his life, which is *not* good enough for either of us." My anger began to boil at the thought of him on the loose, free to find her again. My jaw clenched, teeth grinding together. "It would be safer for him if he was in jail, because if I ever see his face in the world again after the trial, I *will* kill him."

Lila placed her hands over my balled up fists for a brief moment before standing. I looked up at her but didn't find the expression I expected. There was no fear. I'd just told her there was a possibility the man who'd tried to kill her more than once could be out in the world in a few short years, and she was smiling at me with tears in her eyes.

She sat down on my lap and grabbed my hands, wrapping my arms around her.

"Thank you," she whispered. Her hand cupped my cheek and her fingers caressed my skin, lighting the familiar tingle of warmth I always got from her touch.

My eyes closed and I leaned into her hand, sighing as she soothed the beast in me. "For what?"

"For loving me that much."

I blinked up at her. "Do you still not understand how much I love you? That I would do anything to keep you safe?"

"I do, but I also have my moments of doubt and disbelief. Fears that you're a dream and I'll wake up in hell again."

My grip tightened, pulling her closer. "I'm not a figment of your imagination. Do you really think your mind would create someone so fucked up?"

She massaged the back of my neck with her fingers, making me groan. "Maybe. Why wouldn't my mind think the perfect person for me is just as fucked up as I am?"

I smiled and leaned forward so that our foreheads were touching. "We are perfect together."

Her lips met mine, but not in the soft kiss I was expecting. Nails scratched at my neck as her tongue asked for mine. I moaned—she was changing my mood in a *very* unexpected way.

"We fit perfectly together physically as well," I said as she pulled away. Ideas of hauling her into the store's bathroom began milling around my head. My hand moved up her thigh, grabbing the flesh beneath.

Yeah, I could use a quickie.

She rolled her eyes. "Such a horny bastard."

"But I'm *your* horny bastard. And you should know, after all this time, what kissing me like that will do."

She smiled at me all innocent-like, her bottom lip trapped between her teeth. My head was spinning, all the blood from my brain draining down to my dick.

Fuck—the things she did to me.

Nothing told me how much better Lila was getting than when Noah, Lila's foster brother, opened the door and she hugged him. Granted, she'd known him for a long time and trusted him, was open with him in ways only myself and few others knew of. It really shouldn't have surprised me. Lila was reserved, except with those she trusted.

The only other time I'd seen him was that day with Adam, and I was too concerned with her to get a good look at him. Noah was average, overall—a little shorter than my six-two and about my weight as well. Dark brown hair was thick on his head, and his brown eyes were soft as he looked down at her.

When a short little brunette came to the door, I was shocked when Lila wasted no time wrapping her arms around her as well. It was obvious I didn't know everyone who made up her very short list.

"Nathan, this is my wife, Camilla," Noah said.

I held out my hand but was knocked back by the small woman practically tackle-hugging me. "It's so wonderful to meet the man who was able to open up our Lila." She pulled back, smiling at me.

I blinked at her, too stunned to find words. Lila wrapped her hands around my arm and kissed my shoulder.

Noah ushered us into the living room, offering up drinks as we went, and based on his tone months ago, I knew I'd need one.

"Thanks," I said as I took a bottle of beer from him. A squeal drew my attention, and I turned to find Lila and Camilla going through the wedding photos we'd brought with us.

"You look so beautiful," Camilla said to Lila. "I wish we could have come, but with the twins, money's tight."

"It's okay. It would have been great if you could have made it."

Camilla sighed, a wistful look on her face.

"She wanted to go so bad," Noah said from next to me, drawing my attention back to him. "But Mari was just in the hospital for a lung infection. Medical bills were and *are* piling up. Plus, there was no way I could get off with the short notice."

"No need to explain. I know you would have dropped everything to be there for her."

He stared at her, watching. "She's changed so much in the last year, and I know that's all due to you."

"Even I can see the change." I glanced over at her and smiled. Damn. She was so beautiful when she was smiling and at ease.

"It's so much better than the sickly skinny, mousy girl who ran from the room as soon as Armando or I entered."

My teeth mashed together. "After seeing the monster, I can understand why."

Noah nodded. "She still had the bruises and cuts when she came to live with us." I turned to him, and his eyes seemed far away. He turned to me, back to the present, and sighed. "Her arm was in a cast, and she favored her left side. It took over a week for me to hear her voice because she wouldn't speak. Even though she was safe, she was afraid she'd be hit."

I was reeling, my hand tightening on the bottle. She'd alluded to what Noah said, but never delved into it.

"Fuck… Dealing with walking on eggshells all the time, I have no clue how she could stand to be near my ass." I blew out a breath. "I was a bomb waiting to explode, only to detonate and recharge."

He took a sip as he contemplated. "The difference with you is that Lila knows what makes good and what makes evil. She could tell you were good long before she knew it. When she first came to us, her reactions were due to habit rather than fear. Granted, there was fear, but more because of the unknown."

My gaze flickered back to her. "It's amazing she had the strength to get herself out. Most don't."

"No, they don't, but Lila's an observer. That last attack only proved to her that if she didn't get out, it would be no time before she was in a shallow grave and labeled a runaway. She was never going to get away—he'd never let her."

The thought sickened me, even more so since she said okay to starting a family. Her hesitancy made more sense—she never thought she'd live long enough for a future. Her youth wasn't about popularity contests or the clothes she wore. It was about survival. Getting through one day in order to wake in another. Every day since probably felt like borrowed time, so she never dreamed.

It was like Jack said—going through the motions, but not living.

I wanted to go to the jail and beat her fucking stepbrother with a crow bar, bash his skull to a pulp, then drive out to the fucking shack in the middle of nowhere that she grew up in, cut off her father's balls, and burn it to the ground with him and his bitch wife inside.

The beast liked that idea.

Five babies. Grace miscarried four, and the fifth was lost in the accident. I'd lost five of my own, while he was helping his only one into an early grave.

"She doesn't talk about that time, at least not in this much detail."

He nodded. "I figured, but I also felt these were things you need to know. I can tell you know her better than anyone, but at the same time, you're missing key pieces. Her scars weren't a one-time thing. Adam is sick and twisted, out for her blood. He would have killed her, if you hadn't gotten there."

"I know." I swallowed and dropped my head a little as my stomach twisted.

"The trial is going to be very rough on her. What I told you is going to come up. Every haunted memory of each hit, slap, threat… It'll all come out."

I glanced up from my beer. "You've been through this before."

He stared at me and pursed his lips before letting out a sigh. "I put my father in jail for life."

My head bobbed up and down. "Lila said you were in a similar situation."

Noah stared out across the room, then took a sip. "He beat me and my mother all the time. When I was fourteen, he finally hit her so hard it killed her. I lost it. All my life he'd been taller than me, but at that time, we were the same. He was stronger, but I was still able to beat him unconscious."

"So sorry."

He shrugged. "It's over and done. Now, I have a beautiful wife and kids. I only wish their grandmother was alive to see them. It'll get better with time."

"It's going to be rough over the next few months, but I can't wait until the trial is over."

Noah's expression changed, and his eyes flickered to Lila, worry filling his face. "The danger isn't over then." I tensed, remembering one of the reasons we were here— Noah had news on the Marconi. "They're still watching you."

I blew out a breath and pulled on the back of my neck. "Has it been recently?"

Noah nodded. "There are some dirty cops out there that are more interested in money. There's a big case being launched against him, so he's got tails on everyone involved in the case."

"But I'm not involved."

"No, but who has the most information against him? Who does he still hold a grudge against?"

"Fuck." I understood then—we would never be safe.

CHAPTER 11

"That's it, Nathan!" Jared, my instructor, said, slapping his padded, gloved hands together. "Again."

Left, right, left, elbow, knee—breathe and repeat. Ten times each side. I was counting in the front of my mind, but in the back I was going over everything Noah had told us over dinner.

Dirty cops were being bribed by Marconi to turn a blind eye and destroy evidence in a new case against him. He'd hired men to follow around those involved in the case, including me. The longer I thought about it, the more my anxiety grew, because they could already know about my marriage.

I'd put Lila in danger.

I punched at Jared's gloved hand, channeling the crippling fear that was starting to creep in. Over and over, harder and harder I threw my body against him. My muscles protested, but I couldn't stop—I needed the outlet before I spun out. I couldn't hear anything but the thoughts rattling around in my head.

Would they come after us? Would I be able to protect Lila? What happened if I couldn't?

My fist slammed hard against Jared, knocking him back. "Damn, Nate. Can you even hear me?"

My lungs were burning from harsh, labored breaths. "Sorry," I managed to get out between pants.

"Man, what is wrong with you tonight?" he asked, undoing the straps on my gloves and pulling them off.

Sweat poured down my face, and my chest constricted until a strangled noise was released, tears filling my eyes.

What if I lost Lila?

My knees gave out, and I fell hard to the ground. I cried out in pain when I hit the concrete floor below me, but it was nothing compared to the pain in my chest.

Fuck.

I couldn't deal with a fucking panic attack, so I tried to calm myself.

Jared kneeled down next to me, his hand on my back. "What can I do?"

My airway was constricting. "M-my w-wife."

The world was closing in again, the snake around my body squeezing tighter.

"Nathan?" Lila's voice cut through the dark fog. She wasn't there, and it took me a moment to realize Jared was holding the phone to my ear. "Baby, are you okay? Jared just called me. Do you have your meds with you?"

Hearing her voice was enough to halt the panic attack that was seizing me. My chest expanded, allowing for a deeper breath. It began to ease off—my vision started to clear and my muscles uncoiled.

"Nate, say something."

"S-something."

She let out a strangled giggle on the other end of the phone. "Is it getting better? Do you need me to come get you?" Keys jingled in the background.

"I just needed to hear your voice." I took the phone from Jared and sat back on my haunches. Looking around the room, I found more than one person staring at me, aside from my trainer. "I'll be fine."

There was silence on the other end, and I knew she was worried. "Is it about what Noah said?"

I ran my free hand over my face. "Yes."

"We'll get through whatever happens," she said.

"As long as we're together, right?"

"Right."

I blew out a breath. "I'll be home soon."

"Okay. I love you."

"Love you, too." I ended the call and took a bottle of water from Jared's hand. "Thanks."

"No problem. You good now?" He patted my shoulder.

"Yeah."

"So, this is one of those situations you were telling me about?"

I nodded. "Sorry."

He shook his head. "It's cool, man. I'm just glad you warned me when we started and gave me your girl's number. Fucking freaked me out."

I scoffed. "And that was mild."

He stood up and held out a hand to help me up. "We'll call it a night. Go home and relax. Pick it back up on Thursday?"

I clapped onto his hand and hauled my ass up off the floor. "Sounds like a plan."

I grabbed my stuff and headed out, driving as fast as I could, happy to get home to my wife. My hands ached to touch her. Only she provided the peace to calm the storm within me. The beast prowled back and forth, restless for her soothing touch.

As soon as I parked the car, I was in the lobby, waving hello to Mike and calling for the elevator. My hand tapped on my thigh, nervous energy coursing through me. I fumbled with my keys as soon as the doors opened and burst into our condo.

I threw my bag on the ground, locking the door behind me, and went running to find Lila. My foot caught on the floor, nearly tripping when I rounded the wall into the living room.

Standing in the middle of the room was my wife, wearing nothing other than the sexy little set I bought her for Christmas.

"Fuck." My cock immediately rose to attention. The black and purple lace of her bra contrasted against her pale skin. She turned, a little minx smile on her face, and showed off her fuck-perfect ass.

I groaned. Yeah, her ass would make me feel better. Tight and snug around me, squeezing me, pulling out every last drop I had to give.

It only took three steps to be on her. I grabbed onto her hips and pulled her back, hard. My mouth latched onto her neck, my teeth nipping at the skin beneath.

"You will do as I say, and you will fucking enjoy it." Power poured through me as the beast took control, ready to take her, fucking pound her.

She moaned and pushed her ass back against my cock. "What do you want me to do?"

I pushed on her back with my hand and she leaned forward, resting against the arm of the couch. My fingers grabbed onto her hair and pulled. My sexy girl moaned. I fucking loved that I could let go, and she enjoyed it as much as I did.

"I want you to be my dirty little slut. I'm going to fuck you hard." My free hand ran along her hip and over the curve of her ass. "I'm going to squeeze into this tight ass, and you're going to milk all the come from my balls."

I pushed the lacy material aside, and slipped a finger into her already wet pussy. When I moved to press against the tight opening I was about to bust into, there was something blocking me. I leaned back and looked down.

"Fuck!" I got even harder at the image of the sparkling purple jewel on the end of the stainless steel butt plug I'd gotten her, sitting where her fuck-tight hole was. "Already worked yourself open a bit, I see."

I'd bought it to go with the set she was wearing, and I'd eagerly waited to see it peeking at me from between her cheeks. Her timing couldn't be more perfect.

It took every bit of restraint to not just pull it out and push my dick right in without prepping her more, but I

111

wasn't that kind of an asshole. Just the garden variety with a hard dick and a craving for an insanely tight ass.

Fuck, I needed some lube, because I wasn't going to get her as far as she needed. I pulled on the end, shuddering as I watched her stretch around the widest part. When the tip was on the verge of coming out, I drove it back in all the way. I stared down in perverse fascination as I moved it out again.

I looked down at my leaking cock, begging to be pressed between her ass cheeks. It was trying to get out of my shorts, dripping to be surrounded by her. She was so fucking tight that I couldn't think about anything but the sight and memory of my head popping through her tight ring of muscles.

She let out a sexy whimper sound and relaxed into the pumping toy in her ass.

As if she knew what I was thinking, her hand reached behind her, the bottle of lube in her palm.

"Fuck, yes," I hissed, releasing her hair and taking it from her.

In my impatience, I yanked her panties down to her knees, then pulled my shirt off and tossed it to the ground.

I pushed two of my lubed fingers inside. I had to feel exactly how tight and ready she was. I sucked in a tight gasp when her ass pressed back into my hand. The deeper I went, the more she seemed to pull my fingers inside her.

It was fucking perfect—my fingers disappearing inside her.

With my other hand, I stroked my cock. I couldn't take anymore—I was going to come all over the backs of her legs.

112

"What was that?"

"I didn't say anything," she said, her voice hoarse.

I leaned over, bit her shoulder blade, and then I was right fucking there, slicked up and ready to decimate her ass—the hole I worshiped more than my very heartbeat in that moment.

"It's not going to be gentle—more like a two-bit whore," I said in warning as I lubed up my cock.

One hand held onto her hip while the other gripped my cock, lining up and pressing against her slightly gaping but tight asshole. She whimpered a little—my cock was bigger than the plug. I was bad in my need and continued on. Lights flashed in my eyes, a strangled breath escaping as I made it through the her fucking tight muscles and halfway in.

It was the escape I needed, washing over me as her body crushed around mine in tight, cock-strangling bliss. My hips rocked, pushing my cock further in, curses flying at the mind-numbing pleasure that enveloped every cell as she moved up and down my shaft. With each thrust, I pushed harder, faster, driving my way to the release I desperately needed.

I looked down to watch her spread around my cock as I plunged in. The sight made me shudder, glued to the hypnotizing view. Fuck, it was perfect. Goddamned exquisite.

"Such a good girl." My fingers tangled in her hair, pulling her head back. It was the perfect leverage needed to pound her hard.

I needed to fuck her into oblivion. Destroy her—destroy us both.

I yanked back on her hair as I thrust forward, slamming hard, pushing her into the arm of the couch. It was relentless fucking, the friction on my dick driving me harder and faster. Every muscle was tense, every nerve tingling as I let go and took what I needed.

I released her hair, both hands bearing down on her hips, holding her still. I couldn't stop plowing into her or even slow down. There was nothing in me, my mind fuzzy, with only the need to come driving me.

A shudder rolled through me, every muscle coiled tight. My hips slammed hard against her, jerking as I exploded. I shook with each spurt firing off.

Pure bliss and white, mind-numbing euphoria.

Peace.

CHAPTER 12

Ever since we'd talked to Noah, I'd been on edge. My life was turning into a happy place again, but the threat I lived with for years was reawakening, trying to ruin it all. The vibrating anxiety pumped through my veins again, and the beast inside me prowled, growling at me to take Lila and run.

Matters were made worse when an old, familiar tingling sensation from someone watching me reared their forgotten head. I wasn't certain, but it wasn't the first time since the New Year it'd happened, and now I knew why.

Lila's eyes watched me, probably waiting for me to burst. Not that I could blame her—*I* knew I was losing control. I could only guess how I looked on the outside. It was so bad that Darren wanted me to try meditation.

Meditation.

Fuck that. They only meditation I needed was my dick in Lila's pussy. It was the only way to calm my ass down. Unfortunately, getting off inside and on my wife wasn't providing the relief it used to. I wasn't getting the mind-wiping hours of clarity that normally accompanied it. I had a suspicion the added stress of the trial was the culprit and was making me a bigger time bomb than ever before.

I rubbed my face as I stared at the computer screen. The client was driving me mad, reminding me about the good that was working on contracts—no customers. Their plight seemed trivial to the shit-storm in my life.

There was a knock on my open door before Drew walked in and sat down in front of me, a stupid grin plastered on his face.

"Man, what is up with you?" He'd been acting strange ever since we got back.

"Dana," he said with a smile.

My brow twitched, and I stared at him. "Who's Dana?"

The lovey-dovey look in his eyes cleared, and he leaned forward. "The woman I met in Aruba."

He gave me a look like I should've known who he was talking about.

"You met someone in Aruba?"

He chuckled and leaned back. "Yeah, you only had eyes for Lila and were blind to the rest of us."

"Can you blame me?" I asked. He shook his head. "Are you doing a long distance relationship?"

He shook his head. "Kinda, but not the distance you're thinking. She lives in Bloomington. She's an English professor at IU."

"All right, I can see you're dying to tell me, so spill." I sat back in my chair and watched the lovesick fool in front of me.

"She's perfect. I mean, beautiful and intelligent. When she smiles, everything lights up." His own smile brightened, and I wanted to look for my sunglasses. "When I'm with her, nothing else matters. It's like we're the only two people in the world."

"All that in just a few weeks?"

Drew gave a shy smile. "Actually, she was on spring break when we were in Aruba, and since we got back, we've seen each other almost every day."

"You drive down to Bloomington every day?" It was an hour and a half drive from the north side where our office was, which was about the same distance from his house.

He shook his head. "No. She doesn't have class in the afternoon a couple times a week, so she comes up here on those days. It's a little hard to go on dates, so we kind of fell into a living together type situation."

My brow shot up, and I chuckled. "Damn, that was fast."

He shrugged. "It's what we have to do."

"Things are going good, then?"

He nodded. "She's amazing. Absolutely…wow. I've never felt like this. It's kind of scary." I laughed a bit, Drew's face turning from spacy and glowing to glowering. "Shut up."

I held my hands up. "No, man, good for you. That's awesome. I just never knew you were such a sap."

He grimaced and flipped me off. "I thought you of all people would understand. You know, with your obsessive love of Lila."

"Obsessive love?" I thought on it for a moment, then nodded. "Okay, you got me there."

"If it wasn't for the fact that she feels the same and I know you, I'd fear for her safety."

I glared at him. "What the fuck does that mean?" Did he really think I'd hurt Lila?

"It means you're a jealous asshole who is super possessive of her. Borderline psycho."

"Fuck you." I leaned back and blew out a breath.

"Just stating the truth."

"Yeah, I fucking know," I grumbled. I hated when people pointed out my negative personality traits. They always made me wonder if I was always like that, or if I really was a completely different person than I was before the accident. Was I a blend of the two—Nathan and the beast?

Drew pulled me from my thoughts. "What's the plan for lunch?"

I glanced down at the clock on my monitor—it was only ten, still almost two hours before our normal lunch time. My gaze moved to the open chair next to Drew, and I stared knowing what I wanted for lunch.

"Not sure. I have a meeting at one I have to get ready for, so I may just get something to go and eat in here."

"Okay." He pushed against the arms of the chair and stood. "Let me know if something changes."

"Will do."

The moment he was gone, I pulled out my phone. **Lunch. My office, 11:30. No panties.**

I had a little over an hour to finish up my preparations before what I was hungry for arrived. Before I dug in, I pulled out some menus from my desk drawer. Flipping through, I found Lila's favorite Mediterranean place. They weren't open yet, but they took online orders ahead of time. I set up an order for eleven and shoved the folder back into my desk.

One hour to finish up before my meals arrived.

<hr>

The smell of grilled chicken permeated my office as I finished up my contract and waited for Lila to arrive. What to eat first warred in my mind—gyro, or Lila.

At that moment, the door to my office opened and Lila stood before me. Her face was flushed and her legs were rubbing together.

"Sit." I pointed to the chair in front of my desk. She didn't hesitate. The air was thick with both our wants. "Spread your legs."

Again, she didn't hesitate, only taking an extra moment to draw up the hem of her dress to her hips and scoot to the edge of the chair. The gained movement allowed her to open her legs fully, exposing her panty-less, bare, glistening pussy.

Fuck.

All I needed was her.

I continued to stare at her, watching the effect take hold of her. She was flush, a small, whining moan slipping from her as her hips tilted. Her mouth was parted and her eyes were heavy, locked on me.

119

"Stop teasing me."

I licked my lips. "You're the one teasing me, showing off your wet pussy."

"Because you told me to."

"That's right. I like it when you do what I say and having you sit there, getting turned on, begging me to come to you."

She moaned, her hand slipping down, finger brushing over her clit.

I pushed my chair back and stormed over to her, slapping her hand away. She blinked up at me and whimpered.

"Did I say you could touch?" I glared at her hand. "Never forget that pussy is mine to play with."

She looked up at me in glorious want. "Fuck, Nate, please."

"Please what?" I was almost snarling, losing myself in the game.

"Play with me." Her voice was barely above a whisper.

My teeth clenched. "Ask nicely. *Beg.*"

She bit her finger, hips moving, whimpering. "Please, play with me."

"Why should I?" I palmed my cock, which was a fucking rock from watching her undulating hips and wet pussy calling. "Tell me, my little slut, why should I play with you?"

"I'll do whatever you want."

I arched a brow at her as I smacked the inside of her thigh. "You'll do that anyway."

A high rushed through me, my spine tingling. I fucking loved when she stalled following directions. It made me want to punish her more, and I knew that was exactly why she did it. It was our game, our high, the way we pushed each other further.

"Please! I've been a good girl."

I quirked my brow at her. "What about that barista that was flirting with you this morning?"

Her brow scrunched in pain and worry. "He was only being friendly."

I smacked the inside of her thigh again, groaning when her pussy twitched. "He was being too friendly, and so were you."

Fuck. The game was spiraling out of control, and so was I. I'd only intended to work her up a bit more before eating her out. Now I was seconds away from flipping her over, spanking her ass, and fucking her so hard the entire building would know.

She licked her lips as she stared at the outline of my hard dick. "I'm sorry. Please let me make it up to you. I'm a good girl. Let me show you."

A shudder rolled down from my head to my toes. "Grip the back of the chair and don't let go."

She followed my directions again, and I knelt down between her thighs. I reached out and rubbed her clit with my thumb. She arched her hips up into my hand. I could smell her thick, needy scent. It drove me wild, making me need her—the strongest aphrodisiac.

I pressed down on her abdomen. "Keep your hips still."

She nodded, and I bent down, licking all the way up her slit and sucking her clit in between my teeth. Her head was tilted back as she gasped for air. That was just the teaser.

I pressed against her clit with my thumb, then opened up her pussy lips with my other hand before covering her with my mouth. My tongue savored her taste and I dug in deeper, licking and sucking all I could get.

High-pitched squeaks came from her, back arching and her thighs closing in around my head. I pulled back and pushed her legs open and down with my forearms, pressing them against the arms of the chair.

"Stop moving." I pinched her clit, and she bit down on her lower lip.

Moving back down, I stuck my tongue as far in her pussy as I could. My cock was weeping, begging to replace my tongue, but I wasn't done yet. I scraped my teeth against her clit, flicking it with my tongue.

"Do you want to come?"

She whimpered at me. "Yes."

"You're going to come on my face, so I can taste and smell you all day long. *Then* I'll fuck you."

Her pussy was all swollen and pink. It took everything in me to keep my dick in my pants. I flicked her clit with my finger, picking up speed. Her head thrashed from side to side. I continued and moved back to licking and sucking her juices. My fingers dug into her thigh, her muscles tensing, back arching so much I was having trouble keeping up the pace.

With a wail her pussy twitched, and her whole body spasmed under me as she came. Her juices flooded my face, and I drank her up. Eating her out had me so fucking hard that pre-come leaked onto my pants.

I licked my lips and sat back, deftly pulling at my belt to get my pants down enough to get my cock out. Her pussy was soaking wet, letting me easily slide in. There wasn't a lot of friction, but she was still tight from coming and fluttered around me as she built up for a second orgasm.

Quick, no frills, just my cock pistoning in and out until I fired off.

"Fuck." My balls pulled up tight, and I shuddered. I dug my fingers into her hips as I slammed into her.

Lila cried out, her body shaking, on the verge of coming again. I thrust hard a couple more times, and she arched against the chair and clamped down on my cock. I pushed all the way in and held my cock there, jerking with each spurt.

Once done, I looked down at Lila and snickered between breaths.

"You're a mess."

She flipped me off, then gave me a lazy smile. "Best lunch break ever."

CHAPTER 13

I chuckled to myself, earning a quizzical look from Lila.

"What?"

"Your hair is a beautiful fucking mess."

She reached up and her fingers combed through it, trying to straighten it and get out the knots I'd made. My wife looked thoroughly sexed—a look I loved to see her wear. Unfortunately, we were at the office and had to at least look presentable before we opened the door to the sixth floor conference room.

The quiet little corner became our occasional afternoon delight spot. With the trial closing in, we both needed the physical reassurance and calm that came from touching each other.

"I was thinking about having roasted chicken breast and red potatoes for dinner."

I thought it over as I pushed the tails of my dress shirt back into my slacks. "Sounds pretty good. Maybe some salad as well. My stomach hasn't been right since that weird Indian place Drew took us to on Monday." She smiled, laughing to herself. "What?"

She shook her head. "Nothing."

I threw my jacket back on and walked over to her, pulling her to me. "It's not nothing."

She bit her bottom lip, a blush creeping along her cheeks. "We're just weird."

"We're weird?"

"I mean, I don't watch sitcoms, but I've seen some when I dated Drew and spent time with Caroline. The things the people talked about were often strange to me." I quirked my brow at her, and she sighed. "You know I have warped perceptions on reality, and our conversation was oddly similiar to those shows. I didn't realize we'd become so mainstream and domesticated."

I laughed out loud. Normalcy was weird to her, and we were engaging in a normal, everyday couple conversation—the type we'd had hundreds of.

"Baby, we're married."

Her brow scrunched. "And?"

"And we're evolving as people and a couple. Life isn't only about the crap we've been through anymore. The everyday shit, sharing it, and living life is the new us."

"I didn't say it was bad, just…weird." She tucked her head. "And I kind of like it."

I wrapped my arms around her and held her close. "You'll get used to it, and it won't be *weird* anymore." She snuggled into my chest, a content sigh coming from her. "Dinner sounds great."

"You can make the salad."

I smiled and kissed the top of her head. "One of the few things I can make."

"You've gotten better at other things."

I nodded. "I have."

"You can make lasagna tomorrow."

"Mmm, that sounds good."

"Tomorrow. I'm making chicken tonight. Besides, we'll need to stop at the grocery store."

I opened the door and held it for her to walk through. One of the few locals of the floor passed by, giving us a knowing look.

I didn't care who knew. Was it unprofessional to have sex at the office? Hell, yes. Was that going to stop me? Not a fucking chance. Discreet was what we strived for, but sometimes it was inevitable that someone heard us.

"Your tie is messed up." She reached up and adjusted it as we rode the elevator back up.

We were walking down the hall back to her office when I noticed Caroline standing in front of Lila's office, tapping her foot with her arms crossed in front of her. What had her so pissed?

"My God, Nate, can't you wait a few hours until you get home?" She huffed as we neared.

I grinned at her. "No."

She rolled her eyes, then pointed at her watch as she looked at Lila. "Tick-tock, girl. We have lunch plans, and you're eating into them with your sexcapades."

"Oh, crap!" Lila looked down at her watch and headed into her office to get her purse and coat.

"Yeah, you forgot, didn't you?"

"No, time got away from me."

Caroline quirked her brow. "How long were you two getting it on?"

I checked out the time, doing the math of when we left. "We were pretty quick."

"Nate!"

I peeked in and saw that Owen had already left for lunch. "I know it's no secret from her, so stop acting embarrassed. Besides, baby making has no schedule." I grinned.

Caroline's head snapped to me. "Wait, what was that? *Baby* making?"

I glanced at Lila, who was glaring at me. Hadn't she told Caroline? Weeks had passed, and Caroline was out sick for a week in there, but I thought she would be the first person Lila told. Caroline gave me a "I hope you know what you're doing" look.

Lila sighed. "I was going to tell you about it over lunch."

"You sure as hell are."

"I'll see you later," Lila said as she gave me a kiss and headed down the hall.

Once they were out of sight, I headed down to my office. As soon as I entered, I slammed my head against the door. Was I forcing my desires for a family on Lila? Did she even want children, or was she placating me? There was the possibility that the trial on Monday was consuming her thoughts—perhaps that was why?

The answer was clear to that one. Her demeanor told me the stress of the trial was getting to her—hence the romp this morning. She was the one who called me to meet—an unusual occurrence.

I was hard.

Then again, I seemed to be hard all the time.

Fucking PTSD. It affected my mood, often in a bad way, and heightened my already high-demanding sexual needs. At its worst, I was an asshole who needed his dick wrapped in warmth twenty-four-fucking-seven.

Our addictive dependence on each other wasn't considered healthy, but it was what we needed to function. We craved each other to calm the storm within.

Getting off only gave me a moment of peace, but it was a moment.

I had to get it all out, because in the morning, I needed to be strong for Lila. The trial was starting, and my shit needed to take a back burner.

Staring at the TV, I palmed my cock as thoughts of fucking her unconscious took hold. She wasn't home. Her art class, or, as I liked to call it, separation-of-her-dependency-on-me class, was going on until eight.

Another fucking hour.

My cock couldn't wait that long. My balls ached and the head leaked, begging to explode. If I didn't get myself in check, she was going to come home to something destroyed, and that would make her worry. Then she'd let me fuck her until I felt better.

The problem with that scenario was I'd feel worse because I knew what she was hiding below the surface.

She couldn't hide from me.

The pain, the fear—it shook her to the core to an almost debilitating degree. Yet, she went on, putting on that damn face, telling me everything was all right when it fucking wasn't. It was a left-over defense mechanism that I didn't even think she realized she'd been doing for the past week.

My fist slammed down next to my side, and I yelled out a curse. Frustration didn't even describe my situation.

I wanted to be selfish. I was dying to push my cock into her mouth and fuck her face, her throat swallowing around me; to slam my cock in her pussy, making her cry out as I fucked her hard, releasing all of my pent up rage and fear; to feel her tight ass constrict around me. I wanted to tie her to the bed and pound into her over and over until she came so many times she passed out. Make us both forget what was coming.

My tongue swiped across my lips, muscles flexing as my hand opened and closed on the couch cushion. Hips, toes, hands—all curling in *need*.

To taste, to take, to *devour*.

I flipped the front edge of my shirt over my head and pushed my shorts down enough to pull my cock and balls out. The head was red and angry, my dick begging for Lila to make it all better. When was the last time I'd gotten off by my hand? It had been few and far between since I'd met her, so much so that my cock was practically trained to come from Lila and Lila alone.

I moved my hand up my shaft and hissed as I hit the underside of the sensitive head, setting up a slow, teasing, steady pace. It wouldn't take much to come.

I recalled some of our favorite escapades, one of my favorites coming to the forefront—the alleyway in Noblesville. The thrill of being seen, watching as my cock claimed her pussy...

I was lost on the edge of coming. Every muscle was so tight, statue-like as my fist flew up and down my cock. My mouth was open, eyes cloudy. I didn't hear her come in, but she stood before me, fuzzy.

The realization she was watching was too much. With a strangled cry, I tipped my head back and tightened my grip on my cock as the first pulsing shot from my balls exploded onto my stomach.

Everything was gone, quiet, except the ecstasy that filled me with each spurt that left my body. I pulled the last drops out and relaxed back into the couch, spent. My vision cleared, though my lids were still heavy as I tried to catch my breath.

Lila was still watching me. The beast was satiated, my muscles relaxed. I stared back at her. "Come here." I beckoned her over, holding out my hand.

As she got closer, I reached up and cupped her face, guiding her lips down to mine. It was soft, and through her touch, I knew sex wasn't what she needed.

I grabbed some tissue and wiped up the mess I'd made before pulling my t-shirt back down and tucking my cock away. Once that was done, I tugged on her arm, positioning her over my lap, straddling me. Her arms wrapped around my shoulders, while her head rested in the crook of my neck. It felt so good to have her close, but I needed closer, and I held her as tight as I could, breathing her in. I released my grip and swept my hand up, then down her back.

"How was art class?"

She shrugged in my arms. "It was okay. I'm not very good, though, so I think when it's up, I'll stop. Maybe find something else."

"Anything catch your eye?"

She hummed against my neck. "Not really. Maybe I'll just take more swimming or dance classes, just so I can keep up with you."

I kissed the side of her head. "You'll be caught up in no time."

She looked so down. "I really just miss being with you."

"I know. Me, too. But, I also understand why Darren wants us to have separate activities, even though I hate it."

She nodded. "I missed you."

"I missed you, too."

She heaved a sigh and sat back. The crushing anxiety that plagued her earlier in the day was gone, but what replaced it was almost as bad. It was like she was preparing for battle. Shutting herself down, closing in. The way her arms were held in tight and wrapped loosely around her waist told me everything.

I reached out and tilted her head up so I could look in her eyes. "Don't shut me out, baby." Tears started to pool in her eyes, and she wetted her lips before she looked down. "Hey, none of that. Look at me." The sight of tears brimming made my chest clench. "I love you, Lila, and I'm here for you. I know tomorrow is going to be difficult, but you're not alone anymore."

Her body jerked in my arms before a whine clawed its way out of her chest and broke into a sob. The sound tore at me, shredded me to pieces. There was nothing I could do. I felt helpless, and I hated the feeling. I wanted to take away all her pain, but had no clue how.

Tears streamed down her cheeks. "I need lovey hugs."

I drew her in and held her tight as she cried into my chest, letting out all of her fear. She was strong, but I also knew how fragile she was. My only hope was that the following days didn't break her.

CHAPTER 14

When the alarm went off, neither of us moved to turn off the blaring sound. We stared at each other, gathering up the strength to leave the bed. Knowing that as soon as the alarm was silent, we had to get ready.

She sighed and curled against my chest. I wrapped my arms around her, wishing I could keep her there—that she didn't have to go through what was coming.

The volume of the alarm grew to an almost deafening level, and I couldn't take it anymore. I slapped down on the snooze button to shut it up.

Five more minutes.

I went back to my position of trying to pull her inside me. When time was up, we reluctantly separated and moved to get up.

A low pressure front had come through overnight, and we both groaned in pain. The first steps were rough—my leg didn't want to move right. Another reminder of what lay beneath the scars all over my body. Lila was the same, and her hand covered the opposite wrist.

My whole body ached and was stiff. Mornings like this sucked and made an already difficult day that much worse.

We showered and got ready, our pace slower than normal.

Lila's eyes were clouded and unfocused. She wasn't ready for today, but she never would be. The day was a means to the end, and I'd be there, helping her get through it as best as the court would allow. Being a witness meant we'd be separated, testifying without each other in the room.

It was going to be a shit day, but we'd get through it together.

That was, if my ass didn't end up in jail for killing the fucker.

My blood still boiled over it, and the image burned in my mind. I honestly wasn't sure I could keep myself in check and the beast on a leash. Everything in my being wanted to beat the shit out of him, to break every bone in his body for everything he'd ever done to her.

I glanced over at her. The light was gone from her—she was just a shell—much like when we first met. Her hands shook as she pulled a shirt from its hanger and slipped it on. I stepped forward and helped her get it over her head, smoothing it down her waist.

"I can't do this," she said, looking up at me.

She was so afraid and so lost.

One of my hands sat on her waist while the other cupped her cheek. "You can. You're stronger. They can't hurt you. Don't let fears bring you down."

"What if my father is there? Bad enough I have to tell an entire court room what they did to me, reliving it over and over again as they dig in deep. Having to have my past brought up to all those people. But to deal with him as well?"

"I'll be with you."

She shook her head. "No, you won't. You'll be in another room. Cut off."

"No, not cut off. It'll only be a few feet and some walls between us, but I'll be there. You'll be able to feel me."

A tear slipped down her cheek, and I wiped it away. "I need to be able to touch you. How can I get through this day without you?"

"By remembering that by testifying, you're sealing his fate. You'll be able to say the words, knowing I'm not far away and that there are witnesses and a bailiff there to protect you from him."

She sniffed and drew in a shuddered breath, then nodded.

We finished getting ready and headed out. The drive was silent and a bit unnerving with how locked down Lila was. I reached out and took her hand in mine. Her fingers twined with mine, a long breath coming from her as she relaxed, even if it was just a little.

Her grip tightened as we walked up to the courthouse—a death grip of fear. Heading down the hall, we saw Lawrence, the prosecutor, standing in front of the courtroom, with Noah next to him.

Lawrence looked between us and settled on Lila. "Are you ready?"

She shook her head, her voice soft and small. "No, but I never will be."

He pursed his lips and nodded, then ushered us in.

She reached out and grabbed Noah's hand. He stepped forward, giving her a hug and kissing the top of her head. "I know. But it will get so much better after this. I promise."

She nodded, and we moved to find our seats.

I hated that we had to be at the courthouse so early, and hated that we spent the morning doing nothing but waiting as the jury was selected. Waiting to get the damn show on the road and get this the fuck over with so we could move on.

One less threat to deal with. One less monster on the streets.

There was no doubt in my mind he would go to prison. What I did waver on was if we could get all the major felony charges. Not getting one could mean around five or more years less on his sentence.

I didn't even get to see the cleaned-up version of Adam. A bailiff came for me. I wrapped Lila in my arms and kissed her hard.

"You'll be okay. I'm here."

The fear was clear in her eyes, but she nodded. Everything in me wanted to run away with her, to keep her from the pain, but it was a necessary evil. I was shuffled back to my "holding cell," Lila's fingers slipping through mine as we were led away to separate rooms.

⸺⸻••❖••⟨❖⟩••❖••⸻⸺

My knee bounced as I stared at the clock, watching as each second ticked by. It was almost five—they would end for the day, and I could see Lila again.

Fucking stupid rules that kept me from her. I'd never hated them before, because they were often to my advantage in my work, but it was a burning anger when they were forced upon *me*. A brief period at lunch was the only time I'd touched, seen, or talked to her since we'd arrived over eight hours earlier. I was crawling out of my skin knowing she was even in the same room as him, being grilled about all that he'd done to her.

The beast was exceptionally uneasy.

I stood, pacing, prowling the drywall cage those rules locked me in. Every cell in me was vibrating. My nostrils flared, and the urge to slam my fist into a wall was great. The pent-up energy was calling for me to destroy something.

If day one was this bad, how was I supposed to survive day two?

The door clicked open, and my eyes snapped up.

"They're done," my guard said.

He didn't need to tell me any more—I was out the door and headed down the hall. Walking wasn't fast enough, so I began running past people who gave me dirty looks, but I couldn't give two shits about what they thought.

Lila needed me, and I had to get to her.

I rounded the corner and slowed my pace as I approached the open doors of the courtroom. The few stragglers left behind were trickling out. Lila came into view, her head down and arms crossed as if she was holding herself together.

By the time her head rose, I was only a few steps away. She collapsed into my arms, completely drained.

"I've got you, Honeybear," I said as I locked her tight in my arms. My lips pressed against her forehead as my gaze rose.

A couple exited a few feet away, and the man looked in our direction. My eyes locked on his, and I tensed. Flames of hatred ignited and raged through me. I ignored the woman, because I knew instantly who he was. After all, he bore the exact same interesting gray-green eyes as my wife.

Stephen Palmer wasn't the image I'd drawn in my mind, but then again, I'm sure time and age had changed him. He was bald, and shorter than me. What once looked like a solid frame was thinner and weaker thanks to his near sixty-year age.

His lip curled up, utter disgust on his face as he looked at Lila.

A hand clamped down hard on my shoulder as the words "don't do it" were whispered in my ear. It was then I realized my whole body was tense, ready to storm down the hall and deck the bastard.

Noah was standing next to me, his gaze also locked on Lila's father and stepmother. Together we watched as they walked down the corridor and out of the courthouse.

Once they were out of sight, I walked Lila over to a nearby bench and sat down, moving her to my lap. My hand made soothing motions wherever they touched as I looked down at her. She wasn't crying, but I couldn't decide if that was a good or a bad thing. She looked completely beaten down.

Lawrence, the prosecutor, walked out of the courtroom and toward us, followed by Andrew. The rest of his team continued on down the hall and out.

"It was a hard day," Lawrence said as he stopped in front of us. "I'd order in and have a relaxing night. It's going to be another hard one tomorrow. "

"Is she done?" I motioned down to Lila.

He nodded. "We were able to finish up in time. Noah's went faster than I anticipated, leaving lots of time for her. You and Andrew are up tomorrow, along with the doorman"—he opened up the file in his arm—"Michael Cline."

"How do you think it went?" Drew asked. Sadness washed over his features as he looked down at Lila curled on my lap, not moving.

"I'm hopeful." Lawrence gave a slow nod, then sighed. I was caught in his sights, and he motioned in my direction. "A reminder—you are not to talk about the case tonight."

My lip twitched. Yes, I knew the rules, but I wasn't about to let Lila suffer until after the jury deliberated. She was my wife. It was in my job description as her husband to make her happy. Plus, I couldn't stand to see her so distraught.

Lawrence walked away, and I brushed Lila's hair behind her ear. "Are you okay?"

Her fingers flexed against my lapel and she turned further into my chest, her head resting in the crook of my neck. Little wisps of breath tickled my skin.

"You better just take her home," Noah said.

Drew held out his hand. "I'll go get your car."

I dug my keys out of my pocket and handed them over. "Thanks."

He nodded and headed down the hall.

My hand ran up Lila's arm, but she didn't react when I tickled the soft skin on the back of her arm. "She's so out of it."

Noah pulled out his cell phone and keys. "Run her a bath, get her to eat something, and remind her you're there. I'm sure she'll come out of it then."

"Will do."

"I'll see you in the morning."

I held out my hand. "Have a good night."

"You too." He smiled and shook my offered hand.

I stared after Noah, then looked back down to Lila.

"Come on, baby, let's get you home." I didn't make her stand. Instead, I snaked my arm under her knees and pulled her close as I stood.

Lips pressed against my neck as we walked, and the hand on my lapel loosened, wrapping around my neck. I smiled—she'd be fine. The day took a toll on her and she needed a recharge, but it hadn't damaged her. I worried about her, but I should've known by now how resilient she was.

Neither of us said a word the entire way home, which wasn't very far—we lived close to the courthouse. Her head rested on my shoulder as her arms wrapped around mine.

After parking the car, I picked her up again, her body limp. Mike saw us through the door as we walked up and held it open.

"Is everything all right, Mr. Thorne?" Concern was etched into his features. I'd always known that Mike had a fondness for Lila. He once told me how she reminded him of his daughter.

"It was a rough day, that's all." He walked with us to the elevator bay and pressed the call button for me.

Mike nodded in understanding. "Sorry I couldn't be there today—work and all."

"It's fine. We'll see you tomorrow."

Mike pursed his lips and hiked his belt up higher on his protruding beer belly. "I've never been in a courtroom before, but I watch a lot of court dramas."

My lips quirked. People always thought it was like what they watched, not remembering it was staged and they were actors. "It's not like what you see on TV. It'll be a lot like the deposition. They'll ask you a bunch of questions, and then you're done, only this time the audience is larger."

He nodded. "I just hope we get the guy put away forever. After what he did…" He trailed off, lost in the memory. I knew by his expression he felt guilty that Adam got past him.

The elevator arrived and we got on, Mike pushing the button for the fourteenth floor. "Lemme know if you need anything tonight, okay?"

I nodded. "Thanks. We'll see you later."

"Night."

The doors closed and the car jerked as we headed up. By the time we entered our condo, Lila was still unresponsive, so I sat her on the bed. I went into the bathroom and started the water in the tub, letting it fill as I pulled off my clothes.

I was down to my boxer briefs when I stopped and knelt down in front of her. "Lila, do you want to take a bath?"

No response. I sighed and pulled her arms through her jacket, then lifted her sweater over her head and through her arms. It was a good sign that she helped by lifting her arms and leaning back, giving me better access to take off her skirt.

I went to check on the water—it was full and steaming warm. I picked her up again and lowered her feet first into the water. She drew in a sharp breath when the hot water soaked into her skin, but she sat there, waiting.

I climbed in behind her, hissing at the temperature as well. Once I was all the way in, I pulled her back to relax against my chest. She was still so pliable and vacant. There was only one way I knew how to get through to her.

I scooped up the warm water and drizzled it on to her cool, air-exposed skin, wiping it around. One hand moved around her ribs, caressing her breast and pinching her nipples as it trailed to the front and down her abdomen. When she drew in a breath and arched against me, I knew I was on the right track.

I licked her neck, nibbling and kissing down to her shoulder. My fingers slid against her clit, and she jerked against me. I moaned as I found her pussy lips and spread them open, giving me access and pressing one finger inside.

She was warm and silky wet, making my breath go ragged and my cock rock harden at the thought of drowning in her. I pushed another finger in and her breath hitched as she arched against me, then relaxed.

My fingers slipped out, then back in, my thumb circling around her clit. I repeated it, moving faster, harder, teasing her as I pinched her nipples with my free hand. Her chest rose and fell in a staccato rhythm, her back arching further, pressing her harder against my hand as I sped up, pounding my hand against her pussy. Little guttural whimpers and moans slipped from her lips. Her eyes widened for a quick moment, then screwed tight.

I couldn't take it anymore—her reaction had me too wound up. I reached between us and began stroking my cock at the same speed I fingered her.

Water sloshed out onto the floor as my arms moved at a furious pace. I bit down on her shoulder and her body seized, pussy clenching around my fingers. She shook and shuddered against me as my body tensed, fist pumping furiously.

My jaw locked down harder, screaming into her skin as I exploded into the water. I jerked with each spurt, my mouth releasing her neck as my fingers slipped from her pussy.

I pressed my lips against the mark I'd made. It was deeper than usual and already an angry red, but it was my teeth—my mark. I loved to see her covered in me. It was hot, possessive—how much I needed to see it and have others see it.

She was *mine*, and nothing was going to take her from me.

Once I was calm, I leaned all the way back against the tub wall, hissing as I hit the cold portion of the tub that was not submerged in the water.

"Better?" I kissed her temple, and she tilted her head to look back at me. Our foreheads bumped as I slumped into her, happy to see life in her eyes again. Her hand cupped my cheek, and I leaned into her touch, not realizing how much I needed it.

"Thank you."

"That's what I'm here for—to take care of you."

Her head stretched up, and she pressed her lips to mine. "I'm here for you, too."

"We'll worry about me later." Fuck, she was so selfless when it came to me. "How was it today?"

She sighed and took my hands in hers, wrapping my arms around her waist. "It was so hard. I kept having flashes." She paused, slipping her fingers between mine. "But at least I got some satisfaction out of the whole ordeal."

"What was that?"

"When I had to state my name." She turned back to me and smiled. "Adam stood up and screamed out that I was a fucking whore when it registered that I'd gotten married."

My eyes widened and hope flooded my body. "And that reaction could only hurt his case."

She nodded. "Mm-hmm. It was hard to talk, to answer their questions, but his constant state of aggravation was noticeable to everyone, especially the jury. At another point, he called me a lying cunt."

I smiled wide. "Shit, his defense attorney should have sedated him."

"I doubt he knew. Adam learned a lot from my father on how to spin things. I think he really had his attorney convinced I started it. Once the questioning began and Adam started going off, he changed his mind."

Good. Adam's fake innocence couldn't combat his destructive nature.

"He was flustered when it was his turn to examine you, wasn't he?"

Even Lila was smiling. "Very. He looked like a newbie, and even the judge was short with him."

"He wasn't expecting what his client really was." I stroked across her arm over and over, drawing lazy patterns.

She pursed her lips. "We aren't supposed to be talking about it."

"No." I drew circles around her breast and down her stomach. "I'm supposed to be making you forget."

Her lips pressed against my neck. "You're on the right path."

After we got out of the tub, I carried her into the bedroom and laid her down on the bed. Then I did what I always did when she was upset—I lavished her body with mine, showing her my love through touch. Words would never do for her. They could never convey the truth my hands, mouth, and cock could.

CHAPTER 15

As I was led into the courtroom, I couldn't help but look around. I locked onto Adam, and he actually looked reserved. After everything Lila told me, I scoffed at his act. It was probably advice from his lawyer—to look repentant in front of the jury.

They'd dressed him up in a suit, shaved him, cut his hair—anything to make him look like a good boy. It was the way he held himself and the expressions on his face that gave him away.

It was odd being on the other side of the bench. I was used to being in front of the judge, not beside him. I took a deep breath to even myself out and looked at Lawrence. My hands gripped the chair in an effort to keep me calm as I braced to go through the usual retelling of events from my eyes.

Lawrence walked to the center of the floor. "Why were you going over to Delilah's house that night?"

"We were going to have dinner."

He looked around the room, trying not to focus solely on me. "Did you eat together every night?"

"Yes."

"Did you notice anything strange or different that night as you approached her condo?"

I blew out a slow breath. "There were screams coming from inside."

Lawrence stared at me, and I knew the hard hit was coming. "Tell me—what did you see when you opened the door?"

Fuck.

My heart was racing as the image popped into my mind. I let out a hard breath to steady myself. I had to answer and do so in a calm manner. The problem was that calm could be found nowhere within me in that moment.

My muscles flexed, ready to jump out of the stupid box and run to Adam so I could slam my fist in his fucking face. I wanted to reenact the events of that day in order to show the judge what little I'd done to him compared to what he did to her.

"Lila was on the ground with him on top of her."

The prosecutor continued to lead me on. "And what was he doing to her?"

I knew where his questions were going—I'd been in his place and tried to prepare myself for them. It didn't make it any easier. I could anticipate his questions, but not the searing emotions they evoked.

"He had her hands pinned above her head. Her shirt was ripped open, and he was pushing her skirt up." My whole body was shaking, rage enveloping me.

The prosecutor stared at me, begging me to cool down. "What made it different from sexual play?"

My teeth mashed together as I fought for control. "Her face was covered in blood."

I forced myself to stop the words "from him hitting her," because I knew the defense would object.

After a while, the prosecutor glanced at the jury and back at me, then sighed. I wasn't making a very good impression due to my anger seeping out.

"Tell me, why are you so agitated being in this room today?"

A good question. It would make the jury understand why. Who wouldn't be angry, sitting across from the man who almost took your world away?

"Because *he*..." I couldn't say his name, and I was so close to calling him a name the judge wouldn't approve of "...hurt Lila. He tried to take my *wife* away from me. My love and reason for being."

I took great pride in the murderous look that flashed on Adam's face after calling Lila by her marital title. Lawrence smiled and continued on.

After a grueling fifteen minutes and more than one warning from the judge, the defense took over.

"Mr. Thorne, you and Delilah Thorne weren't married when you first encountered Mr. Mitchell, were you?"

"No."

"Neither were you engaged, is that correct?"

"Yes." If I thought answering the prosecution was bad, it was nothing compared to the "yes" and "no" answers for the defense.

"Were you living together?"

"Yes."

"But you still retained separate residences?"

"Yes."

"And that is because your employer did not allow fraternization between its employees, correct?"

"Yes." I shifted in my seat, but made sure it wasn't noticeable.

"Is it true that you destroyed all the drywall in your entryway in a fit of anger?"

"Objection," Lawrence called out. "Irrelevant to the case."

The defense attorney didn't flinch. "Mr. Thorne also has a history of violence. I am strictly trying to show that, your Honor."

"What relevancy does it pose?" the judge asked, his voice clipped in annoyance at the defense attorney. Lila was right—the judge didn't like him.

"That Delilah Thorne is the instigator of violent reactions."

The judge thought on it for a moment. "I'll allow it. Please answer the question, Mr. Thorne."

I sighed, unhappy with the twist. "No."

"No, you did not destroy your entryway."

"Yes, I did, but not—"

"You blamed it all on your coworker, Delilah Palmer, isn't that right?" He cut me off, keeping me from elaborating.

"No."

"Weren't you angry at her?"

"Yes."

"You've shown us your anger today. Have you ever hit Delilah?"

"No." My gut was tied in knots at even the thought of it, and I somehow managed to keep from flinching.

"Never?"

"*Never.*"

"The defense rests." He wore a smug look as he moved back to his seat.

The prosecutor stood, and I knew they wanted to redirect after some of the questions posed by the defense.

"Mr. Thorne, you destroyed your entryway, but not in a fit of anger?"

"I tore down the drywall in a fit of *despair* after separating myself from Lila in a futile effort to keep her safe from a mob boss who wants me dead—because I prosecuted his daughter, and she's in jail." I sat up a little straighter.

"And why were you angry with Lila?"

"Because ever since my wife and child were murdered, I didn't want to fall in love. I didn't want to care about anyone. If I cared, they could kill them as well. But, Lila worked her way inside me without me even knowing it, and it made me angry at her for reviving feelings in my dead existence. I didn't want to love her, but in the end, I couldn't fight fate." My jaw tightened with each passing second, making it increasingly difficult to get the words out.

His lip twitched as he fought a smile. A quick glance to the jury confirmed that my honest and passionate answer hit many of them in the heart.

Afterward, I was led back to another room, forced to be separated from Lila again until the jury left for deliberation. It was a grueling time. Thoughts that maybe I'd feel lighter once I got it out to the jury and others knew what he'd done was a myth.

The knot in my chest was weighing me down like chains wrapped around my body, dragging me to unknown depths. I'd fucked up, unable to control my anger. It looked bad and could undermine some of my good testimony with the jurors.

My skin itched with the need to feel it marring Adam's flesh while simultaneously begging to be all over Lila. She was my oasis in the giant sea of fuckery.

When the bailiff came to let me out, I ran right into Lila, who was waiting for me. She threw her arms around me, and it was then peace started to settle in. The hard part was done—now it was up to twelve people.

———— •••◐●◑••• ————

The jury couldn't come to a decision in the short amount of time left in the day, so we arrived at the courthouse bright and early the next morning. We didn't have to wait long—an hour later, the jury was done deliberating. The short time could be a good sign, or a bad one. Either way, our group filed into the room and took a seat.

We'd waited so long, gone through so much, and the moment was finally upon us. My arm was around Lila's shoulders, holding her close, our hands entwined. The whole room was tense as the jurors entered and took their seats.

The judge entered a moment later, read over the findings, and settled in.

"Will the defendant please rise."

Prompted from the judge, the jury foreman stood, and my breath halted.

"On the first count of Aggravated Sexual Battery, how do you find the defendant?"

The world stopped, time stopped, and the entire room held its breath.

"We find the defendant guilty."

I scooped Lila up in my arms, holding her tight as we cried out in joy.

The judge called for order, and we settled down. I looked into Lila's eyes and for the first time in days, there was life and light. We didn't pay attention to the judge, only every single "guilty" that rang out from the jury foreman.

Adam was found guilty on all five charges.

"Sentencing will be held on April twenty-first. Court is adjourned."

I couldn't help smiling as I watched the bailiff approach to take him away.

"You fucking cunt!" Adam screamed out, garnering the attention of the room. "I will fucking kill you!"

I pulled Lila behind me as Adam jumped over the banister and charged toward us. The beast in me smiled, ready to get a good swing in, to pulverize his face, but Adam was subdued by the bailiffs before I got the opportunity. He continued to act out as they hauled him away.

After he was gone, I used my hands to direct Lila out into the aisle, then to the hall.

Smiles lit up everyone as we exited. Hugs were spread around.

I couldn't wait to celebrate.

My mother hugged me as Lila made her rounds. "Now?" she asked, and I nodded. "Okay. I'll be right back. I'll have her text you the information."

"Thank you." I kissed her cheek and moved back over to Lila.

We said goodbye to everyone, thanking them for coming and for their support. The sun was shining as we exited the courthouse, smiling down on us.

"Joan?" Lila blinked at an older woman standing outside the door.

She stood, and I got a good look at the woman who freed my love from possible death. There was more gray than brunette in her well-kept hair, and her suit was from another decade but fit her age well. A kind smile graced her face as she stood.

"Oh, Lila, look how beautiful you are." Joan wrapped her arms around Lila. She sighed as she pulled back.

Lila blinked at her. "How did you know?"

"Teresa called me." She took Lila's hand. "And this was one of my cases I needed to see the verdict on."

"I didn't even see you."

"I didn't want to disturb you, so I sat in the back."

I stared at her in amazement. "After almost fifteen years, I'm shocked you still remember her." I know I didn't remember all of my cases.

She turned to me and smiled. "I remember all the children I've saved, but some stick out more than others. Lila's was one of the very few calls I've ever received from a child." She pursed her lips and stroked Lila's hand. "A very broken sixteen-year-old asked me for help when no one believed her."

"What made you?" I'd always wondered what her lawyer saw.

"As soon as she walked into the principal's office that afternoon, I knew. One look at her, and I knew what she'd told me was the truth."

"Do you have time to stay for lunch?" Lila looked at her with hopeful eyes.

Joan shook her head. "I'm sorry. I have a hearing in a few minutes, but I wanted to see you and tell you how amazed I am at you."

Tears formed in Lila's eyes as she smiled at Joan, then threw her arms around her. "Thank you for everything, for believing."

"You're most welcome." Joan drew back. "I'm so proud of you." She glanced at me, then back to Lila. "Congratulations on your wedding, by the way. I'm filled with joy, knowing how happy you are and that you're taken care of."

Joan held her hand out to me, and I shook it. She then gave Lila another hug before turning and heading back. I noticed my parents and Drew looking over at us from a few steps up. Drew gave Joan a hug on her way back into the courthouse.

Between the verdict and running into Joan, Lila was glowing. She still seemed to be in disbelief as we walked down the steps, but there was a lightness coming over her, blanketing her.

We were basking in our victory, talking amongst ourselves, when a venom-laced growl came from behind us.

"You little bitch." Lila's father stared at her, sneering. She gripped onto my arm, nails digging deep as she froze. "You were always a fucking disappointment. I never wanted you in the first place, then your whore of a mother had to die and I got stuck with a miserable little brat." He moved forward, reaching out to grab her, but I intercepted him, stepping between them.

"Step back." My teeth clenched tight, the words escaping my throat with a growl. He was *not* even going to get close enough to touch her. He was lucky I allowed him to breathe the same air.

He glared up at me. "She a good cocksucker? Is that how she roped you in?"

I stepped forward, looking down at him, towering over his aging frame. "Say another fucking word, and I will punch you so hard you won't remember your own goddamned name."

"Are you threatening me? What lies has that little bitch been spreading to get you to defend her?"

"No lies—just the truth of a verbally and physically abusive father who encouraged his stepson to abuse her as well, to the point of almost killing her on more than one occasion. Should I go on, asshole?"

"Don't you fucking call him that!" The stepbitch saddled up next to him, ready to fight.

My icy glare turned to her. "Don't even get me started on you."

He stepped forward, inches from me, and sneered. "Little bitch deserved it. She needed to be broken if anyone was ever going to take her off my hands. Just needed Adam to pop that cherry of hers, train her up a bit, and she'd be ready for the highest bidder. That's all she was good for."

My fist slamming into his face was pure gut reaction. It sent him sprawling on the ground. I was seething, murderous rage pumping in my veins. I wanted him dead.

I wanted to kill him.

Trash like him didn't deserve to breathe. I dove down and grabbed on to his shirt, picking him up a bit. There was screaming around me, but my focus was on the piece of shit in front of me and how I was going to tear him apart.

His daze wore off and he lashed out, his fist glancing off my cheek. I cocked back and exploded on him. The euphoric feel of his flesh being pummeled by my fist lasted longer than the split second it was in reality. After the third punch, I was pulled back.

"Fucker! You piece of fucking trash! I will fucking beat you within an inch of your life!"

He was bleeding—I'd busted the skin on his cheek and split his lip. It wasn't enough.

The evil bitch-mother started wailing as she knelt down next to the bastard. "You asshole, what have you done?"

I pulled against whoever was holding me, ready for round two. "Only a fraction of a taste of what he did to his own daughter. You make me sick. You're not even human if you can do that to a little girl."

"Come on, Nate, calm the fuck down." Drew pulled against my arm.

Drew had my left arm, while my father had my right.

My father's eyes were pleading. "Calm down."

I looked back down to the man who needed to be dead as he tried to sit up.

"You are nothing but a pile of shit," I spat down at him. "Don't ever touch her, don't even look at her, and don't ever think of her again."

A couple of police officers were rushing over, alerted to the altercation, and began asking questions. They even asked the shithead if he needed an ambulance.

Realization hit me.

Her father planned to sell her off as a slave. He was going to let Adam rape her over and over. If she survived, he was going to trade her and who the fuck knew what they'd do to her before she wound up dead.

I felt sick.

I looked over to Lila, who stood frozen, wrapped in my mother's arms and staring at her father.

Everything lifted from me, leaving me with only the need to protect her. I opened up my arms, and she stared at me for a split second before running straight into them. I pulled her as tight to me as I could.

"It's okay, baby. I won't ever let him near you."

She was shaking in my arms. No tears, but obviously just as sickened and frightened as I was. If she hadn't gotten out... There was no doubt how horrible the outcome would have been.

"I've got you. You're safe."

One officer walked over, pulling out his notepad. "Sir, can you come over there with me?"

I nodded, keeping Lila attached to me as we walked about fifty feet from where the bastard lay.

The bitch-monster was still screeching, making my ears hurt and my anger boil again. "You monster! He's bleeding, you psycho son of a bitch!"

The officer blinked at Lila, noticing she'd come with me. "Miss, can you give us a moment?"

Lila shook her head, her eyes filled with fear as they flickered back to her father.

"He'll get me. Don't let him get me."

My chest clenched at her words. He'd reduced her back to a child almost, clinging to me for safety from the monster that hunted her.

The officer's mouth popped open, seeming to get an understanding of the situation. He cleared his throat and began his line of questions.

"What happened here?"

I took a deep breath to calm myself—much needed since adrenaline was still pumping through me, and the beast was begging to go back and kill him.

"We were coming out of the courthouse after the verdict on an aggravated sexual battery case against that woman's son." I pointed to the hell-bitch leaning over the asshole, then motioned to Lila. "He began verbally attacking her, then me, before attempting to grab hold of her. He then moved to attack me and I acted in defense of us both." Lila trembled in my arms, burying her face further into my chest. "The man was her father, who admitted to everyone within listening distance to battery of her and plans of human trafficking of his own daughter."

The officer's pen stopped, his hand still as he looked at us, a horrified expression on his face. I felt sick.

What if she'd been given to Via Marconi's operation? She had a far reach for her girls. I'd seen the women there, and death would be preferable to what they went through.

I pulled out my wallet and handed him a business card. "You can reach me here for anything further, but I really need to get her out of here."

The officer nodded as he looked over my information. "We'll be in touch, Mr. Thorne."

I glanced down at his name badge. "Thank you, Officer White."

The moment he stepped away back over to his partner, I pulled out my phone and texted Noah. I sent him the officer's name and badge number, also giving him a heads-up on what happened.

Drew was done with his statement, and we waited for my parents, slowly inching toward the parking lot.

"Well, you now have grounds for a restraining order." Drew leaned forward for a second to take a quick look at Lila.

I nodded. "Can you file one?"

"I'll get with Caroline this afternoon. We'll have it drawn up and submitted ASAP."

"Thanks, man."

"No problem." He clapped me on the arm.

I looked down at my phone, noticing the text message I'd been waiting on along with the time. "Want to join us for lunch?"

He shook his head. "Sorry. Dana's meeting me back at the office."

My parents stopped in front of us, and Drew said his goodbyes before walking off.

"Lila, honey, are you okay?" My mother dipped her head down to look at her.

She nodded against my chest, her iron grip still digging into me. It didn't matter, as long as she felt safe.

"I just need to get away from him."

My father patted my shoulder. "We'll let you go and talk to you soon."

Lila let go of me enough to walk to her side of the car, her eyes glancing back over to where the cops were still talking to her father. She sighed, mumbling something under her breath as we sped off.

It almost sounded like "I wish you'd killed him."

I wished I had as well.

CHAPTER 16

W e sat at a table in Lila's favorite hole-in-the-wall
Mexican restaurant a half hour later. I ordered her a
margarita—a well-deserved drink after the morning we'd
experienced. We were supposed to be having a celebration
of our victory, but instead we sat in the booth with a
somber aura, and I was icing my aching knuckles.

She was lost in thought, but not vacant or detached.
I was happy with that, and the fact she didn't need my help
but only my presence to pull her from the debilitating fear
that took hold of her thanks to that asshole father of hers
opening his mouth.

She blew through her first drink in minutes, and I
found myself shoving the chips and salsa at her before I
had a drunk on my hands. After all, I had plans.

"Baby, you need to slow down."

Her eyes flipped up, almost as if she was just
noticing me, and her lips twitched. "Sorry, it's just been
a…day."

I nodded. "Lots of highs and lows."

She blew out a breath and dipped a chip in the queso I ordered. Her teeth bit into the edge, nibbling on it instead of stuffing it in her mouth.

"What would've happened to me?" She tilted her head at me.

I knew the answer, a little too well for my liking. Her inquisitive eyes bore into me. I shifted in my seat and cleared my throat.

"Nothing good, and everything bad." I took the ice off to look at my hand, flexing my fingers as I determined nothing was broken—just inflamed and sore.

She thought on what I said for a moment. I almost didn't know what to do with her reactions—they weren't normal for her.

"I never would've gotten free, would I?"

I shook my head. "Only by death."

She hummed in agreement. My jaw flexed. I was not comfortable with this conversation. The thought of her continuing on that path was excruciating.

"I know you called Joan, and she got you out of the house, but how? Why didn't you call Social Services?"

She sighed. "I didn't know at the time. I only knew I could be emancipated from him and you needed a lawyer for that."

"There was no way a judge would have agreed, and you would have continued living with him through that process."

She nodded. "I was only sixteen—I didn't know anything, only that I had to get away."

The waiter chose that moment to arrive with our food. My stomach rumbled with the wonderful sizzling smell coming from my fajitas. I dove in, waiting for her to gather her thoughts while she cut up her food.

"Joan arrived at the school not two hours after I called her. I'd found her number in a phone book in the library that morning." She cut into her chimichanga and took a bite. "When she arrived, I was called into the principal's office. The moment she saw me, she started yelling at him for no one noticing what was going on." She stared down at her food for a moment, thinking as she cut off another bite and ate it. "The principal was friends with my father and told her I was just clumsy and shy. That set her off. His inaction ultimately led to him losing his job."

My brow rose in surprise and satisfaction. "Which was well deserved. He should've known the signs. Friend or not, he took an oath to protect his students."

She nodded. "My father was a charismatic man of the community—they never knew the man he hid behind closed doors or the disdain he had for me. He painted them a pretty little picture, and if I did anything to mess it up, there was hell to pay." She took a long pull of her margarita. "That all changed that night after Joan arrived at the house with Social Services."

"I didn't know they worked that fast."

"They did after Joan showed them the damage. My bruises were fading, but still very visible. She took me into the nurse's office, had me take off my shirt, and took photos of it all. After developing them that afternoon, she took them to a judge along with my medical records, and I was pulled."

"I'm so happy you had the courage to contact her. Otherwise... I don't like the alternative future you would've endured."

"Me, either." Tears welled in her eyes. "I never would have met you."

We stopped conversation, both needing a moment to decompress and eat. After I finished stuffing myself with fajitas, I placed the ice back on my hand and looked down at my watch. Time was passing a little too fast.

I reached across the table and took her hand. "So, what do we do now?"

She shrugged. "No idea. Go back to the office?"

I shook my head and smiled. "No, Honeybear." I laughed. "First off, you've been drinking. Second... What does everyone say when they win something?" She quirked her brow at me, then looked at me like I was insane. "I'm going to Disneyworld!"

She stared at me, her brow scrunched. "What?"

I sighed and took her hand in mine. "We're going to Disneyworld."

She continued to stare at me, possibly wondering if I'd gotten another lobotomy. "Huh?"

"Delilah Thorne, you and I are flying down to Orlando in four hours and spending the rest of the week at Disneyworld."

She blinked at me. "But we have work."

She was still confused, and I tried not to laugh. Then again, I did broadside her. "No, we took the week off for the trial, remember? We weren't sure how long it would go."

Her head tilted. "So…we're going to Disneyworld?"

My lip twitched—she was catching on. "Yes."

"Really?" The confusion cleared from her face and was replaced by disbelief.

I nodded. "Yes."

"But how did you know we'd be done today?"

"I didn't."

"Then how? I've been with you this whole time."

"Mom had it all waiting in the wings with her travel agent for me. When we were leaving the courthouse she called her, and the agent texted me our flight information."

"We're going to Disneyworld? Now?"

I laughed, unable to keep it in any longer. "Yes, we're going to Disneyworld."

Her eyes widened and she bounced in her seat. "Oh, my God! We're going to Disneyworld!"

"Now, *that* is the reaction I was expecting."

She jumped up. "We need to get packed!"

We headed home and began to pack like maniacs on the run. I pulled out a few pairs of shorts and t-shirts and threw them in a small suitcase. Lila was flipping clothes everywhere into a larger suitcase. She was a planner, so the sudden need to pack was driving her a little insane and she was over-packing.

"How long will we be there?" She stared down at the pile of sundresses she pulled from the closet.

I pulled out my phone and looked over the information again. "We fly back on Sunday, so three full days."

After sorting through the stack, she picked two and left the rest in the middle of our bed. She then went through the clothes she'd already accumulated and weeded some out, making the mess on the bed bigger.

Half an hour later, we were packed and ready to go. Well, Lila was still going through a mental list to make sure she remembered everything.

"Did we leave the oven on?" she asked as we were driving to the airport.

I quirked my brow at her. "Were you using it any time this week?"

She blinked at me. "No."

"Then I'd say no."

She turned back to the front and looked out the window as we neared our destination. I took her hand in mine and kissed her fingers.

"Relax. That's the point of these days off. We've just been through the gauntlet and won. Adam's in jail. It's time to celebrate."

She let out a hard breath and sank back into the seat.

"He's really going to jail."

"Yes, he is."

Her lips twitched up and grew into a smile that lit up her eyes. Nothing but happiness.

———— ⟫⟫⦿⟪⟪ ————

A few hours later, we checked into the Grand Floridian. It was an iconic, out of time hotel. With as late as it was when we finally got there, and with as long of a day it'd been, we ordered room service for dinner.

We were unpacking, going over the park information, when Lila threw open the curtains and looked out. Her eyes widened as she stared out at the park in the distance and the castle lit up in the middle. I walked up behind her and wrapped my arms around her waist.

"You know what else we could do while we're here?" I kissed her neck and ground my hips against her ass.

She relaxed back into me and let out a contented sigh. "I think I know where you're going with this."

"Yeah, where's that?" I nipped at her skin.

"Baby making practice."

I pulled back. "Practice?"

She nodded. "Practice makes perfect."

"Well, it's always perfect, but why are you calling it practice? You're not on birth control anymore, right?"

"No, I'm not."

I turned her in my arms. "Am I pressuring you?" She was silent as she looked back at me. "Lila, do you want to have kids?"

Her brow scrunched and she let out a hard breath. *Fuck.*

I held my breath, waiting. I couldn't explain my want—*need*—for a baby. It was visceral. Every part of me wanted a family with her, as if it was an attempt to get even closer to her. I wanted to see the mix of her and me in our child.

Men didn't have a biological clock, but it felt like I did. Maybe it was because I was someone new, who understood better than the old me how important and special family was. Grace was the driver then, and now it was me. I'd wanted kids then, wanted the American dream—and more than to appease Grace—but with Lila it was more than all that.

"It's not that I don't want them, it's that it scares me to death. Would I love to bring our children here? Yes. I want the family experiences I've always seen but never had." She leaned forward and rested her head on my chest. "But I can't shake the fear that I'll fuck up, be a terrible mother. I…I don't know what to do. I don't even know if I can hold a baby, because I never have."

I let out the breath I'd been holding and chuckled, the tension leaving me as I pulled her closer.

"Honeybear, I know it's scary, but it's impossible for you to be a terrible mother."

"You don't know that."

I tilted her head up so I could look into her eyes. "Yes, I do. You've changed before my eyes, but your capacity to love has only grown." She let out a shaky breath, and I turned her so we could both look out the window again. "Look out there, out at the castle that has you entranced." I looked down to make sure she was, and she was locked on, her hand reaching out and settling on the window. "Now imagine coming back here in five years and sharing it with our little girl. Imagine her face lighting up."

Lila's voice was barely a whisper. "Anna."

My heart stopped and a sense of déjà vu took hold. *Anna.*

Flashes of a dream, a nightmare long ago, came back to me. The smiling face of a little girl who called me Daddy.

I swallowed hard. "That's a beautiful name."

"It was my mom's."

I kissed her temple. "I think it's a great name for our little girl."

She sniffed and nodded. "I think so, too." She tilted her head up and kissed my jaw. Her lips continued up my jaw, nipping as she went. "Let's make our baby girl."

I growled and took her mouth with mine. "I love you."

CHAPTER 17

Lila was not the woman I knew. No, the woman before me was a little girl—wide-eyed, smiling, full of bouncing, hyper energy and wonder.

We were starting out our trip in the Magic Kingdom bright and early. Her attention was all over the place as she took in Main Street. When we were almost to the end, I pulled the map from my back pocket.

I didn't even get to ask where she wanted to go before she nearly tugged my arm out of the socket and I tripped over my feet, almost face-planting onto the stone below. Her pace was almost a run, her gaze fixed on one thing in front of her. She was practically dragging me on her quest.

When I looked up, I saw what had her so excited—Cinderella's Castle. It was the iconic Disney view. She blew past people, only to stop in front of it and stare. I wrapped my arms around her waist and stood behind her, cradling her against my chest.

"It's so pretty." Her voice was low, reverent almost. I nodded against her shoulder. It was what had given me the idea in the first place—the Cinderella story. Lila mentioned in the past how it was her favorite growing up. It wasn't until we were standing in front of it that I was reminded how much she lost out on growing up with her father.

We probably stood there for a half an hour, Lila soaking it in, memorizing every detail. The chiming of a bell seemed to wake her up and remind her where we were. She straightened and grabbed my hand before turning and taking off again.

"Someone excited?" I laughed as I took an extra step to catch up. Her head was bouncing around everywhere, trying to take everything in at once, but I wondered if she could absorb anything with as fast as she was going.

She slowed and gave me a sheepish grin. "Sorry."

I shook my head. "No, Honeybear, don't be sorry. Be happy."

"I am happy." She pulled me close for a quick kiss. "You have no idea what this means to me."

We walked around, heading through Adventureland and stopping to watch people on the Aladdin ride. "What does it mean?"

She stepped back and headed toward the Pirates of the Caribbean ride. "I don't remember much about my mom, but I do remember she had a jar above the fridge with money in it." I was surprised at the mention of her mom—Lila never had any stories. I'd often wondered if she remembered her at all. "Every time she put any in she

172

would look at me and say, 'We're getting closer to Disney.' I would pick up every piece of change I found on the ground and give it to her to add."

"How close were you?"

She shrugged. "Who knows. She died before we got to go, and I was sent to—"

"The bastard asshole motherfucker."

She elbowed me and glared. "Sssh!"

"What?"

"We're in Dinseyworld."

I smirked at her scolding me like it was the most obvious answer and held up my right hand. "I will attempt to refrain from cussing out loud for the duration of our time in the park."

She smiled at me and linked her fingers with mine.

A little while later, we were done with one ride and climbing onto Splash Mountain. The faux log swayed as I stepped on, and I held my hand out to help Lila on. She leaned her head on my shoulder, her arms tangled around mine, as we began moving.

I couldn't help but stare down at her chest and the view I had of her soft breasts.

"What?" She grinned, her brow quirking, knowing exactly what I was looking at.

I shook my head. "Nothing."

"It's not nothing, so what is it?" She prodded my side with her finger.

I leaned, trying to get away. "You're wearing a white shirt."

"And?" Her brow scrunched.

"We're going on Splash Mountain."

"And?" She was so fucking adorable when she was confused. I grinned at her and licked my lips. Her eyes widened. "Oh."

I slipped my hand up her thigh and squeezed as we took off.

Full-blown giggling filled my ears as we twisted, turned, and dipped, followed by a high-pitched scream along with my own yell as we plummeted down the final hill. She was laughing as the ride slowed down, and we took stock of our water-soaked, dripping bodies.

After exiting, I looked down and groaned—her *white* tank top was thoroughly soaked and giving me a nice show of her sexy little bra. I pulled her close, grabbing her ass as I pushed my tongue into her mouth.

Surprise filled her eyes, her cheeks turning pink.

I leaned down, my lips ghosting her ear. "Tonight I'm going to get you wet in a whole other way." Keeping to my promise of no spoken cuss words, I adjusted what I wanted to say. "I'm going to eat you out, stick my fingers inside you, and suck on your nipples until you're begging me to stop. If you're lucky, I'll stick my man meat in you and thrust until we both come undone."

I smirked down at her as I pulled back. Her eyes were heavy, mouth open, and her face was flush—all her telltale signs of arousal.

"How about a picture, you two?"

I looked up to find a park photographer holding up a camera. "Sure." I stroked her cheek with my finger. "Look at the camera, baby."

She did as I asked, but I had a feeling I'd pushed her over the lust edge and she was no longer aware of what was going on. My dick got hard just thinking about it. I was tempted to find some little corner for a quick fuck, but I didn't want to get thrown out of the park for sexing up my girl in such a wholesome place.

We continued on, taking a train ride in a western town, stopping for lunch, and taking in a creepy trip through It's A Small World before walking around toward the Haunted Mansion.

A shop window caught my eye before we got to our next destination, and I pulled us in. It was filled with little girls dressed up as princesses with their hair and makeup done while wearing frilly dresses.

Lila's brow scrunched as she looked around. "What are we doing in here?"

I read over the signs around the register. They talked about different princess packages. "I think you should be a princess."

"What?"

I grinned. "Don't you want to dress up? Be a princess for a day? I'll be your faithful man-servant, Cristoff."

"This is for little girls."

"Ah, you were thinking it would be fun." Her face turned pink and she looked down to the ground.

"This is stupid."

I grinned at her. "No, it's not. Come on." I tugged on her arm.

"No."

"Why not?"

She huffed. "It's for little girls! Besides, they aren't going to have adult-sized dresses."

"Then we can stuff you into something too small."

She pushed on my shoulder. "You just want to see my ass hanging out."

My mouth dropped open. "We're in Disneyworld! You said a dirty word!"

Her cheeks got even redder and she beat on my back, pushing us out the door.

We walked around, taking it all in and looking for our next adventure when it dawned on me.

"Do you like rollercoasters?"

She nodded. "Mm-hmm. Teresa and Armando took Noah and me to Kings Island one time."

"What was the first ride you went on?"

She grimaced. "Well, Noah was a bit sneaky. I told him I wanted to try, but was scared. So he convinced me to go on the Vortex, saying it was a pretty easy one."

My eyes widened. "What? Are you kidding me?"

"Nope. I screamed, probably cried a little, and told him how much I hated him."

"You saw it before you got on, right?"

She nodded. "I was freaking out the whole time we were in line. Once I calmed down, I realized it wasn't that bad, so we went on the Beast next. After that, I was in love with the thrill. I guess you could say it was the first time I'd felt alive in many years."

At the beginning of her story, I couldn't decide if Noah was a little shit back in the day, but by the end, I had a feeling he knew it was exactly what she needed at the time.

"Teacups!" Lila's face lit up and she pulled on me again, heading straight for the end of the line.

After spinning and spinning and almost making me sick, we got off. My stomach turned a few times, but after a drink and a snack, it settled back down. We sat at a café and watched the people walk around, taking a nice break. I stretched—my body snapping, crackling, and popping. We still had a lot of park to cover, and I couldn't wait to take her to Space Mountain.

After another pass of Cinderella's Castle and a few other small attractions, we entered the line for Space Mountain.

"Okay, now you're the one that's full of excitement."

I realized then I was bouncing on the spot and shrugged at her. "Mom and Dad brought Erin and I here probably twenty years ago. Erin and I went on it about five times. It is by far the best coaster I've ever been on. It's awesome."

"What is it?" She snickered at me.

"It's awesome!" I threw my hands up in the air and did a little dance.

And it was. As soon as we were off, Lila grabbed my hand and ran back to the end of the line. By the third time, the sun was setting and we were both dragging. We decided the day was done.

"Oh, wait!" I pulled the photo ticket from my pocket on our way out.

"What's that?"

"The photo number."

"We had a photo taken?"

I grinned. "Oh, yeah. After we got off Splash Mountain."

She blinked at me, confirming that I was right—she was lusted out and not paying attention to anything but what I'd said to her.

We walked over to the photo booth, and I handed the attendant the ticket. It took him a moment to find it, and the moment it popped up on the screen, I knew I had to have it. Lila gasped.

"We can't get that!"

It was fucking perfect. She was so alluring my dick was getting hard just looking at it. Her cheeks were pink, lips slightly parted, eyes heavy-lidded.

"Oh, yes, we are!" I reached into my wallet and pulled out my credit card.

"No!" She tried to wrestle the card out of my hand, but I held it high up.

I nipped her neck, and she squeaked, backing up enough for me to get the card to the sales associate.

"I'm putting it on my desk so I can look at it all the time."

Her eyes bugged out of her head before she jumped onto the counter and tried to grab the card back. I wrapped my arms around her waist and pulled her down, laughing at the lengths she was going.

"You can't."

"Oh, yes, Honeybear, I can and I will. You can't stop me."

She folded her arms across her chest. "I can burn it."

I pouted and gave her my best puppy dog eyes. "Would you really do that to something I love so much?"

She pursed her lips and whimpered. "But it's so embarrassing."

"Think of it this way—I've never asked for naked pictures, so let me have this."

The sales clerk snickered. He'd been having as much fun as I was, laughing at her reactions. Her bottom lip jutted out and she looked to the floor.

"I'll buy you mouse ears."

Her gaze narrowed on me as she thought about it. "All right, but I want some Minnie ones with a pink bow."

I smiled. "I saw a princess one with a tiara."

"Don't push it."

Once she saw a crown on some purple printed Minnie ears, she changed her tune and forgot all about the photograph I was carrying around.

When we got back to our room, we pulled up the room service menu and picked a few items. We were both too tired to get dressed up and go out. Besides, we had another day ahead of us.

Lila was sitting on the bed, staring out at the park and the castle while we waited. "Today was the best."

I nodded as I shed my clothes. "It was. But I'm not sure who those loonies were."

"What loonies?"

"The ones that looked just like us, but acted nothing like us."

She threw her head back and laughed. "I don't know who they were either, but they sure looked like they were having fun."

"Fantastic time."

She smiled and played with my fingers. "Thank you."

"You don't need to thank me." I moaned as I lay down on the bed. It felt so good to get off my feet.

"Yes, I do." She crawled next to me.

I moved my arm behind my head. "Why?"

"Because you're always so good at knowing what I need."

"I think that's luck."

She shook her head. "No, it's more than that."

"You always know what I need."

She snorted. "A pussy?"

I chuckled. "Well, there is that, but there is also so much more."

Her fingers caressed my cheek. "I love you."

I captured her lips with mine. "I love you, too."

⟡

The sun was blinding me, waking me from my nice Lila-in-a-Playboy-bunny-outfit dreams. I grumbled and reached for her to snuggle with, but all I felt were cold sheets. I propped myself up on my elbows and looked at the empty spot where my wife should've been.

"Lila?"

"Yes?"

I turned around to find her sitting at the desk with her laptop open. She had one of the hotel robes on, her hair wet from a shower. I rubbed my face, then sat up, a yawn escaping as I stretched.

"What're you doing?"

"Well, I had an idea."

I stood and walked over to her. "Yeah?"

She turned the laptop toward me. I blinked at the screen, my brain still foggy with sleep. It took me a second to put the letters together into words and then for it to sink in.

"Universal Studios?"

She nodded. "I had my day, and now it's your turn."

I shook my head. "Baby, I don't need a turn, but I would love to go there."

"Ride some big coasters."

"They have that Marvel section?" A smile grew on my face as I looked at all the coasters. "Okay, I take that back—I need a turn."

We spent the day going on every coaster we could, and some more than once. I was going to be even more sore when the day way done, but it didn't matter. We had a great time, and it was worth a little pain to have such fun, carefree moments where we could be kids again.

The next day was filled with fun and relaxation around the hotel pool. We needed it after two hard days, and the water was great at relaxing sore muscles.

"You keep taking me on vacation to warm, sunny places and then making me leave," Lila grumbled at me on our last morning.

I chuckled. "Sorry, but we have to go. I'm just happy we were able to take a couple of days to get away."

"Me too." She leaned against me, yawning.

There was a whole new woman beside me when we returned home. I loved the new side of my wife. I loved seeing her happy, and I'd do anything to keep her that way.

CHAPTER 18

Lila was stuck in a strange state between relief and fear for the weeks following the trial. Adam had been found guilty on all charges, but there was still sentencing to go. She was teetering on an edge, and I knew things would tip when the ruling came down.

Our little getaway helped, but the countdown to sentencing was excruciating. We were both ready for it to be done, over. Put the crap in the past and move on to the future.

"Lunch today?" Lila asked as we rode the elevator up to the office.

My face scrunched up a bit at the uncertainty in her tone. "Of course. Why wouldn't we?"

She looked down to the floor. "I just didn't know what your schedule looked like."

"Sunny with a chance of afternoon Honeybear." I winked at her.

That got a smile to peek out and an elbow into my ribs. The damn dark cloud was washing over her again. The effect it had on her was hell to watch, and harder every day to combat.

One fucking day left before Adam's blackness wouldn't be able to touch her anymore. I hoped the judge would give him the full extent of each charge.

The elevator opened, and I linked my fingers with hers, pulling her along and out of her head.

"Sorry." She sighed and leaned against me as we walked down the hall.

"Don't be. Stop being sorry. It's his fault. He's the one who should be sorry."

"I hate that he still has a hold on me."

I stopped, and she looked up at me. I caressed her cheek, giving her the reassurance she needed. "He won't after tomorrow."

She leaned into my touch, relaxing and even resting against me. The wall she was unknowingly building between us was collapsing. "I'm not paying you the attention you deserve. It should be you who consumes my every thought."

"Me and my dick."

Her eyes widened and she looked around, then smiled and nodded when she saw no one was watching. I couldn't stop myself from leaning forward and kissing her. She let out a small gasp before gripping my jacket and pulling me closer, deepening it, opening her mouth and seeking out my tongue with her own.

"PDA! Ewwwww." Owen laughed as he passed us by.

I broke away from Lila and flipped Owen the bird as he continued on down the hall. Even Lila was snickering. I couldn't think of a better replacement for me. Owen was a good guy and had a way of keeping the atmosphere light—something Lila needed.

"Come on." She pulled on my arm, and we continued.

I kissed her again at her door before continuing down the way to my office. Twenty-four hours. Things would change then—we just had to make it through the next day.

There was a clink as I threw my bag onto my desk. I'd almost forgotten that I remembered to bring a photo for my desk. I already had one from our wedding, one taken at my parents' house, and another from the holiday party, but the newest one could possibly be my favorite of all.

I pulled the photo set in its new frame from my bag and placed it on my desk, next to my monitor. It was bound to get me in trouble, causing a constant hard-on looking at her lust-filled face every day.

Lila still pleaded with me to keep it at home, but I was set on what I'd said at Disneyworld. I wanted to be able to see it, see *her*, all the time.

I needed the good times to help me get past the days like today, when the world weighed down on my shoulders.

⇒ ⚫⚫⚫◉⚫⚫⚫ ⇐

It was a beautiful day, which hopefully meant good things were coming our way. The late April day was not filled with showers, but rather a crystal clear blue sky and bright sun. Even the temperature was perfect for the day—sixty-five degrees.

"We just have to get through this, and it's done. Over," Lila said to herself in the mirror as she did her makeup.

I wanted to say something, anything to reassure her, but at the moment everything failed me. We were both wound tight. The last few months had been a constant up and down, and we both desperately needed Adam to be gone and our lives to even out.

My mind couldn't stop playing out the devastation of Adam getting the minimum, which would have him out in less than ten years. I honestly couldn't gauge my reaction if that happened. Would I crumble along with Lila, or would I fucking lose it and do anything I could to kill him?

Part of me wanted that. His death would make her world a better place, and I would do anything for her.

Darren was very concerned about that reaction— afraid I might go off the deep end and snap. What was worse was that I could see it playing out in my mind. The satisfaction of watching the life bleed out of him, out of his eyes.

The need to protect her at any cost, even above my own life, was severe.

I pulled my suit jacket on and straightened the collar in the mirror. "Ready?"

Her reflection froze still as a statue. I turned toward her, waiting.

"Tell me everything's going to be okay."

Fuck. I was already failing her today.

"Everything's going to be great. In a few hours, Adam will be in prison for a very long time." I couldn't even convince myself with the tone I spoke in, so how the hell was I supposed to convince her?

Adam would be out of our lives, but for how long? Could I handle the decision if it wasn't as good as we hoped?

She turned to look at me, her demeanor shut down, and I fell apart.

I covered the few steps between us and scooped her up in my arms, crashing my lips to hers. She shook in my arms, fingers scratching at me as they wrapped around my neck, teeth clacking as the frenzy built.

How could I forget the easiest, most simple way to get us out of our heads?

Touch.

Hands, bodies, mouths—skin against skin.

I turned her and threw us down on the bed. We were both fully dressed and ready to leave, but there was no way we could go as we were.

I was driven with need as I pushed her knees open and ground my hips against her, my cock begging to be inside. My teeth dug into her skin as my fingers tangled in her hair, pulling back. Lovey hugs weren't strong enough on a day like today, and not when we both needed a connection.

She was moaning, her legs wrapped around my waist, pulling me closer. I reached between us as I claimed her mouth again and pulled down the zipper of my pants to get my cock out. I moved her panties aside, happy to find her soaking wet and ready, and shoved my dick into her pussy.

My eyes rolled back, and I grunted as her tight warmth surrounded me. Fucking perfection. I could spend every moment of every day between her legs.

There was no time to waste. We were both going crazy. No words, no talk, just our moans and groans of want filling the air. I drove my hips into her harder and faster, trying to force the demons out of us. Lila was screaming, pleading with sounds, begging me to take it all away.

Everything was static except the pleasure. A crescendo in her sounds sent a ripple through me. My balls were pulled high, so close to giving me the release I needed. Her pussy tightened, her walls clamping around me. So close.

Harder.

Teeth clamped down on my neck, and my cock fired off without warning. I bucked into her, my whole body tingling in an almost pain.

Everything was gone. The whole world ceased to be. All that was left was fuzzy, tingling, white nothing and Lila caging me in.

Strength failed us both and we collapsed onto the bed. Heavy breaths, satisfied bodies, and clearing minds. After a minute, I tilted back to look at her.

"Hi."

Her lips twitched. "Hi."

"I think we may have to change."

She let out a giggle that made the last of the tension fleeing from me.

"Considering your come is sliding down my ass right now, I'd have to agree."

"Fuck." I sat up, both of us moaning as my cock popped out, and stared down, watching me seep out of her. I licked my lips, loving the sight of pearly white covering her pussy. My cock twitched, wanting to do it again.

"Get back in." She pouted at me. "I wasn't ready for you to leave."

I smiled at her and slid my still hard but softening cock into her. "Sorry. You know that's one of my favorite things to see."

"Pervert." She nuzzled my neck, and I hissed when she moved over her bite. It was going to be a dark one.

"I almost feel bad for the drycleaner."

She let out a small laugh. "Yeah, I'm on my third one since meeting you."

"Third?"

"The first gave me dirty looks every time she saw one of your spots. You need to learn to aim better."

I laughed out loud and kissed her hard. "I get so excited I can't contain it."

She kissed me, and we sat there for another moment, taking in the peace. When we pulled apart and looked down, I was also covered in a mixture of us.

"Looks like we're both changing."

"That's what happens when you don't push your pants down. But I also love seeing you with just your cock sticking out of the opening."

"Me too." I glanced at the clock. "Shit, we're late."

She tilted her head to look over. "No coffee then."

I shook my head. "Nope." I held my hand out to help her stand. "Come on, Mrs. Thorne, we need to get out of here."

A half hour and one clothes-change later, we walked into the courtroom and sat down behind Lawrence.

"Good morning," he said with a smile. "Ready for this to be over?"

I blew out a breath. "You have no idea."

"I have a good feeling."

I let out a nervous chuckle. "I'm glad one of us does."

He gave an understanding nod and turned back to the file in front of him.

Lila was silent beside me. I wrapped my arm around her shoulders and she leaned in to me, her lips pressing against my neck.

It was just the two of us as everyone had already taken time off for the trial. The sentencing was so short that we promised everyone we would call them when it was over. There were only a few sparse people sitting around. So few, in fact, that Lila's father and stepmother made up nearly half.

I tried not to look over at the bald fucker across the aisle, but I couldn't keep my glare away. He stared straight ahead, not even giving a hint he noticed our presence. It was a good idea on his part, because I was more than

189

prepared for another beat down of his ass. It was probably due to the restraining order. He was allowed near us at that moment only because the case involved his stepson.

The bitch on the other side of him, however, was shooting daggers.

It was then I finally took a good look at Cheryl Mitchell-Palmer. She looked like a cross between suburban wife and trailer park trash, which was a strange combination. Her once-black hair was riddled with gray. She was almost sickly thin with long, fake nails, overdone makeup, and an overpowering smell of cigarettes.

The smell had me craving a puff or two, but I'd been good and avoided smoking for the past few months. I wasn't going to let her of all people make me fall off the wagon. If Lila could squash the nicotine call, so could I.

A smile crept onto my face as the door opened and Adam was let in wearing a bright orange jumpsuit and shackles. It was fitting, and the image gave me a much-needed boost. He kept his gaze down, barely glancing at his parents. I was getting wound up at the idea of him looking our way and imagining ways to hurt him if he did—waiting for him to so I'd have an excuse to let loose.

The judge entered a few minutes later and sat down. My grip on Lila tugged her closer just as her fingers locked down on mine. He took a moment to look over some papers in front of him, then turned his gaze to the room.

"We're here today for the sentencing hearing of Adam Mitchell."

I tensed, my breath almost stopping. Months boiled down to the next words out of his mouth.

The judge cleared his throat, then looked over to Adam. "Mr. Mitchell, you have been found guilty on multiple charges by a jury of your peers. As I reviewed all the charges again in combination with the testimony, it was shocking to me."

My muscles tightened, hope rising from his words. Lila was the same, leaning forward a bit in anticipation.

"Your all-consuming hatred for Delilah Thorne is profound, and I can find no basis for it. After she was taken from her father's home years ago, you were sent to jail for attacking her. Once released, you continued in your violence against others, unrepentant of your actions."

It felt like I was about to burst, begging him to get to the damn point. Was he drawing it out to torture us?

"Thirteen years passed in which you had no contact with her, and yet you still hunted her down. You tricked your way past her security and brutally attacked her."

I flinched, a memory of that night flashing.

"Your lack of remorse is astounding. It is my ruling that you need to serve the full extent of each charge against you, reaching a total of twenty-seven years. It is *your* actions that have put you here, and no other's. Take responsibility for yourself."

A harsh breath left me. Disbelief followed by relief filled my body all in the same moment.

We did it.

Lila was still staring at the judge, almost as if she was waiting for him to change his mind. When he stood and exited the room, she remained silent.

I stood, smiling, and held out my hand.

"Thank you so much, Lawrence, for all your help."

"I think I should be the one saying that. It's not often I get to work with other lawyers, and it's usually a disaster when I do."

I laughed at that. "Yeah, lawyers don't make the best clients."

"But you did."

We waited a moment for Lila's father to leave first, then walked out with Lawrence. I waved goodbye as he headed off, but Lila wasn't beside me.

I looked over and froze as I stared at her. "Baby?"

Lila's whole body shook and she leaned over, one hand pressed against the wall for support. A choking sob came from her. Her reaction confused me, and I rushed to her side.

I pulled her face up to look at me and sighed in relief when I saw a smile on her face—it was a cry of joy. Her nightmare had the fairy tale ending we hoped for, and the evil monster was banished from the kingdom.

She threw her arms around me and cried into my chest. Happy tears.

CHAPTER 19

L ila was different. That was the only word I could come up with to describe the change. Over the past few days, she'd shed a lot of the crap that held her back for years. It always dwelled in the back of her mind, ever since she left her father's house—when will he come for me?

The unsurmountable weight that pressed upon her was lifted. Chains that held her down released, shedding away the girl like a cocoon and opening up the woman inside. Adam was going to be in jail for a long time, and the judge had approved the restraining order on her father.

It was the first time in over a year I felt like my words really penetrated her. After years of suffering, others finally saw the monster that Adam was. It was validation.

Life returned to its normal pace. It was hard to believe how fast the days were passing. Even more unbelievable was how even we were—no more ups and downs. I was thankful for the change, for the monotony of getting up, going to work, and coming home with my wife—dinners together, talk of what to do on the weekend.

"Hey! That's mine." Lila swatted at my hand, knocking the fry away.

I snuck another one and popped it in my mouth. "We're married—what's mine is yours and vice versa. Right?"

She glared at me and moved her plate away. "You're right. What's yours is mine, but what's mine is mine as well."

"Oooh, man, you better step back from her plate." Drew cackled from across the table.

Caroline was howling in laughter, and I felt like I was being ganged up on. I needed to change my tactics if I was going to get any more fries. Though, I had to admit I was cracking up on the inside watching Lila guard her plate as she ate, giving me the stink eye.

"You said you'd do anything for me, baby."

"You finished your fries. These are mine."

I gave her my best puppy dog eyes. "Just one or two?"

She moved her plate further away. "No."

More snickering from across the table.

"Just think when she gets pregnant. All food will be hers." Caroline slapped her hand on the table as she tried to talk between snorts of laughter. "Try stealing food from a pregnant lady, you'll draw back a bloody stump!"

Drew's jaw dropped. "Dude, what if you end up with the cravings?"

"And lose his taut bod?" Caroline gasped.

Lila joined in, giggling with them but still guarding her plate. The back of my head tingled, like someone was watching us. Granted, with all the commotion, I was certain half the restaurant was staring at us in annoyance.

Drew pointed a fry at me. "You better watch it or you'll end up gaining weight with that sweet tooth of yours."

I glared at him and snatched a fry from his plate.

His eyes narrowed at me. "What the hell?"

I shrugged. "Payment for your jabs at my expense."

Drew pulled his plate back and leaned over it, one arm blocking the front.

I looked over at Lila, who was conversing with Caroline and not protecting her plate as much. It wasn't that I was hungry, but it was now a game, one I was determined to win. With my wife distracted, I planned my attack. I slithered my hand in the space between her arm and ribs. My fingers grazed her breast, and I cringed when metal slapped across my knuckles.

I pulled my hand back, hissing as I shook it out.

"No!" Lila glowered and pointed a fork at me.

I stared at her in shock for a moment, then shook my head. "Oh, hell no."

I grabbed hold of the back of her neck and pulled her to me, kissing her hard. She squeaked and tried to pull back, but I held her tighter, kissing her deeper until she melted against me. There was no way she could resist me.

When I pulled back, her eyes were glassy and unfocused. I reached over and grabbed a few fries and tossed them on my plate.

Drew shook his head.

I stuffed one into my mouth. "What?"

"Nothing."

Caroline snorted. "And that's lunch, boys and girls." She pushed back from the table and stood up. "I have a meeting in half an hour." She grabbed Lila's arm. "Come on. Walk with me while your husband pays for lunch."

"Me?"

Lila stood, then grabbed my head and crashed her lips to mine. My cock jumped, lust coursing through me as her tongue lapped against mine.

Fuck.

She was pulled away by Caroline, who rolled her eyes. "You two are like teenagers. Sheesh."

Drew nodded. "It's Lila's turn, but since you had to lust her brain out for a few fries, it's yours. After all, what did you say? What's hers is yours."

I sighed and pulled out my wallet, placing my credit card on the check.

"Where are you going?"

Drew turned back to me. "Gotta call Dana."

I waved him off and waited for the waitress to return for payment. While I was sitting there, I watched some basketball game on one of the TVs. I smiled up at the waitress as she took the check and returned to the screen.

After a moment I turned, looking for the gaze I felt drilling a hole in my head, but there was no one. It happened multiple times over lunch, and I didn't like the feeling of being watched.

I thanked the waitress when she returned a moment later, and signed the slip before putting my card away. I took one last sip of soda and stood before heading to the door.

"Nate!"

I turned toward where my name was being called. A group of people were being seated, and walking toward me with a familiar smile that greeted me was Tom Preston. We'd worked together in the prosecutor's office. As my mind compared the image in my memory to the man in front of me, I noticed that the years hadn't been the best to him. He had to be in his mid to late forties. His once black hair was more than salted with gray, and what had once been fine lines were now carving deep into his skin. Even his once well-kept physique had added a good twenty or so pounds.

"Nathan Thorne. I'll be damned," he said as he walked up to me and stuck out his hand.

I gave his hand a stiff shake and smiled at him. "It's been a long time."

"Yeah. Last time I saw you, the judge was throwing you out of the courtroom, a bailiff on each arm dragging you down the aisle." He let out a harsh chuckle. "I thought they were about to drag you off to the nut house."

My lips were set in a thin line. "Well, it wasn't the best time in my life." I was certain there'd been much talk about me after that.

"I had a lot of hope for you." His eyes scanned me up and down. "What are you up to these days?"

"I'm working for Holloway and Holloway."

His head tipped back as he nodded. "Ah, your father-in-law. How's that going?"

"Pretty good. I spent about a year as a transactional attorney after a few years off, and now I'm in the real estate division."

"Quite different areas."

I shrugged. "It was necessary. I wasn't ready to go back into the courtroom."

"Well, now that you're back in the game, maybe we can get together. I could really use you."

"On what?"

"I'm building a case against Vincent Marconi."

It felt like the blood rushed from my body, and I began to sweat. Why hadn't I looked into who was working on the case Noah told me about? "I don't want anything to do with your case."

"What? How can you say that?" He frowned at me, his arms crossing over his chest. "Nate, you have all the information we need. No one has ever gotten a conviction, and *you* did. I know you have more information on them. Help us."

I shook my head, my jaw set. "I can't."

He leaned toward me, his expression imploring, and I stepped back. "These are bad people who need to pay for their crimes."

"You don't need to tell *me* that. I understand, more than anyone, but I'm sorry. I can't help you, Tom."

"Why not?" he asked, complete confusion in his aged features. It didn't seem like he could comprehend my reluctance. Couldn't he put two and two together?

I leaned in closer, almost spitting on him between my clenched teeth. "Because the last time I was involved with them, my wife and son were murdered and, for a few seconds, they killed me as well." It dawned on me that we were both being watched and our innocent conversation was being noted. "Fuck. Even talking to you now is bad."

He shook his head. "You've become paranoid. Do you really think they're keeping tabs on you? They've induced you with fear." His arms relaxed, waving around in defense. "I'm not downplaying what happened. It's a tragedy what they did to Grace. She was a wonderful woman, but they aren't still watching you. They hurt you. They got what they wanted."

I gaped at him, stunned. "You really have no idea what you're getting into. Don't you realize they're watching your every move? They're watching mine as well, and this little meeting could very well get my family killed. So, back the fuck off!"

"You've gone off the reservation, Thorne." He looked at me like I was out of my mind.

"Don't be cocky. That's how I was, and you know what happened. You think a family like that doesn't have connections or the money to buy people? They know. I was informed by a third party they were tailing me again and anyone working on the case. Probably waiting for a meeting like this to crop up."

I pulled at my neck, the tension rocketing to sky-high proportions.

"I'm not cocky... I'm realistic." He looked at me with sad eyes. "You should look at seeing a psychiatrist. There are obviously some issues left over from your accident."

I scoffed at him. "I have a therapist, but thanks for that. I assure you, I'm quite sane, and my paranoia comes from truth."

He stared at me for a moment, but then his eyes flickered around the restaurant. "What do I do?"

"You walk away before they come after you or your family."

Tom lost his fight, his voice lowering, as it seemed to dawn on him that I was right. "What are you going to do?"

"I'm going to do *everything* I can to keep my wife safe."

He looked at me like I was insane. "Grace is dead."

I shook my head and gave him a small smile. "Not Grace. I'm not that crazy, Tom. I got married a few months ago. Her name is Lila."

A genuine smile lit up his face. "Congratulations. I mean it."

"Thanks." I held out my hand. "I need to get going. Take care, and think about what I said."

"You, too."

I turned to walk away.

"Hey, Nate," Tom called, making me turn back around. "At least think about what I said as well. Do the world a little good to get a man like him gone."

I pursed my lips and nodded, glancing to the corner of the restaurant as I pushed the door open and walked out. Lila was waiting for me at the edge of the parking lot, Drew and Caroline already gone.

"Who was that?" she asked when I got closer.

"No one."

She grabbed onto my arm and halted my steps. I turned to look at her, the playfulness of lunch gone and replaced with concern.

"What's yours is mine, and that includes your burdens."

My chest tightened, the truth in her words almost strangling me. It wasn't right to keep him or my concern bottled up from her.

"His name is Tom Preston. We used to work together. He's the one building a case against Vincent Marconi." I pulled at my neck, trying to work the growing tension out.

She stared at me, then nodded. "He wants your help."

I swallowed hard. "Yes."

"You told him no." She looked into my eyes. I nodded. "Because of me."

Again, I nodded, unable to find the words.

She wrapped her arms around me and held me close, kissing my neck. "It's all right. I'm here."

I was confused by her words until I realized I was shaking. A harsh breath left me, and I pulled her close.

She agreed to be with me, knowing the danger, but was I so selfish to risk her life further?

CHAPTER 20

The next day, I was a wreck.

Meeting Tom was a mistake.

Granted, it wasn't like I planned to run into him. That was what made it worse. If Marconi had someone watching us at that moment, I was screwed. It was a chance meeting that could get Lila killed.

An innocent fucking errand that brought the devil down.

After what Noah told me, I knew it wasn't an "if" someone was watching. I'd recognized one of his men sitting in the corner as we talked. Marconi probably thought I was working the case.

I needed to figure out a way to keep Lila safe.

My mind was cracking, and the beast paced, whimpering. Everything was spiraling out of control. I was losing my grip.

It was times like this the beast in me was let out. Nothing calmed it more than Lila. My body ached only for her touch. I needed it to survive. I'd die without it—without *her*. She let me ravage her, letting go in ways no other would. Euphoria and comfort—the soothing balm to my screaming agony.

I couldn't go hunt her down and drag her off. I needed her to come to me, so I picked up my cell phone and texted her.

Need you. Now.

I tossed it back down on my desk and rubbed my face. My foot tapped on the floor as I listened to the tick of the clock, waiting for her response. Wound tight, my muscles locked down. I needed to relax.

There was a light knock on the door, and I sighed. I didn't even have to say anything before the handle spun and Lila walked in. She flicked the lock on my door, a devilish smirk on her lips.

In her hand was a fresh cup of coffee, which she set on my desk as she walked up to me. She was silent, reserved...*submissive*. Exactly what I needed.

I turned my chair, following her movement as she sunk down to her knees in front of me. I wet my lips as I leaned forward, my hand gripping the back of her neck as I kissed her. It wasn't soft—it was rough and needy.

I stood up and moved to free my aching hard-on. Her eyes followed my hands as they moved to my crotch. I palmed my cock and groaned at the hungry look in her eyes as she stared at it.

"See how much I need my cock slut?"

She nodded, licking her lips as I pulled down the zipper and reached inside. My cock was hard and hot, ready to mark her as I pulled it out. I moaned, pumping it in my hand as I looked down at the sexy sight of my wife on her knees before me, looking up at me, eager for my cock.

"Stay still." I adjusted my stance and ran the head across her lips, my mouth open as her lips parted, tongue teasing my slit.

My eyes rolled back and my toes curled when her lips wrapped around the head of my cock, the sensitive edge overstimulated, making me shake. Nothing in the world was better than Lila wrapped around me. Her sweet mouth moved down, making me shake as my entire length slid in and the tip eased down her throat.

I hissed out a "fuck." She'd gotten so good at deep-throating me over the last year.

My fingers tangled in her hair, fisting it as I guided her luscious mouth up and down my hard shaft. I was seconds away from holding her head still and fucking the shit out of her mouth. The twisted and sexy thing was that she'd let me, and she'd enjoy it.

Lila made it all disappear. Being inside her, all my thoughts and worries were replaced with white, mindless bliss.

My balls were so tight, cock so hard—I was about to come.

My eyes flickered around, trying to take my mind off the intense pleasure of her mouth. I needed more, needed to last longer. Her coffee cup was sitting on the edge of my desk, steam coming off the top. It was black, and not the way she took her coffee.

A wicked grin formed on my face, and I looked down at her.

"Do you want some cream in your coffee, slut?"

She hummed around me and tried to speak—the vibration made my eyes close and almost tipped me over the edge. I was so close to exploding. My hands released her hair, and I leaned over, my cock popping from her lips as I grabbed her cup. She chased after me with her mouth, her tongue lapping at my tip.

I grabbed my cock and gave it a tug, then slapped it against her lips. She smiled up at me as my hand worked up and down, teasing the underside of the head, getting me that last little bit further before I popped.

Her mouth was open and waiting. My whole body tensed, every muscle coiled tight. The first explosive bursts landed in her mouth, then I pulled away and let the remainder land in the cup.

"Don't swallow," I said with heavy breaths. She did as I asked, her mouth open as I finished off, emptying into her coffee.

When I was done, I held the mug in front of her as she let my come roll off her tongue into it. I set it back down on my desk, a hard shudder running through me as she sucked the last drop from the tip.

I felt lighter and a bit sleepy as I slumped back down in my chair. "Fuck, I needed that."

She grabbed a tissue from the box on my desk and wiped away any leftovers. My hand reached out and ran through her hair, straightening out the mess I'd made. "I have a meeting, but don't worry. I'll get you tonight."

She smiled and stood up, then leaned forward for a kiss. "Can't wait." She turned and headed for the door.

"Don't forget your coffee," I called after her.

Turning around, she picked it up and brought it to her lips, taking a sip. She let out a little moan, smiling as she licked her lips.

"Perfect." She winked at me and took another sip, then headed out the door.

Fuck, she was naughty. I fucking loved it.

<hr/>

My little afternoon tryst with Lila helped calm me, but didn't disperse with the threat hanging over me. Making it worse was that it wasn't just me anymore—I had Lila to protect. With my dying breath, I would make sure she was safe.

Which led me to my current dilemma.

I walked into my home office and sat at my desk, swiveling the chair around to face the closed closet door.

It was mad…crazy…*insane* for me to think about what was in there and what I could do with it. The box was buried under other file boxes. A label reading "Taxes 2008" was affixed to the exterior.

The only tax documents inside were Via Marconi's. My insurance resided there as well.

Phone records, witness accounts, photos, etc.— enough evidence to tie Vincent Marconi to over five deaths and seven felonies. It only scratched the surface, but it was enough to get him put away for life and begin having his operation dissected, which would lead to his empire being torn apart.

I wasn't going into the situation again believing that everything would be fine. His daughter still had five years left to serve before even the possibility of parole. Until then, and probably even after, I was a marked man.

What pissed me off was that the little bit of invisibility I'd had, the shadowing from his vision, was blown away because someone in an office where I no longer worked was forming a case against him. Marconi knew what I had on him—I was stupid enough to gloat in his face that he was next. Between that and the death of Grace and my baby, he was satisfied for the time-being. Happy to keep me scared and buried in my own personal hell.

It was to the point of being damned if I do, or damned if I don't. Seeing me with Tom would raise a red flag to Vincent. His first intuition would tell him I was working with them.

I was a dead man.

"Nate?"

I looked to the door to find Lila standing there, a worried expression on her face. "Yeah?"

She walked into the room and stood in front of me. "Didn't you hear me calling?"

I shook my head. "Sorry, I was lost in thought."

She pursed her lips. "What's wrong?"

I sighed and pulled her close, leaning forward to rest my head on her stomach. "Running into Tom Preston has fucked things up, and I'm afraid for us." Her fingers moved through my hair, nails scratching, calming. I pulled back to look up at her. "What do I do to protect you?"

"Protect me?"

"You know from who, and now I'm left with this decision. We're at a fork in the road, but which way will kill us?" My chest clenched, and I nuzzled into her. "I'm not sure there's an alternative at this point." I looked back up at her, pleading to anything that would listen. "The most important thing to me is keeping you alive."

Her brow scrunched up, and she shook her head. "There is no life for me without you."

My chest tightened, and I pulled her to my lap, holding her close. I didn't know if there was enough hope and prayers to deities above to keep her safe, but I'd do whatever it took. Even if it meant killing the devil myself.

⟫•••◐◖◗◑•••⟪

The next morning, I pulled three expanding files along with a manila file out of my bag and set them on my desk. After soaking in my wife, I'd broached the box that haunted me and emptied its contents. They stared at me, and I stared back. It hurt me to even touch them, to bring them back out into the light of day.

Memories and heartbreak tore at me all evening. Nightmares that were too real haunted my dreams. I couldn't stop touching Lila, my worst fears killing me from the inside out. My heart begged me not to do it, but at the same time, it wanted justice—the files could help with that.

I sat at my desk, my fingers running across my lips as I looked at their worn edges. Sending them to Tom would make things worse. Then again, I was already on the Marconi hitlist. The information would help in his case—I had no doubt about that—but I had to be discreet about delivery. There was no way I could walk up to Tom and hand it to him—we'd both be dead that day.

I sat back and rubbed my face.

Sending the files could help keep Lila safe. If Marconi was convicted, he might leave her alone. He might stop keeping tabs.

I stood and picked up the files, heading out of my office and down the hall. I needed help and guidance. Who better than someone I trusted and had lost the same person I had?

"Hey, Cassie, is Jack available?" I smiled down at his secretary.

"Hi, Nathan." She looked down at her computer. "You're in luck. He's got a break right now and he just got off the phone."

"Thanks." I stepped forward and knocked on the door.

"Come in," Jack called from inside.

I opened the door and walked through, closing it behind me. He smiled at me from across his desk, his gaze narrowing on the files in my hand.

"How are you doing, Nate?"

I sat down in the chair across from him and placed the files on the edge of his desk as I leaned back.

"I ran into Tom Preston the other day." I jumped right in.

"Oh yeah? How's he doing these days?"

"He's working on a case against Vincent Marconi." The smile slid from his face. "Jesus."

"I'm pretty sure we were spotted together."

"How do you know?"

209

"Lila's foster brother is a cop. He told me Marconi's men, along with some dirty cops, were tailing those involved with the case. The list includes me."

"But why you? You aren't involved with it."

I leaned forward and placed my finger on the stack of files. "Because of this."

His face paled. "All of your information on them." He looked back at me. "You kept it all?"

I nodded. "It was a bit of insurance, along with not knowing what the hell to do with it. You know how bad things were back then."

He leaned back and ran a hand through his white hair. "Nathan... What do you want to do with it? Why is it here?"

I pursed my lips. "That's the big question I've been struggling with. Grace died because of them. If there's a strong case against them, I want to give them more ammo. But..."

"You're afraid." A pained look crossed his face.

"They already saw me talking to Tom, even if it was only a chance run-in and small talk. They know I have all this." I waved my hand at the file. "Pretty certain the whole fucking thing red flagged me. If my life is in that much danger because they think I'm helping them, I'd rather someone put this to use."

"Do we have to go through all this again?" His head was down, shaking. "You're so happy now."

I tried not to think about Lila, but it was useless. The road was about to get very rough, and I'd need her strength.

"I'm not resigning myself to death. I have too much hope for a future to do that. But I'm not going to live like everything is fine, oblivious...not like last time."

"Have you talked to Lila about this?"

I sighed. "A little. She caught that something was off. She's been so happy since the trial, and I made her cry last night. We've even been working on a b-baby." I stuttered on the word. My chest was tight, and I rubbed at the spot.

Jack's eyes were soft. "What can I do to help?"

I let out a shuddering breath. "I can't just hand this file to Tom."

"You'd be dead before the day was over."

I nodded. "I need a way so it's not traceable to me."

Jack stared at the files, humming as he tapped his fingers on his desk. "You know, Mary has a niece that works for Michael Lawson. Last I was down there, his office was two doors down from Tom's." My eyes grew wide, hopeful. "And Jenny, Mary's niece, just so happens to be coming over this weekend."

"Is that far enough removed?" Bad enough I was involving Jack, but my former mother-in-law and her family as well?

He lips set into a thin line. "No, you're right. We need another step."

My brain fired off ideas, each wilder and more extreme than the one before. "What if she put it in a courier envelope with a random address and sends it to Tom?"

Jack thought it over for a moment. "Do you want to risk it with this information?"

I blew out a breath. "What other choice do we have? Besides, I asked around, and Michael Lawson's name did not come up as being associated with the case against Marconi. No one would be watching his office."

Jack scratched at his jaw as he stared at the files. "I'll get it wrapped up in a code-locked courier bag and have her send it that way."

"How do we get him the code?"

"Leave that to me. I'll figure it out."

I was silent, unsure of how to thank him. "I can't let it happen again, but I don't know what to do to stop it."

Jack's eyes were soft, full of understanding. "This will help. And try to stay calm—Lila needs you."

"Not as much as I need her. She's stronger than I am."

Jack shook his head. "When it comes to you, Lila is the weakest woman on the planet."

I blinked at him. Fuck. He had a point. We were so codependent on each other that it was almost debilitating to even think of life without the other.

CHAPTER 21

Days passed and…nothing.

Well, not *nothing*. I was a mess. A fucking disaster.

High anxiety, nightmares, and a constant popping of pills got me through the day. Lila got me through the night.

She made microwavable popcorn one evening and I flipped out, tackling her to the ground. I did laugh about it later, but it still had me on edge. I knew she was worried about me. She wouldn't say it, because she didn't want me to flip out even more. Conversations of the file and Marconi were taboo in our home.

Every day, she sucked and fucked me in an attempt to keep me calm. It worked, but I wasn't stable. Highs and lows led to more forceful, selfish, but mind-blowing sex.

"Fuck, you're so fucking good at that." She had me panting as she swallowed around my cock.

I held her head down, nose pressing against my skin, cock down her throat. Her fingers flexed against my skin, but I kept her there. The overpowering sensations of her gagging around the head forced me to pull out.

Lila was panting, almost gasping for air, her hand wiping at her mouth. Tears made her makeup bleed black down her pink cheeks and her lips were swollen and red. Her hair was a mess, thanks to my hands.

"You're a fucking gorgeous mess."

She smirked up at me and licked her lips.

"Do you want me to fuck you, little whore? I'm so fucking close. Or do you want to drink me?"

Her tongue flicked against the tip of my cock, and I hissed. She was lucky I didn't push her back down right then and fuck her throat raw.

She sat up straight and opened her mouth, ready to receive. It was tempting, but I wanted to feel her pussy clamp down on me.

"Hammering your pussy it is."

Her mouth closed some and she glared at me. "Why the fuck give me a choice?"

I walked around her and pushed her head down, leaning over her. "To make you think you had one."

I was an asshole, but I'd make sure she enjoyed it.

My cock slipped easily into her wet pussy, and we both moaned. She hissed out a "fuck" and a sharp intake of breath when I slammed into her.

All of me curled into her, fingers digging hard into her skin. It was the only way I could get it all out.

She was crying out, screaming each time I bottomed out in her. Shaking, she looked back at me, and I almost lost it under the lust in her eyes. When her eyes rolled back and she fell forward, I smiled. Her fingers clenched into the sheets, fisting.

Her pussy clamping down finished me off. I shook, my hips thrusting, trying to reach deeper with each spurt of come that exploded out. Her pussy pulsed around me, drawing out the last drops. My legs gave out, and we fell to the floor in a tangled mess.

⸺ ⋆⋆⋆◉◉⋆⋆⋆ ⸺

Before we married, we made a pact to have a date night once a week. It was to take the place of our bar night and help us get out of our hiding tendencies. Thanks to the wedding and trial, we'd lost a few. There was still a nervous edge in the back of my mind that one of our coworkers would see us and report us. Even after we were married, it caught us both at times. I loved being out with her, whether to the grocery store or a movie—it was great being able to live life again.

Adam was locked away, and Lila was glowing, despite the danger that was encroaching.

"You're wearing that?" Lila asked as she came out of the closet.

I blinked at her and looked down at the charcoal slacks and black button-down. "Yes."

Her tongue peeked out to wet her lips, and it was then I understood that I didn't just look bad. It was good—I looked edible.

The same could be said about her. The few dresses she had for work were always the perfect combination of sexy and sophisticated. Conservative, with body hugging lines. They looked great on her, turning me on and creating the easy access I craved. I still blamed the flirty hemline of one of her skirts for my inability to control myself that night a year ago.

We rarely went out for a nice dinner, but she always seemed to surprise me with a dress she pulled out of nowhere, and the one she had on was *not* a work dress.

My lip twitched up and I stepped toward her, needing to touch her. I reached out, my hand resting on her hip, the deep red satin silky and soft beneath my fingers. It was classy and elegant, showing off just enough cleavage to draw my cock's attention. It made me want to rip her out of it and wonder why we ever thought to leave the house.

"Do we have to go to dinner? I could easily eat my dessert right now."

She rolled her eyes at me and smiled. Her hand reached out and she pressed her palm against my dick, making me groan. Her other hand slipped under the collar of my shirt as she stepped forward to whisper in my ear.

"Something you want, baby? Do you want to fill my pussy, make me cream, and scream your name?"

"Fuck yes!"

She stepped away from me, her touch gone. My eyes opened to find a wicked grin.

"Too bad. I'm already dressed, and we're going."

My gaze narrowed at her. "I can rip it off you."

"You do that, and I'll be a dead fish for the next month."

My jaw dropped. "My dick is magical, baby. You can't resist the feelings it brings you."

She didn't flinch, her expression the same. "No anal, no blowjobs."

"Now you're just being mean."

"I really like this dress."

"I really like that dress, too. I'd like it better on the floor." I smirked and my cock twitched. It liked that idea quite a bit.

She sighed and shook her head. "You're incorrigible."

I adjusted my cock so it wasn't tenting in my pants so much. "Okay, you win. I'm picking my battle. Dessert after dinner."

"I knew you'd come around."

"But…"

She glared at me. "What?"

"You can suck me off on the way to the restaurant."

"It's a two-and-a-half block walk."

I held the door open for her. "You've got your work cut out for you."

She rolled her eyes and walked through the door. "Yeah, I have to learn to levitate by the time we reach the lobby."

We headed out, walking down the street with our fingers entwined.

"I love that the weather has finally warmed up."

I reached out and touched her bare shoulder. "Me too."

She looked at me, trying not to laugh, but just shook her head.

A few feet later, we were walking into the restaurant, and I attempted to behave.

Attempted.

The rich, dark woods that adorned the walls coupled with the low lighting provided a warm and romantic setting. How was I supposed to stave off my desires in a place that was asking me to grope her under the table?

We were seated at a table and not at a booth that would give me easy access to her. I wanted to pout at how far apart we were, even though our legs were touching under the table.

The host handed us our menus, along with the wine list, before departing. I was almost salivating as I read over the different types of steak. Ruth Chris was by no means cheap, but they were worth every penny.

"Hello, my name is Brian, and I'll be your waiter this evening. Have you dined with us before?"

I looked up from my menu and was about to speak when Lila beat me to it.

"I haven't."

He smiled down at her. "Welcome, and thank you for coming."

He was a young guy, mid-twenties, with the all-American boy look about him. Probably played sports and got in all the girls' panties.

My jaw twitched as he pointed things out to Lila on the menu and explained that it was all à la carte. There was a difference between friendly and flirting. She was oblivious to it, but his smile was a little cocky for my liking, as was his staring down her dress.

I cleared my throat to gain his attention, and his head snapped up. "We'd like a bottle of the Chateau St. Jean, Reserve Merlot."

He nodded, then looked back down to Lila and licked his lips. "Is there anything else you'd like?"

I couldn't take any more. I grabbed her chin and turned her to me, kissing her so hard our teeth hit. She gasped before melting, like always.

"That's all." I held out the wine list for him, Lila's hair still tangled in my fingers.

He gave me a tight smile as he took it and left.

Lila looked at me, her brow quirked as she sat back.

"What? He was too friendly with you."

She pursed her lips. "He was being polite."

"He was flirting."

She leaned forward and nipped at my bottom lip. "So possessive."

"Damn straight."

She smiled and shook her head. "I'm your wife. Taken."

I took her hand in mine. "Yes, but fuckers like to look and salivate and think about screwing you. That pisses me off. You're mine. I need to hurry up and get you pregnant. Then everyone will see what I do to you."

My cock twitched, reminding me it wanted another go at knocking her up.

She ran her hand up my leg, her fingertips brushing my cock. "You'll get a chance to fill me after dinner."

Our waiter returned with the bottle I ordered and poured two glasses. He kept his eyes off Lila. We placed our order and happily munched on some bread while we drank.

Dinner was perfect. My stomach was filled with the most delicious and perfectly cooked steak I'd ever eaten. I rubbed my stomach, patting it.

"That was the *best* steak ever, and I've been here before."

"I hope you saved room for dessert." Lila stretched her hand out to me, and I slipped mine over hers.

"You'll probably need to give me and hour or so and then I'll be up for it."

She let out a small chuckle. "I was talking about the sweet pastry kind."

"You can eat more?" She'd devoured her steak just as I had.

She frowned at the thought. "Well..."

The waiter stopped by, but instead of asking if we needed anything, he set a cake covered in candles on the table in front of me.

Lila smiled at me. "Happy birthday."

I stared at her for a moment, then my eyes moved down to the cake. Yes, it was my birthday dinner—May 30th. I'd agreed to celebrate it this year as a way of moving on. It was a little easier, because the one I hated to think about was on a different date, a date I'd never forget—June 21st.

It was the first time I'd celebrated my birthday in five years. I was trapped between moving forward and being stuck in the past. The candles flickered at me, waiting. That was the signal that jostled me to the present, and I thought about the wish I would make.

The year started out terrible and ended up beautiful—Lila and I were married.

But we still had one more obstacle that was looming over us, and it was hovering much closer than I liked.

I took a deep breath and blew out.

I wish that I can keep Lila safe, that she will be free from danger.

In one breath, all the candles were extinguished and my wish was out into the cosmos. I didn't really believe, but it couldn't hurt. We needed all the help we could get.

The cake was white almond with buttercream icing—my favorite.

"You got this from that cake place in Noblesville, the one we went to last fall." She nodded, and I moaned as I took another bite. Yes, I was full, but nothing was going to stop me from eating the best cake I'd ever tasted. "When did you sneak this?"

"Sarah picked it up for me and delivered it to the restaurant."

I chuckled. "Conspiring with my mother now."

"You do it all the time."

"Yes, but she's *my* mother."

She swiped her finger across the icing and stuck it in her mouth, sucking it off. Suddenly the best place for the icing wasn't in my stomach, but on my cock.

"Well, it's hard to surprise my caveman husband who can't stand an hour without me."

I gave her a pout. "Makes me sound like a dependent pussy."

She laughed and patted my hand. "Dependent? Yes. Pussy? Hell no. You can be a controlling asshole... You're so possessive of me."

"Because you're mine."

She bit her bottom lip and smiled. "Because I'm yours."

I leaned forward and kissed her, savoring the taste of her mixed with the buttercream frosting. When I sat back, my eye caught a familiar onlooker staring at us. I'd seen him before, but had no clue who he was. That didn't matter, because I knew why he was there.

"Where are you going?" I asked as she moved to stand.

She smiled down at me. "I'll be right back. I'm just going to the ladies' room."

I nodded, watching her go as I finished up the last bite of cake. I was mid-sip when my stalker sat down in front of me, a smile on his face. "Hello, Mr. Thorne. How's your driving these days?"

The blood drained from my face as I remembered why he was so familiar—he held the gun in the car that ran us off the road.

It took every ounce of will in me to keep my reactions cool and calm, but inside I was trying to keep the anxiety from exploding, though anger and fear prevailed. My hands twitched, begging to wrap around his throat and choke the life out of him.

Dead men couldn't talk.

I would do *anything* to keep her safe.

"Get the fuck out of here." The words barely made it past my clenched teeth.

He wasn't even fazed. "Getting rid of me won't stop *him*."

Fuck. How could I be so stupid? I'd relaxed, taken a breath and enjoyed the moment, and gotten comfortable with a deadly man so close.

"Why are you here, talking to me?"

He smirked. "How's your wife?" Hatred flamed in me, my muscles flexing and ready to destroy. His smile broadened. "Mr. Marconi would like to congratulate you on your marriage." His gaze flickered over to the restroom entry. "She's beautiful."

My teeth clenched tight, and my whole body vibrated. "Don't you fucking touch her."

He laughed as he stood and walked away just as Lila returned. Her gaze moved to him and then to me.

"Nate? What's wrong?" Her hand reached out to touch me, and I shot up from my seat.

I ran to the door. He hadn't gotten far—just a few steps ahead of me. It only took a few strides for me to catch up to him.

He turned just as my fist collided with his face, knocking him back against the brick wall. I didn't waste a second before hitting him again.

His skull was hard, splitting my skin.

Beat him bloody.

Beat him dead.

Protect Lila.

The surprise wore off and his fist swung forward, connecting with my ribs. All breath left me as pain flooded in, giving him the opening to smash my face. My vision blurred, and he hit me again.

Lila screamed in the background, and I swung out, hoping to strike. My hand scraped against the brick before connecting with the side of his head. He stumbled back, and we both got a moment to catch our breath. He cursed when he noticed the crowd around us.

He spit the blood that filled his mouth out onto the ground and glared at me. "You knew, Thorne. I'll let Vincent know you said hello."

Before I could get to him, a car pulled up and he got in just as Lila grabbed hold of my arm. I watched them tear down the street and out of sight.

I grimaced in pain, bending over as the adrenaline started to wear off and the effect of his hits settled in. When I turned, Lila was staring at me, eyes wide in shock. I stepped forward and scooped her up in my arms.

"I won't let them hurt you. I'll protect you."

She nodded against me, her hands fisting into my shirt.

Murmurs from the gathered crowd brought me back. With her close, we headed back toward the restaurant. The manager gave me a dirty look and blocked the doorway, but I shut him down from speaking when I pulled out my wallet. I slapped three one hundred-dollar bills into his hand and continued walking.

"Should we call someone?" Lila asked as we headed home.

I couldn't stop scanning the street, waiting for someone to pop out at us. "Who could we trust?"

The list was short, and possibly getting shorter.

CHAPTER 22

─────⟨●⟩─────

The event alarm pinged on my computer, opening a window in the middle of my document. I cracked my neck, stretching it out. I'd been staring at my screen for more than two hours without moving and was happy for the distraction of the end of the workday.

I saved my progress and shut my computer down. There wasn't much time, and we needed to get going. I slipped my jacket back on and grabbed my phone before heading out the door, locking it behind me.

A few feet later, I popped my head into Lila's office. "Are you ready?" It was almost five-thirty, and she had an appointment with Darren in half an hour. It would take nearly that long with traffic to get there. "Honeybear?"

Both Lila and Owen failed to acknowledge my presence, still typing away. I shook my head and sighed.

"Yo! Wife of mine, come on."

Her head snapped up, eyes blinking in confusion. "Fuck," she hissed as she noticed the time. "Give me a sec."

"It's never a sec in this black hole."

She held her finger up, not even looking at me anymore. I licked my lips, thinking about giving her a little spanking for that later.

Leaning against the door frame, waiting, I took a good look around the room. It wasn't my first view since I'd vacated it months ago, but it was broken in with Owen. Not much had changed, with the exception of Owen and his personal belongings. A photo of him and his girlfriend sat next to his monitor along with a Scooby-Doo figure.

Any trace of the nearly one year I'd spent there was gone. I kind of missed that time—missed being so close to her.

She closed up the file in front of her and played with her computer before shutting it down. There was a frazzled edge to her as she located her purse and stood to face me.

"Okay, ready."

She stepped toward me, and I grabbed her face, pulling it close as I licked her lips and kissed her. When I pulled back, her lids were heavy and she was leaning into me.

I grabbed her hand and started down the hall. She pouted.

"That was mean."

My lip twitched. "What?"

"You know what, mister."

We stopped at the elevator bay and pressed the button. I leaned down, kissing her neck as I squeezed her ass.

"Just wanted to show you how much I missed you."

The moment of fun was just what I needed at the end of a long day.

During the drive, she took my right hand in hers, placing kisses on my busted-up knuckles. She swiped her fingers across mine, soothing us both.

I'd gotten a good five or six punches in on the bastard, but he matched me. The hit to the brick wall behind him had me hurting the worst.

As we pulled up to Darren's office, three police cars sat outside with their lights flashing. Red and blue lights bounced off the building.

My stomach dropped out, and I grabbed for Lila's hand, encasing it in mine. We walked up to the office and found Darren standing outside talking to an officer. His eyes widened, only for a second, but it was enough that I noticed.

"Darren, what's going on?" I asked as we approached.

He spoke to the officer and turned toward us. "Someone broke into my office over lunch."

Lila's eyes widened. "What?"

"Did they take anything?"

His gaze flickered away from mine. "No."

I didn't believe him. I'd known him long enough. His poker face wasn't that good.

"What did they take?"

He pursed his lips and looked between Lila and me, then let out a long breath. "They took your file…and Lila's."

Dread washed over me. "Is that *all*?" I needed to know the answer. Needed to know that it was just a break-in for files and not mine specifically, because I knew who it was.

"They only took yours and Lila's."

I cursed under my breath, my hand tightening around Lila's as the world began to crash around me. This couldn't be happening—not again. Maybe he'd been right. Maybe I should have listened closer. Maybe I should have run with Lila when he sat down next to me at the restaurant.

They were coming back. They were going to kill us, and every fear I'd had since I met her, since I met my Lila, washed over me, enveloping me. My hands began to shake—something that Darren noticed.

"You have to stay calm. I didn't want to tell you because I knew this would happen."

"Of course it was going to happen." My stomach turned, and I pulled Lila close to me, my arms wrapping around her as my body bent in on itself.

Her hands ran soothing circles up and down my back, her nails digging in slightly, scratching. The small bit of pain reminded me she was there.

Darren put his hand on my shoulder. "Take a deep breath." I took in as much air as I could and slowly let it out. "Lila, could you go inside and get a bottle of water from the vending machine down the hall?"

I reached out as she walked away and grabbed onto her arm. "No."

Darren placed his hand on mine and waved an officer over. "Can you escort her inside to the break room for me?"

Lila caressed my face. "I'll be right back."

I whimpered as she walked away, but I couldn't take my eyes off her. "How did they know to come here?"

Darren sighed. "I don't know, but I think it's obvious they're tailing you again."

My head snapped to him. "You think?" I flashed my busted up knuckles at him. "Every fucking place I go."

He cursed under his breath, eyes wide as he stared at my hand. "When?"

"My birthday."

"Have you thought about hiring a bodyguard or getting police protection?"

I shook my head. "Police are in on it, and what the hell is a body guard going to do against them?"

"Protect you."

My jaw twitched. "How the hell will one guy, or even five guys, be able to protect us round the clock for the rest of our lives?"

Anger built up, and the urge to punch something skyrocketed, but there was nothing to hit. I exploded, yelling out and up to the heavens.

"There has to be something."

I was breathing hard, tears filling my eyes. "There's only one thing. I'm dead, but I can still protect Lila."

Devastation.

The email said it all—*bang!* You're dead.

I couldn't stop staring at the screen, at the photos of Lila and me coming and going from the condo I was sitting in.

When did I become so lax? I didn't even notice it happened, so blissed out with Lila the threat that hung over me wasn't even a blip on my radar.

I'd tried to live a life, be happy, start over with the woman I loved.

"Nate, you there?" Tom's voice rang out through the receiver.

"Y-yeah, I'm here."

"We've gotten three of his men arrested and are close to getting him. The files have been instrumental to that. Not much longer."

My hand rubbed over my face. "I don't know if it'll be soon enough."

"Why? What's going on?"

I swallowed hard. "They know I'm helping you."

"How?"

"They know."

I hung up the phone and clenched my shaking hand into a fist. My eyes scrunched closed, and I tried to hold it in, but that was impossible. I swung out, hitting the lamp on my desk and sending it smashing into the wall.

I yelled, hard and harsh, the sound bouncing around. Anger coursed through me. I stood up and tossed my chair across the room. Every muscle was tight as I

231

searched for more to destroy, to quell the overwhelming pain consuming me.

I wanted Lila to be mine in every way, and she was going to pay the price for my selfishness with her life.

Should we stay, or should we run? They'd still find us, so we'd only be delaying the inevitable, but there was always the small chance they wouldn't. There was also the fact that my family would be put in danger.

It was the end of days.

I picked up something from my desk and hurled it, indifferent to what it was, then found another object. I was lost in a sea of destruction, searching for the way, pushing past it all. A chair leg in my hand crunched as it slammed into the monitor, cracking through the photos and turning it black.

I then took it to the walls, beating them in as I begged a higher power to take it all away.

"Nate?" Lila stood in the doorway, staring at me.

I stopped, my breath coming out in heavy pants, and looked around. Papers, glass, and wood splinters were spread out all around me.

I said I would protect her with my life, and the fates were going to take me up on my offer.

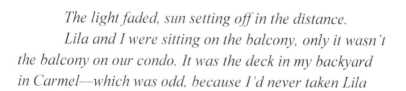

The light faded, sun setting off in the distance.

Lila and I were sitting on the balcony, only it wasn't the balcony on our condo. It was the deck in my backyard in Carmel—which was odd, because I'd never taken Lila there. I didn't even own the house anymore—it sold two years ago.

I hadn't even lived in it since before the accident. I couldn't after Grace died.

Two stories, nearly four thousand square feet, over a half acre lot—suburbia.

Lila smiled at me, her hand running over her baby bump. She sipped her lemonade and stared out at the sunset. I reached out and ran my fingers down her arm.

A shiver ran through me as her image flickered, changing. Blue eyes turned to me—Grace.

"Do you really think it will be any different this time?"

"What?"

"Miscarriage after miscarriage—do you really think that will change with Lila?"

The scenery shifted, the sky darkened, and I was in my condo. Moonlight filtered in, exposing the starkness that was life before Lila.

There was no furniture in the living room, only a box—the box.

My chest tightened as I stared at it. Why was it there?

"Will you make another box of secrets? Another place to hide the evidence of your past?" Grace walked over and kneeled in front of it. Her fingers ran around the edges and then she flipped the clasp.

My hand shot out. "Wait!"

She turned to me. "Wait for what? Don't you want to see what's in here?"

No. I was certain I didn't want that.

She raised the lid and set it back.

"Wow." Grace went silent as she looked at whatever was on top. She turned to me and held up a photo of my wedding with Lila. "You really were meant for each other."

I began to shake, the tightness around my chest squeezed. "W-why is that in there?"

Grace blinked at me. "Why wouldn't it be? She's dead, just like me."

I shook my head. "No. No, she's not."

Grace stood and walked forward, another photo in her hand. My eyes widened, tears filling them as she held up a photo of Lila staring blankly at me, blood everywhere.

"Of course she is. She's married to you. Don't tell me you really think you can keep her safe." Her hand caressed my cheek, her eyes sad. "Nate, she was dead the moment you met her."

My eyes squeezed tight, and I shook my head. "No! I can keep her safe."

She stroked through my hair. "Really? I thought you weren't going to be naïve any longer."

My eyes snapped open, and I stared at the pain in hers. She leaned forward and kissed me. When she pulled back, it wasn't Grace, but Lila who stared back at me.

"Do you really think you can keep me alive? Keep us alive?" She looked down, her hand running soothing circles on her round stomach.

It felt like there was a vice locked down around me. "I will do anything to keep you safe."

She stepped back, pain filling her face. "Why aren't you seeing it? Why are you blind?"

My brow scrunched. "I don't understand."

The air swirled around, lightning cracking. She closed the distance between us in the skittering blink of an eye, her face inches from mine.

"Lila will still be dead."

I sat up. Confusion filled me, and it took me a moment to realize I was in our bedroom. My breath was coming out in hard, harsh pants as I took in the darkness.

Dream. It was all a dream.

I looked next to me to find Lila inches away, staring at me with wide, worried eyes. The constriction around my chest loosened and a strangled croak escaped me. She moved closer and wrapped her arms around me, holding me close.

"Shhh, I'm here. I'm with you, baby. We're going to be okay."

That was the moment I knew Lila held my weight on her shoulders. I was dragging us both down, and it made me face with the horrible truth I'd denied—Lila *wouldn't* live without me.

The only way to save her was to save myself, and there was no way to do that.

CHAPTER 23

⟫••◉◉◉••⟪

The day was long, and I was ready to get home. My workout with Jared left me exhausted and in desperate need of a shower. He was pushing me harder, to beat all the pain, fear, and anxiety that consumed me out and into the pads and the bag.

It helped a lot, and I was thankful for another physical release, but it didn't change the truth. Marconi was coming for us.

In the back of my mind, I'd been working on a contingency plan—a getaway. Working it out in real life without them finding out was harder than I imagined. Who could I trust, and of those few, who wasn't being watched?

When I stepped into our condo, dread washed over me.

Silent.

Black.

Nothing.

"Lila?"

I closed and locked the door behind me, then set my bag down. Silence remained. Her car was in the parking lot, so I knew she had to be here.

The echo of my footsteps on the tile accentuated the quiet, along with the hammering in my chest. I flipped light switches as I moved through the condo, scanning rooms for anything out of the ordinary. The anxiety rocketed, adrenaline pumping through me as I fought off my fears.

Everything was right where it was supposed to be. I didn't know if that was good or bad.

Glowing yellow drew me to our bedroom, the light from the bathroom spilling out into the room. Lila sat against the wall. She was biting her lip, her hands tangled together, fidgeting.

"What happened?" I asked, rushing to her side.

She blinked back tears as she slid up the wall. "Nothing... Well, not nothing."

Her eyes fell down, staring at my chest. A buzzing fear wrapped itself around me. Lila usually told me everything. The only time she'd pause was because she was afraid I'd fly off the handle.

I swallowed hard and raised her head so that our eyes met. "Lila, tell me."

She was cautious, her expression pleading and scared.

"I'm late."

I blinked at her, the fear that was building falling from me and my lips twitching up into a smile. The words weren't foreign—I knew them well. It was another life, so long ago, but the weight of them was the same.

"Really? Do you think..."

237

She blinked up at me and swallowed. "I took a test. It was positive."

Her eyes were trained on me, studying my reaction. A smile grew on my face and excitement coursed through me.

Lila was pregnant.

We were going to have a baby.

My hand moved to rest on her abdomen as my mind imagined it ballooning out from her hips, full with my child. The beast in me purred, excited about the development. It was territorial, the possessiveness growing in me—Lila was mine in every way.

Time seemed to stop as reality set in and the duality of the situation reared its ugly head.

The Marconi were watching.

The smile slid from my face. I stared down to where my hand lay. My fingers flexed against her skin as her reaction began to make sense. She was waiting for it, braced for it—my meltdown.

My eyes snapped to hers and I froze, staring at everything I wanted and loved, and feeling the sheer terror of it all being taken away the same horrific way as before. Vincent Marconi wouldn't hesitate to kill my pregnant wife. In fact, I was certain the symmetry would be poetic in his eyes.

A strangled sound escaped me, and I fell to my knees. My arms wrapped around her waist, pulling her tight to me. My heart threatened to beat its way out of my chest. It refused to believe it was all happening again.

"We have to go to the doctor," I said against her skin.

Her fingers moved through my hair, each stroke trying to soothe the crippling fear that was ripping through me, but it couldn't keep up with the waves of despair.

"I have an appointment scheduled for tomorrow."

I took a deep breath, then nuzzled her stomach. Time had changed me, and for the better. The unexpected was expected. I wasn't the carefree, naïve man anymore. This time I could protect my world, and I would.

I had to.

My lips pressed against her abdomen as I looked up at her. "I won't let it happen again." I stood up and cupped her face as my arm wrapped around her. "No one will take you from me. You're mine, now until forever. We're going to be a family. We're going to be happy. I won't let anyone take that from us."

I didn't give her a chance to respond. My lips crashed to hers, silencing whatever she would say. I needed her to believe me. I *would* find us a way out.

The desperation fueled my need to have her, to feel her wrapped around me, to consume her. She whimpered against my mouth, nails digging into my shoulders. I growled as I pushed her up against the wall.

I slammed my hips against her, begging for the friction of her body against mine, the calming release for all my ailments, all my anxiety. Celebration for the life we created.

"Fuck." I pulled back and led her over to the bed. She pulled her cami over her head, leaving herself in only her tiny panties, knowing what was coming next. "Now, bend over, baby." I pushed on her back, and she bent at the waist, her forearms resting on the bed. I tugged her panties

239

off her ass and slipped a finger in her pussy, making her squirm against me. "Good girl. I'm going to make you come so fucking hard. Have you cream on my cock." I hissed as I rubbed my clothed cock against her ass. "Mmm, my good little slut loves it when I talk dirty to her."

She whimpered and pushed back against me. "Yes."

"Turns you on so much when I call you my whore, my cock slut, doesn't it?" I pushed my shorts down enough to pull my cock out and slapped it against her ass before sliding it between her cheeks.

"Fuck, yes!"

"Why is that?" I pulled back on her hair, exposing her neck and making her arch against me. I nipped down the column of her neck and latched on at the base.

She cried out and shuddered. "Because I'm yours."

My cock sunk into her pussy, both of us moaning. "That's right, baby, *mine*. My wife, carrying my child."

I released her hair, my grip moving down to her hips as I rocked into her, my thrusts increasing. Incoherent sounds clawed their way out of me each time my cock bottomed out against her ass. The sight of her pussy stretching out around my cock was hypnotic.

Her pussy walls tightened around me, and I picked up the pace. The angle was always good for her and got her off faster.

"Come for me. Milk me." I was panting then, groaning as she clamped down. A scream escaped her as she shuddered around me.

I exploded inside her—mind-numbing, white release, my muscles contracting with each pulse of come that emptied into her. A bead of sweat slid down my cheek, my mouth open as I gasped for breath.

All strength left me with the last drops, and I released her, falling back onto the floor. She sunk onto the bed, then slipped to the floor, crawling until she could collapse onto my chest.

"I love you to the end of the earth and beyond," I said between pants.

She looked up at me and quirked her brow. "The earth is round."

I snickered. "I love you to the moon and beyond."

She kissed my chest. "I love you to the rock formally known as the planet Pluto and beyond."

I ran my hand down her arm. "That's a long way."

"Yes, and that's how much you mean to me—more than this world and all in between."

I grabbed her face and kissed her, trying to pour all the love I had for her into it. "For all eternity, this life and the next and the one after that, you are mine and I am yours."

"Always."

<hr />

Lila's hand was clutched tightly in mine as we sat in the sterile environment of her OB/GYN. Neither of us said much to the doctor, just answered her questions, both of us anxious. The answer would change everything. If the pregnancy test was right…

My knee was bouncing, hand rubbing a hole in the back of my neck. The tension was thick, both of us waiting.

We'd celebrated, happy to have a baby on the way, but we both needed the definitive proof of a blood test. Maybe then we could make rational decisions on what to do.

Who the fuck was I kidding? I didn't make rational decisions, not when it came to her. If I did, I would never have given in to the lust and fucked her in our office that night. I wouldn't have gone to her time and time again. My door would have stayed closed to her. It never would have gotten far enough to know I couldn't live without her.

Each minute that passed made my agitation grow. What the fuck was taking so damn long?

Another time, long ago, I'd been in the same situation. It was happier then, when I didn't have a threat hanging over my head. How could I be so fucking stupid? It was bad enough that I allowed Lila to come into harm's way by being with me, but bringing a baby into the fucked up situation? What the fuck was I thinking? I was *asking* for Marconi to come after us, more than my actions already had.

But I'd practically begged Lila for a baby. I wanted us to have a family—I wanted everything with her. My nightmares were in full force. The parallel of then and now…

"Mrs. Thorne?" the doctor called from the door, bringing me back from my thoughts.

Neither of us seemed to notice when she entered the small examination room. "Yes?"

She sat down and looked at the two of us. "Well, the test came back. It was negative. You're not pregnant."

"But the test…" Lila trailed off as I stared at the doctor in disbelief.

Not pregnant.

I didn't know whether to sigh in relief or cry. My relief was from knowing Marconi couldn't take another one of my children from me. Yet, it was laced with torturous pain from a loss that was never there. I wanted it, was so excited about us having a baby, and now I felt…empty. Devoid of something we never had to begin with.

"It was likely a false positive. They are extremely rare, but there is that one percent."

Lila's cheeks turned red, likely due to embarrassment, and she looked up at the doctor. "My missed period?"

The doctor nodded. "It sometimes happens if you've been on birth control and go off, to miss one soon after as your body regulates itself again." She gave us a pity smile. "Sorry to be the bearer of bad news."

Lila looked up at the doctor. "It's my fault, isn't it? User error?"

The doctor nodded. "That's usually what happens in these rare cases."

Lila looked between us, distress written all over her face. "I took a shower after taking the test." She looked down, fidgeting with the hem of her skirt. "I couldn't stand waiting."

"Tests read after the time on the instructions can lead to a faint positive."

"Thank you." I held out my hand, and she shook it.

"Are there any questions you have while you're here? Any help you need?"

Lila shook her head. "No, that was all."

The doctor stood. "You still have plenty of time, and if you need anything, don't hesitate to call. Okay?"

"Thanks," Lila whispered.

We followed the doctor down the hall and checked out. Silence filled the space between us. The walk to the car was empty, but as we moved through the parking lot, her head was down, looking to the ground.

"Honeybear?"

"I feel like an idiot." She sniffed, and her bottom lip trembled.

I shook my head as I cupped her cheeks and lifted her face. Unshed tears welled in her eyes. "You're not an idiot."

"Yes, I am! I gave us joy and fear in one announcement that wouldn't have even happened if I hadn't been so scared to wait the damn two minutes." She lost it then, tears spilling down her cheeks. "You freaked out, and I caused you pain."

"Oh, baby, no. That's not it at all." I held her in my arms. "I *want* us to have a baby, to be a family."

"The Marconi aren't going to allow that."

I had no response, no rebuttal.

The reality of life-threatening danger hung heavy around us both.

Lila—my goddess, my sin, my soul mate. Live together or die together. There was no in between, and the odds were stacked against us.

No more hoping, no more dreaming, only harsh reality. It was a time for action. I had to get my plan going, and it had to be soon.

Time was *not* on our side—it was running out.

244

CHAPTER 24

Lila

—∙∙∙❂∙∙∙—

I stared at my reflection in the mirror, at the dark circles that needed more makeup every day. Insomnia had taken control again, and sleep eluded me. I took comfort in my husband's arms, but I couldn't shut my brain off.

What were we going to do? Over a week had passed since we had the pregnancy mishap, and things were only getting worse.

Life was hard for everyone, but it was incredibly atrocious to others. Nathan and I qualified as others. I knew with every cell in my body he was my soul mate. I also knew that fate was a cruel mistress.

"Honeybear, you almost ready?" Nathan called from the bedroom.

"Almost." I closed up the concealer and brushed on some powder.

My hand trembled, and I clenched it into a tight fist, trying to stop it. I had to keep calm, had to show calm, no matter how badly I was breaking on the inside. Nathan needed me to be strong, and I would be his pillar.

"Ready." I smiled at him and held out my hand to take his.

I didn't want to die.

I was happy for the first time in my life. Was it too much to ask to grow old with Nathan?

The tremors got worse with each passing day, and soon I wouldn't be able to rein them in. He would see the fear I fought so hard to keep from him. The show left me more exhausted every day.

My eyes flitted over to the remnants of what was our home office as I walked toward the door. He destroyed it, obliterated it, telling me the end was near.

He pulled me close and kissed my forehead as we rode down to the ground floor. "I have to go to the Hamilton County courthouse today, so I won't be able to go to lunch." His voice was tight.

"Okay." I leaned my head on his shoulder, soaking him in.

We headed out to the parking lot and got in the car. He eyed me and pursed his lips.

"What?"

"Can you order lunch in today?"

I wanted to object. I wanted to tell him everything was okay.

But I couldn't.

"Sure. Caroline and I can take over your office." I elbowed his arm and smiled.

Why couldn't we be left alone? Ever since we'd met, wave after wave of hurdles crashed in front of us and we cleared them all, together. The one in front of us now loomed over, casting a shadow and making it almost impossible to attain freedom.

Eggshells. We were walking around avoiding everything in a strange dance, all out of fear. Part of me wanted them to kill us and get it over with, to end the anxiety that ruled our lives. The other part begged for another day, hour, minute—I never wanted to leave him.

Instead, I squashed both feelings and aimed for calm obliviousness. My act fooled him because he was so trapped in his own anxiety.

When we arrived at the office, I pasted on a smile and wrapped my arms around his arm. "What should we do this weekend?"

Rule one—keep smiling and upbeat. Rule two—always talk about the future, no matter how close.

He swallowed. "I was thinking we could go for a drive. Maybe get away."

"That would be fun." I smiled, trying not to let on I knew the double meaning in his words.

The kiss as we separated for our own offices held an edge as they all did of late—passion—like it would be the last.

"I'll see you later, Honeybear. Love you."

"Love you." I gave him another soft kiss before he turned and headed down the hall.

When I sat at my desk, I leaned forward and covered my face, trying to gather myself. I pulled my phone out and opened up the email app—something I couldn't do with Nathan around.

"Shit." Another one popped up, sent at three that morning—surveillance shots with a time stamp. It was from the same address the other three had come from, each with a photo of Nathan and me coming and going. They'd been coming in for weeks. Marconi's guys knew our schedule.

I marked it as unread and closed out of the app—I didn't want Nathan to know I was reading his email. He kept me in the dark for my safety, but I wasn't going to stay there. He was my husband, my life, and I wasn't going to let them surprise me—surprise *us*.

"Morning!" Owen's smile helped to calm me, his happiness infectious.

"Good morning."

He set his bag down and took off his jacket—it was unseasonably cool.

"Brrr." He shook off the cold. "It's a hot coffee kind of morning. Want some?"

I smiled up at him. "That would be great. Thanks."

"No problem, partner."

The moment he was out the door, I picked up the burner phone Noah bought a month ago and dialed the number I'd called every day for the past few months—Noah's own burner phone. I peered out the door, keeping a lookout for anyone coming.

"Hello?"

"How's it looking?"

There was a pause, then a sigh on the other end—a very bad sign. Usually he had little to report, and it was

248

mostly the changing of guard. A prickling sensation moved across my skin.

"Lila, it's time to consider leaving."

My heart stopped, my body going cold. "What's happening?"

"I don't know, but it's not good."

I swept a hand over my face, unable to keep the façade up, shaking like I was going to come undone.

"Did you get another gun yet?"

I nodded, not that he could see. "It's in my purse."

"Does he know?"

"No." My voice broke.

"Are you going to tell him?"

Tears welled in my eyes. "Not right now."

"You need to, because if you don't, I will." The low tone in his voice told me how serious he was.

Everything was spiraling out of control.

<hr />

I popped another pill, hoping it would calm me before I broke out into a full-blown panic attack. My hand gripped the edge of the sink harder, trying to suppress everything.

Dr. Morgenson didn't like the state either of us was in, or upping both our dosages so we could make it through the day. It was an unfortunate necessity. Even he knew therapy wasn't going to help us, and the drugs would help get us through the days ahead...however many there were left.

The reflection in the mirror hardly resembled me. Maybe it was the florescent lighting of the office's restroom, but the terror clawing at my insides looked like it found an outlet.

My eyes sealed tight as I fought to gain control. Deep, even breaths helped, but they still couldn't stop the shaking. I let out a harsh breath and looked down at the sink, at the phone that sat there, and the message from Noah that stared back at me.

Vincent Marconi is on his way here.

I bent over further as a dry heave ripped its way through me.

What were we going to do?

The door swung open, startling me, and Caroline stepped in. She stopped as soon as she saw me, her eyes widening. Her course changed from the stall to me.

"What's wrong?" She stopped in front of me, worry filling her face.

Tears filled my eyes, and I picked up the phone and handed it to her.

"Did you get a new phone?" She was confused as she searched for the button to light up the screen. Her eyes scanned it, and she gasped as it registered. "Lila?"

"It's a burner phone."

"Burner phone? What the hell? Are you a criminal now?"

I shook my head. "No. With them watching us, I was sure they were monitoring our phones as well. Noah picked this one up for me, and he's the only one that has the number. He's been keeping me up to date on the things Nate keeps from me."

250

"Jesus Christ… I… Does this mean what I think it means?"

I nodded.

Her brow scrunched. "What do you mean by 'keeps from you'?"

I shook my head and let out a strangled chuckle. "You know him. He wants to protect me, keep me calm, so he takes the burden on himself and doesn't tell me everything."

"And here you are hiding a phone from him. Double standard much?"

"Because I have to keep him calm." My face scrunched up and my arms wrapped around my waist. "He's so far gone. Worse than when we met."

She sighed. "Because it's happening again."

I nodded. "He swings between destructive anger, depression, extreme anxiety, and hard passion in a span of five minutes."

She pulled her arms up and matched my stance. "Fuck. I didn't even notice he was that messed up."

"He's not as bad at the office and can hide it better here."

"What are you going to do? If he's coming, you're running…right?"

I sighed. "I don't know. Running isn't going to help. They'll find us."

"Are you sure?"

"Where would we go?"

She threw her arms up in the air. "Anywhere! Just go. Leave."

I sighed. My brain whirled around all the things we would need to do. What was worse was that I didn't even believe myself when I thought it could be done.

<hr/>

The morning was shit, and the afternoon wasn't looking any better, especially when Owen came back from the break room with empty cups. At least the meds I took were helping and the tightness in my chest had eased.

"Let's go get some coffee," Nathan called from the door, startling me.

Shit.

I forced a smile, hiding the festering news as I looked up from the file I'd been buried in, watching him as he strode in. "A break?" I turned in my chair to face him as he walked around my desk.

He nodded. "The coffee machine is broken, so I thought I could pull you away and take a break with my wife."

I quirked a brow at him. "You of all people should know we don't take breaks."

"Yeah, but, as I said, there's no coffee. How are you going to get your caffeine fix?"

I pursed my lips. He was right—I'd go into withdrawal.

We headed out, promising to bring back one for Owen, and walked the few blocks to the coffee shop.

Nathan's smile was forced as he looked down at me. My smile was forced as well. We were both keeping things from each other, and more than just the anxiety.

"So, do I get some special cream for my coffee today?" My attempt at banter sounded like I was trying too hard to my own ears, but his lip twitched. It may have been a poor go, but it did its job of giving levity to the air around us.

"I'm sure we could arrange that." His arm wrapped around me, holding me close as we walked.

He tried not to be obvious, but I caught his gaze moving around, looking for them. I pulled myself tighter into him, knowing time was a precious commodity.

There was a small line when we entered, and I decided to forgo my usual regular coffee and go for something sweeter—a white mocha. Nathan paid, and we moved down to wait. His ring tone blared from his pocket, and he pulled his phone out, his brow scrunching as he looked down at the screen.

"Sorry, I have to take this." His lips pressed against my forehead, then he turned and headed for the door, putting the phone up to his ear.

His back was to me as I stared out the window at him. He'd been so stressed lately. Nightmares, anxiety, anger. Every day he got closer to snapping, and I wondered when it would come, or if the Marconi would get us first. In light of my text from Noah, I knew the answer.

I blew out a breath and turned back to the counter to grab our drinks along with a carrier. My cheeks heated as I set them down to add the creamer to Owen's. Nathan's kinky stunt made me blush every time I'd gotten a coffee since then.

Once completed, I grabbed the cups and headed toward the door, but he was missing.

My heart stopped, and everything began to move in slow motion.

The carrier slipped from my hands, but I was already racing out the door, not caring that the hot liquid splashed on me as they hit the floor.

Panic gripped me as my vision narrowed in on him. His eyes were wide, searching around while his hands shook and his breath came out in clipped pants, face flush with anger. The phone that had once been in his hand was shattered on the ground—the glass cracked, the back popped off, and the battery lying a foot away.

People were staring at him with whispered words, wondering what was going on. There was an officer approaching, and I quickened my pace to his side.

"Nathan, what's wrong?"

His angry eyes snapped to mine, then he wrapped his arms around me, turning us so that his back was to the street.

"I'll protect you."

"From what? Baby, what happened?"

"I'll protect you."

"You're scaring me. What aren't you saying?"

His jaw was clenched tight and he cursed when he looked down at his phone before bending over to pick up the pieces.

"We need to go." He grabbed my arm and took off at a brisk pace that I was almost unable to keep up with.

I stumbled more than once, trying to keep up while wearing heels. "Where are we going?"

"Anywhere but here." He shook his head, cursing under his breath.

I tugged back on my arm, yanking it free. He turned, annoyed, and reached for me again.

"No! What happened? Who called you?"

His face scrunched. "Noah called. Tom Preston was shot at lunch."

I gasped. "Is he okay?"

"He's alive, for now."

Stunned silence took hold. What were we going to do?

"Give me your phone."

"What?"

"I have to call Jack."

I handed it over and got lost in my thoughts as he talked to Jack and our pace picked back up. I didn't understand before, when we met, when I was told, my own naiveté clouding everything. It wasn't just Nathan they were after. Everyone involved was marked.

A chill moved down my spine. Would they ever stop? I knew the answer—it was clear as day.

When we were all dead.

CHAPTER 25

Nathan was silent, his grip on my hand tight on the walk back to the office. It all began to settle in that we'd reached the finale. My chest clenched and I leaned into him as we rode the elevator up.

He refused to let go of me. The office exploded in murmurs—hushed whispers, scared faces, and pointed fingers.

Nathan stopped mid-step and let go of my hand, reaching across my body instead and gripping my arm. It was too tight, panicked. I looked up, and in front of his office door stood a figure.

The man had slick-backed, midnight black hair, deep age lines carved into his clean-shaven face. He had to be at least sixty, if not seventy. The black suit he wore was not off the rack and probably cost a small fortune.

Nathan positioned himself in front of me, blocking me from the stranger, but I could still see. The man's stance screamed elite—legs apart, spine straight, hands in his pockets. He radiated arrogance as his cold eyes surveyed me with an odd curiosity. Our eyes met and his lip twitched, and what looked like a combination of cruelty and excitement flashed.

A shiver ran through me, and my heart began to hammer in my chest. My flight response screamed in terror, pulsing the danger signal through every cell.

I'd never seen a picture of him, but I was certain the man in front of us was Vincent Marconi himself.

Nathan tensed, his muscles strained tight and shaking with suppressed energy. "Stop looking at her." The edge in his tone as he snapped surprised me. "What do you want?"

The anger-filled, intense feeling emanating from Nathan was suffocating. I'd seen him angry before, but the strength was crushing me—a whole new level of emotion.

Vincent's lips curled up, the cruelty I'd seen before shining through in his false, mocking show. "Ah, Nathan, what a pleasure it is to see you again."

"Vincent," Nathan growled. "What can I do for you?"

My airway restricted as my theory was confirmed. The floor began to fall away and the world slipped as my knees weakened. I could barely stand from the weight of it all.

"I just came by to see how you were doing after that horrible accident you were in a few years ago." His fake concern dripped from his voice. "Terrible, really, to be filled with so much titanium and other metals to hold your shattered body together."

I grabbed onto the back of Nathan's jacket, fisting it, anchoring me to him. The man who'd broken him stood in front of us, wanting to do it all again.

His body hardened even more—a rock bracing for the coming wave. "As you can clearly see, I'm getting by."

"And your poor, poor wife. Pregnant, wasn't she? To lose all of your family. Tragic, really. Rumor has it you have remarried." Vincent's gaze flickered back to me.

I locked my knees, fighting to stay strong and not let him see my weakness.

With that comment, Nathan's hand reached out and pushed me so he was standing fully in front of me.

"Is that her?" Vincent asked, fake curiosity dripping from his tone.

Nathan's arm shook as I peeked to look around his shoulder again.

"Hello, Mrs. Thorne, it's a pleasure to meet you." Vincent extended his hand.

His whole demeanor and the conversation didn't sit well with me, and the prospect of touching him sent chills through my body. I leaned into Nathan for support.

"She has nothing to do with this. Leave her alone."

Vincent gave Nathan that smile again. "Nathan, don't be rude. I only stopped by today to see how you were doing after all this time. Nothing more." Vincent sighed, as if put off. "However, I see you remain as arrogant and rude as you always were. Therefore, I'll take my leave." He nodded at me, a strange hunger as he looked me over. "It was a pleasure meeting you, *Mrs. Thorne*."

His stance, his tone, *his presence* was a threat.

Nathan's hands were balled into tight fists, shaking as a low growl vibrated through him.

Vincent chuckled before giving his final goodbye and sauntering down the hall away from us. We both stared after him, as did the entire office. The moment the elevator doors closed and he was gone, Nathan yanked on my arm, moving us down the hall.

"Get your purse."

"What?"

His jaw twitched. "We're leaving. We're not staying here."

The tension was still high, his grip tight, barely letting me get my things before pulling me down the hall. All eyes were on us as we made our way to the elevators, and their own fear could be seen—their pity.

Nathan sped through the streets on the way home, his eyes constantly checking the mirrors to see if anyone was following us. I'd never seen him so shaken, but Vincent Marconi's visit had him on a whole new level of paranoid and freaking out. When we arrived home, he quickly ushered us to the elevator. As soon as we were in the door, he was running to the bedroom.

When I caught up, he was pulling our suitcases down from the closet and throwing them on the bed. The pace as he moved back and forth from the dresser, the closet, and the bed, depositing clothes as he went, was frightening.

"What are you doing?"

"We're going. Leaving now."

I shook my head. "We can't just leave."

"Yes, we can, and we are." He pulled open the dresser, grabbing handfuls of stuff, paying no attention to what it was. "It's the only way I can protect you."

I shook my head and set my hands on my hips, digging my heels into the floor. "There has to be another way."

"Unless Vincent Marconi drops dead, there isn't."

"It could happen."

His jaw flexed, teeth mashing together. "I'm not taking a chance on *if*."

"Nate, we need to form a plan. We can't just take off."

"Damn it! Why won't you fucking listen to me?"

"Because you're being unreasonable." My fingers flexed against my hips.

"No, I'm not." The volume of his voice increased, almost to the point of yelling. His eyes hardened. "I've warned you about my past."

"You're just going to leave your family?"

His motions halted. He stood stone still for a moment, then grabbed my phone from his pocket and dialed a number.

"Mom, I need you to pack your bags… The Marconi… Mom, please don't argue."

I snatched the phone from his hands. "Sarah, we'll call you back."

I forced down my own anxiety as I stared at my husband's frantic behavior.

"I'll call Darren, you work on calming him." The worry in her voice could be heard

I nodded, not that she could see. "Talk to you soon."

I hung up and walked over to him. He was shaking violently as he stuffed clothing into the cases.

"Baby, you need to calm down," I said in a soothing tone, my fingers running through his hair. "We need to work out a plan."

His head snapped toward me. "This is serious. We have to leave. I have to get you out of here. I can't let them... I won't let them hurt you."

"Slow down. Take a deep breath. Please."

"No!" he shouted and turned to me, his eyes beseeching me to understand. "This wasn't a warning. Everything before was, but Vincent himself seeking me out was his way of saying goodbye, of letting me know that we're dead. He wanted to see you, see what he was going to take from me. He is going to kill us, Lila! We have to leave now!"

CHAPTER 26

I vibrated with anger and fear as I stared at Nathan. We weren't right. There was an element that was off in both of us. We weren't working together as a unit, as a family, and it was hurting us.

I picked up a shoe he'd just dumped into the suitcase and hurled it against the wall. "No. This ends now. Stop with the bullshit!"

He stopped packing and looked at me. "*Bullshit?*"

"Yes. Bullshit." I was seething. Not working together made us weaker, and it'd become obvious we were falling apart because of it. "You've kept things from me. I've kept things from you, as well. We can't do that, not now. Especially not in this moment."

He blinked at me, stunned. "What are you keeping from me?"

"What are *you* keeping from *me*? I'm your wife, remember? Partner in this life we have together, including impending doom."

He stepped forward, towering over me, and snarled. "*What* are you keeping from me?"

I blew out a breath and bit my bottom lip before looking him in the eye, my jaw jutting forward. "I knew Marconi was on his way in town this morning."

"How?" His voice was flat, even, and a shiver ran through me.

"Noah."

His face scrunched, and he lashed out, grabbing the nearest thing—a pillow—and tossing it across the room, screaming.

"You didn't tell me? I missed a call from Noah around eight, but I had no idea…" He shook his head. "Why the fuck didn't you tell me?"

I slumped down onto the edge of the bed. "You would've freaked out this morning. I was waiting until after work, trying to form a plan, but he's already here."

"We could've been gone hours ago." He threw his hands up and stomped away, stopping in front of the bathroom door, his back turned. "How did Noah contact you?"

I closed my eyes and braced myself for his rage. "On a disposable phone he bought me a month ago. He's been keeping me up to date as well as keeping tabs on us."

He bent forward, then slammed his hands against the door frame. When he turned to me, I jumped at the fire in his eyes.

"A month? This has been going on for a month and neither of you mentioned it to me? I've fucking talked to Noah multiple times, and he never said a word."

I stared at him and sighed. "You've been so on edge. Between the false positive and giving Tom the file, I've had to walk on eggshells and do everything I could to keep you relaxed."

He glared at me, and icy dread flooded my system. It was anger, and not in a good way. "So, my wife has been placating me like a fucking child."

I jumped up from the bed and stalked forward, pushing against his chest. "You wake up screaming *every* night! Your moods are so heightened and change so fast, I can't keep up, so I keep even."

Anger fled from him, replaced by something I couldn't identify, but I knew it was a jumbled mess of turmoil. His hands ran through his hair, then down to his neck, pulling.

"I never should've proposed. We never should've gotten married."

I flinched, recoiling back as if he'd slapped me. He looked up, his eyes empty. My mouth opened and tears began to gather in my eyes. My chest was tight, and I reached behind me, searching for the bed. Stability as my world threatened to collapse around me. His face morphed, eyes wide in panic as he lurched toward me, grabbing my arms.

"No, Honeybear, I'm sorry. I didn't mean it that way."

"What way am I supposed to take it?" My voice was strained, forcing the overpowering emotions from pouring out of me. Everything was upside down.

His eyes scrunched closed, teeth bared as he squeezed me tighter.

"I somehow thought I wasn't a bother to him any longer. All our therapy toned down my fears, and I forgot and was happy. I *convinced* myself we could have a future, a family, and grow old together." My heart broke at the tortured expression on his face. "Everything that consumes me is you, and I want you in every way, but the one thing I don't want is you hurt because of me. Marrying you tells them how much you mean to me. They can take you away from me."

I swallowed hard, then reached out and grabbed hold of the lapels of his jacket. "You told me to stay away from you over and over again. You said you weren't worth my life, but you were wrong. *You* are my life. If I hadn't met you, I'd still be a zombie."

His forehead fell against mine, and he cupped my face before kissing me hard. "I'm sorry. So fucking sorry. I love you so much. I need to keep you safe, for you and for me. Even if that means keeping things from you." His thumbs caressed my cheek. "I don't want you to worry. It's my responsibility to protect you."

I stared into his eyes as I shook my head. "That's not protecting me—that's leaving me vulnerable. Noah noticed it as well and *that's* why he got the phones. And I do nothing but worry, because I see how everything bothers you. You can't hide from me. Not me." I leaned forward and rested my head against his chest, my arms wrapping around his waist. "Remember what we said, what we promised? We'll never be free, never have a baby, if we continue on this path."

He flinched at my words. "There isn't going to ever be a baby if we stay here, if I don't get you away."

I pulled back. "Where are we going to go? They'll find us."

He shook his head. "I've been getting emails, pictures of us, for a few weeks."

"I know."

His attention snapped back to me. "You know?"

I nodded. "I saw you looking at them when you were on the phone with Tom. After that, I downloaded your email app to my phone and have been checking it."

He stared at me in stunned silence for a moment before turning and kicking a half-packed bag. "Jesus fucking Christ! Who the fuck are we?"

I sat back down on the edge of the bed and let out a sigh. "We're two people in a shit situation, and all we want to do is protect each other."

He turned, hands on his hips. "Fuck lot of good that's done us." He ripped off his jacket and threw it on the ground. He stared off, his face relaxed, almost as if an idea struck him. "Once I take you somewhere you'll be safe, then I need to hunt him down and end this once and for all."

"What? That's crazy! He'll have a dozen guys with him all carrying guns."

"Then I'll get a grenade and we'll all go down."

My jaw dropped open as I stared at him and the determination setting into his features. I got back on my feet and slammed my hands against his chest with all my might. "No! Don't even fucking say anything like that."

He wrapped his arms around me, pulling me tight. "If it's the only way to end this..."

My eyes watered, and I swiped away the unshed tears. It was sinking in that there might not be a tomorrow. *Our last night on earth.*

The thought hit me like a punch to the gut. My whole body began to shake.

I pulled his head down and bowed up to press my lips to his. The surprise, followed by reluctance, threatened to crush me, and he almost did when his hands wrapped around my wrists. He pushed me back, head shaking.

Tears streamed down my cheeks. "I need you. Please, please." Nothing could be more true. I needed him, our connection. It felt like I would rip apart without it, the torturous fate ahead of us burying me in crippling grief.

"We have to go." My own agony reflected in his features.

"If tonight is all we have, give me one last moment with you."

It hit him as well—understanding flashed across his face. His lips met mine again, fierce and desperate, as he reached down and lifted me up by my ass. I moaned into his mouth, a gasp leaving me soon after as we fell onto the bed.

Harsh hands ripped open my shirt as he bit down on my bra-covered breast. He sat up and pushed my skirt up, grabbing my hips and pulling my pussy against his cock. His mouth was parted, lids heavy as he looked down at me.

"Tell me." The lust in his eyes faltered, exposing the fear and sadness beneath.

I reached out, my fingers brushing against his chest. "I love you…more than my own life."

His fingers deftly worked his belt, then moved to his zipper. "More."

"I'm yours for this life and the next." His fingers pushed my panties aside, then he rubbed the head of his cock against my pussy, making me burn and melt around him. "I will always be yours."

He thrust forward, and I convulsed. My eyes rolled back as my nails dug into his forearm. Everything centered around the connection created from his cock being inside me. He leaned over me and wrapped his fingers with mine as he pinned my arms against the bed. Desperation fueled his kisses as my hips met his.

"I would die for you," he whispered against my lips. My heart fluttered in my chest. "I would kill for you." His voice was airy, and he grunted as I clamped around him. "My life is yours." His thrusts picked up, harder, deeper. He stared into my eyes, burning with so many emotions my chest clenched. "My body is yours."

I whimpered, every muscle tense, my body bowing toward his. His name tumbled from my lips in a mantra.

"Forever. In this life and the next, you are *mine*."

I crumbled, the world exploding around me as I came. White nothingness washed over me, my body pulsing as each wave of pleasure ripped through me. Nathan let out a roar above me, his hips slamming against me. His cock jerked inside me, and I writhed beneath him, knowing he was filling me.

His breath was harsh above me, and he leaned forward, resting his forehead against mine. Unshed tears sparkled in his eyes.

"I love you, my beautiful wife."

A tear slipped from my eye, my bottom lip began trembling. "I love you, so much, my husband."

We stayed like that for a few minutes, hoping the danger would disappear and we could remain lost in each other. It couldn't last, and we got up, moving to the bathroom to clean up the mess.

Sex helped to relax Nathan enough to slow down and think a little more rationally, but we still got ready to leave. Silence remained over us as we changed our clothing. He made a noise, drawing my attention.

"I can't believe we've been walking around unprotected all this time when we should have had your gun on us."

I pulled up my jeans and buttoned them. "That's not entirely true."

His stared at me for a moment, stunned, before his gaze became angry, nostrils flared. "What?"

I grabbed my purse from the floor and pulled out the Ruger SR22. His eyes were wide as he stared at it.

"When did you start carrying it around?" He held out his hand, and I gave it to him, making sure the safety was still engaged.

"I got it a few weeks ago."

His head snapped up. "A second gun? How? And why the fuck didn't you tell me?"

"Drew helped me."

He cursed under his breath. "Motherfucker."

"We went over lunch. And I didn't tell you because I didn't want you freaking out and stressing any more than you were."

"Where's your other gun?"

My eyes widened, flickering briefly to the closet. "Nate, I don't—"

"Where?" His jaw was locked, anger radiating from him.

I walked into the closet and sighed as I pulled out the black metal case.

Nathan watched me as I exited and set it on the bed.

"How do you open it?" He set the Ruger down.

I lined my fingers up and set them down. "It's a biometric fingerprint lock." After a moment, the lock sprung and the case opened. "Glock 19."

He reached forward and grabbed the gun along with the clip that was sitting beside it. He looked at it for a moment before sliding the clip in.

"Have you ever used a handgun before?" I stared at him, and he shook his head. "*Any* gun?"

"A shotgun long ago."

I held out my hand. "Give it to me."

He glared at me. "No."

"Nate, you don't know how to use it."

"I've seen it used enough."

"When? On television? This is serious. I went through training classes. It's not as simple and easy as you think."

"Aim and fire, right?"

I huffed and rolled my eyes. "There are safety precautions so you don't shoot someone by accident. You need to know how to use it."

"Then show me. That's why you got a second gun, right?"

"I got it to protect us. I've never had to use it, let alone to kill anyone."

He shook his head. "It's not killing if it's self-defense, and they're coming to kill us."

"Nate…"

"What? Why else would you buy a gun?"

I continued to look at him for a moment before focusing on the two guns I owned. The main reason I purchased the Ruger was for its size and easy portability. It didn't detract from the reality of *why* I purchased the smaller firearm.

I wasn't going to go down without a fight.

"I'm tired of being afraid of the monsters that hide in the dark, of evil things in the form of humans."

He nodded and handed me the Ruger while he stuffed the Glock in the back of his pants.

"Then it's time to end this." He held out his hand, and I slipped mine in.

Together. Live or die, it would be together.

CHAPTER 27

When we got down to the parking lot, Nathan popped open the trunk to my car and not his own. I glanced at him in curiosity, but understood. Switching to mine could buy us some time, because we were always in his car.

The air was heavy as we made our way through downtown to Meridian Street and north a mile to pick up I65. We were both stiff, unable to relax. I watched the Indianapolis skyline disappear in the rearview mirror when the interstate angled west. The IMA sat off to the right overlooking the White River as we passed, streetlamps filling the car with alternating light to dark.

"Shit."

I turned to him. "What?"

His jaw clenched tight, eyes flickered between the road and the mirror. "They've already found us." The engine revved as he pressed on the gas pedal.

I looked into the rearview mirror, but only saw the bright headlights from all the other cars. My heart fluttered in my chest, the beat seeming to increase with our speed. Every time I took a breath, it echoed in my ears. I kept watching, waiting to see what he did. A few miles flew by, and we approached the exit for I465.

Then it became clear, as traffic moved over to the exit lane, and one car accelerated toward us. Nathan's knuckles were white as he gripped onto the steering wheel and hit the gas again as the speed limit increased. The words "Thank you for visiting Indianapolis" flashed by, and we were out of the city. My hands trembled as the safety of population was replaced by the unknown of Indiana's famous corn fields.

Someone had to know. If we didn't make it, someone had to know what happened.

Nathan cursed again and swung the car hard right over two lanes, barely missing the grassy median as he took the exit. Lebanon was written on one of the signs, and the tires screeched as we turned left at maximum speed.

Why is he taking us off here?

I torqued my body at an awkward angle to see if we were still being followed, and I caught their car swinging hard, barely missing the metal guardrail. If nothing else, there was a bit more space between us and them.

I dug my burner phone out of my pocket and pulled up my text messages. A hard jostle of the car from a pothole sent the phone flying from my hand and slipping between the door and the seat.

"Shit!"

My gaze flickered to the rearview mirror—the second set of headlights was much closer.

I shoved my hand in the tight space to get my phone. There wasn't much time left. My fingers clasped around the plastic and pulled it up. I looked for another sign when we took a hard right and typed frantically, hoping he understood.

Lafayette Lebanon CR1300. Chased. Help.

I sent it off and clasped the phone between my hands in a silent prayer. When I opened my eyes, headlights shone back at me. The car honked, long and loud, and we swerved.

No matter which way we zigged or zagged, the car after us kept up.

I was jostled into the door, cringing in pain. The sound of screeching metal filled darkness. We couldn't get away and were hit again, pushed several feet over in the lane.

The metal made a sickening crunching sound as Nathan veered off and took the car into the grass that separated the road from the field. I screamed when he barely missed a mailbox.

The car behind us was undeterred. It kept at us, hell-bent on catching its prey.

Nathan's eyes were focused and his grip on the wheel firm, yet he somehow seemed relaxed. Like he'd done this before.

An eerie chill slid down my spine. He *had* done this before.

The lawyer sat next to me, not my husband, working it all out in his head as he drove. Asking himself questions. Going over past evidence, reliving past mistakes, and trying to come up with a different outcome. I stared at

274

him and could almost see his mind spinning faster than the vehicle we were travelling in.

What was I supposed to do?

Nothing. All I could do was keep my death grip the on the door and count each second, waiting for the ride to stop.

"What are we going to do?" I asked, my voice shaky and feeble. The car jostled again as they slammed into the bumper. I shrunk into my seat, holding on to the seatbelt and trying not to freak out.

"Away from them. Away from everything." His voice was clearer than mine, yet it spoke volumes about where he was at in his head. He was far, far away from here. Imagining some place where he could lock me away.

The wheel jerked as they slammed into us again. The back end of the car swung out, but he kept control, the car rocking as it maneuvered back into a straight line.

Every heartbeat passed in what felt like hours, not seconds. Slow motion in fast forward—a strange sensation.

I wanted the car to stop.

I wanted it to go faster.

I wanted the world to melt away and take my fear with it.

Another minute, hour, *lifetime* with Nathan.

I wanted to catch a fucking break in my shit life and have the future we deserved.

A tear slid down my cheek and time caught back up.

The tires lost traction on the road as they hit us again, sending us careening into a field. My head slammed into the window as we bounced around on the uneven ground. I held on tighter as the car spun out, narrowly missing a tree.

I exhaled, expunging the air from my aching lungs. How long had I been holding my breath?

Nathan pried his hands from the wheel and turned to me. "Are you okay?"

I nodded, unable to voice any of the hundreds of emotions boiling. His head whipped around, searching for our followers. He turned the key, but the engine wouldn't turn over.

"Fuck! We need to get out of this car." He reached out, pointing across the field to a large wooden barn. "There. We have to run."

I reached down to my purse for the Ruger and opened the car door. The darkness made it hard to see anything, but the moonlight created enough light to make our way across the overgrown grass. As we approached the barn a light flipped on.

"Shit." I hissed.

We slid onto the ground behind a stack of hay. Nathan's head popped up to see where our stalkers were. A car door slammed and he turned back to me, sadness and fear flooded his features as he stared at me. His hands grasped the sides of my face and brought my lips to his.

"I'm sorry, Lila. I'm so sorry." His expression broke my heart. "Baby, I need you to do as I say."

I shook my head violently from side to side.

"Please!" He rested his forehead on mine. "Baby, you have to run. I'll buy you some time."

I gripped onto his shirt, fisting it and holding on tight, unwilling to let him go. "You mean your death will buy me some. No! I can't live without you. Please, Nate. Don't leave me."

He let out a shaky breath. "I can't watch you die, and their intent is to kill you."

"Then don't go. We can still make it out of here."

"Come on out, Thorne!"

I gasped, and Nathan froze.

I swallowed hard and looked down at the gun in my hands. "They don't know where we are. We can take them out now."

His eyes went wide and he nodded, pulling the gun out from his pants. "Together." He leaned forward and kissed me, then turned back to the direction they were coming from.

There was a small space between the stack and I peeked through, but it wasn't enough. I popped my head up enough to see that there were two guys, both dressed in suits. Another set of headlights headed down the road toward us.

My eyes widened as I recognized a guy wearing a knit cap—I'd seen him before. Many months before in the dress shop. He was the one I'd told Nathan about—Mack.

"Shit." Nathan hissed as he ducked back down, pulling me with him just as a shot rang out, flying through the hay and past us into the barn. A small amount of light poured out from the new hole.

Another shot whizzed by, and I peered through the small space again. The chubby one was in view and I pulled the gun up, lining up the sight. My finger sat on the trigger, my chest heavy with anxiety and the weight of what I was about to do. I closed my eyes, blew out a breath, and squeezed.

The gun fired, the force of the kick-back and surprise of the shot made me lose sight of him for a moment. A scream of agony pierced the air, and I knew I'd hit my target somewhere.

Nathan shook me and I looked at him, but he sounded like he was in a tunnel.

"What?"

He pulled on my arm. "Come on."

My hearing cleared, and their yells came through. We skirted around the edge of the barn, out in the open, and a bullet barely missed us. My hands wouldn't stop shaking, even when I fired off another round at our attackers.

He pulled me through the large, wide doors of the barn for some cover, just as one of the men came into view.

"Stay down!" Nathan shot off a round just as one of them ran around the corner. The guy screamed out as the bullet clipped his shoulder.

I shook my head at him and kept at it as he began to close the door. If he was going to protect us, then I would, too. We were a team.

He pulled the lever down into its footing in the ground. "Fuck…" He looked around behind us, realizing we were trapped within the barn's large walls, the only other exit being a regular-sized door next to the large one.

A loud bang with some splintering wood filled my ears before Nathan screamed out and clutched his arm. I grabbed hold of him and led him over behind a tractor. He hissed when I pulled his hand off to see—the bullet grazed his arm, but he was fine.

They tried to get through the doors and started firing off, punching through the wood planks.

I gripped his shirt and pulled, yanking us toward a ladder that led to a loft.

Before we could reach it, we were tackled to the ground. Two men began kicking Nathan, and another hauled me up from the ground by my hair.

I dug my nails into my attacker's hand as I screamed in pain. He turned, pulling me by my hair and slamming me into one of the barn's support beams. I fell to the ground, the world spinning and blurry for a moment as my head rang. The need to move was strong, but I couldn't.

"Don't fucking touch her!" Nathan yelled from a few feet away.

Whoever stood over me turned toward him, leaving me on the ground and heading to Nathan. I squinted and saw that the men who'd been kicking Nathan were laying at his feet. In the next moment, Nathan hit the one who attacked me and sent him to the ground, blood gushing from his nose.

I stood, my legs shaking and my head still spinning. The guy in the hat also got up and picked up his fallen gun, raising it in the air.

"No!" I jumped onto him, the force enough that the bullet missed Nathan and fired off into the distance.

He grunted, cursing as he pulled me off. I stumbled back, but before I could right myself, something hard collided with the side of my head, sending me down to the ground. Pain exploded through me, my vision blurring, ears ringing.

"Stupid bitch."

I turned over and tried to get up, but I was weak. I tried again, but it was too late.

The asshole pushed on my back and I lurched forward. One of his other guys had his gun on me, and Vincent stepped forward for the first time.

Vincent stared at me with an eerily happy smile—it was intense. "Hello again, Mrs. Thorne."

He stood in front of me and motioned for his men to stand me up. I turned to look for Nathan as they hauled me up, and he was being held by two men, blood dripping from a large split in his lip. He pulled against them, still fighting. One of them punched him in the stomach until he stopped.

Vincent turned to Nathan, his wide smile becoming even more malicious. "I really wanted to kill you. I killed your wife and son, and at the time I thought that the life you had left was punishment enough. Then, all of the sudden after so long, you're happy, and they tell me you re-married." He sneered at Nathan. "All the while, my daughter is miserable in jail. I cannot allow you to be happy when she is in such a state." His nostrils flared, and his arms opened wide. "So, here we are again. I'll kill your wife in front of your eyes and watch the misery take hold of you again, making me very happy. Restoring the balance back to the way things should always be."

There was only an instant that passed—a click followed by a loud bang that bounced around the metal walls of the warehouse. Something pushed my shoulder back, hard. Nathan howled behind me, but it took a second to register why.

Searing pain ripped through me, time delayed by a few heartbeats as my brain received the signal. My face scrunched up as a scream exploded. My mouth hung open, whimpering, shrill gasps coming through.

As the shock settled, I looked down. Thick, dark red liquid was coloring my shirt and seeping from the open wound. My left arm was cold, hanging limp at my side. I didn't even want to try and move it, afraid of the pain it would cause.

My knees gave out, and I fell to the ground.

"Oh, I missed." Vincent's malicious smile told me it was intended. Torture me to make Nathan suffer more. "Aren't you going to beg for your life? Or to kill you and spare him?"

"No." My voice was steady despite the fear and pain I was in.

"No?" he asked. He seemed a bit shocked by my response. "And why is that?"

"Because even if you don't kill both of us, whoever survives will kill themselves."

Stunned, Vincent's eyes widened, and he stepped back from my kneeling form. My shoulder was throbbing, sticky blood seeping out.

"I will ask, though, if you are going to kill us both, kill him first."

"Oh, but I want him to watch you die. I want him to suffer more."

"But for him to suffer, you would need him alive. And if you leave him alive, he'll just kill himself before dawn breaks."

Vincent continued to stare down at me, and then his gaze flickered between Nathan and me.

"Lila, baby, please," Nathan begged from behind me, struggling hard against his bindings and the men holding him.

I smiled up at Vincent. "Death can't stop us. We'll be together on the other side, because we were born for each other. So do it. Kill me. End this nightmare."

Nathan begged for me to stop, but there was no stopping. Not now. We were at the end of the line. I couldn't live without Nathan, and I knew he couldn't live without me.

Vincent raised his gun and pressed the still-warm steel to my forehead. Nathan thrashed behind me. It was violent—fighting with all his might. The sound was breaking my heart, but it would only be until the trigger was pulled. A tear escaped and ran down my cheek.

"I love you, Nathan," I whispered, his wailing filling my ears.

"A pity to kill a woman such as you, Delilah," Vincent said as he cocked his gun.

I closed my eyes and waited for the last sound I would ever hear. My muscles unconsciously tensed in anticipation, my thumb twirling my wedding bands on my finger as I counted the seconds.

Then the shot rang out, along with Nathan's screams.

I felt no pain.

CHAPTER 28

$\rightarrow\bullet\bullet\bullet\bullet\mathbb{O}\bullet\bullet\bullet\bullet\leftarrow$

My eyes were still sealed tight, waiting for the pain, waiting for the nothingness to consume me. The concussive sound of the gun firing exploded in my ears. Warm droplets landed on my skin.

I waited.

One heartbeat...

Two heartbeats...

The beating continued on.

The ringing grew louder, making me cringe, then was gone, replaced by the thud of something heavy dropping to the ground in front of me.

My breath was ragged as my heart raced, still waiting for the bullet to hit me. I forced my eyes to open, half expecting to see the nothingness of death or the shiny leather shoes of my killer splattered with my blood.

I saw neither.

Vincent Marconi's body lay sprawled out in front of me, his eyes open, the light fading from them. Blood seeped out of his chest, pooling beneath him. I wiped my hand against my forehead and found no hole, but thick, sticky, dark red blood instead.

It wasn't mine.

Everything was silent, or seemed to be. I began to shake, my body trembling and convulsing. Pain radiated from my shoulder as I slumped to the ground, my head falling onto the packed dirt floor. Nathan called out to me.

"Drop your weapons!" someone yelled.

Men stormed into the barn, filtering in and disarming Vincent's men. Shots fired off again, echoing in my ears.

Everything moved in slow motion, the sound muted by a tunnel. I saw the vision of a terrified Nathan sliding to the ground in front of me, then nothing.

<hr>

My eyes flew open, and millions of blinding lights assaulted me.

Warm, large hands brushed over my forehead and then drifted through my hair, calming me. "Shh, it's okay, baby."

I groaned, my brow furrowed as my brain tried to wake from its groggy state. Where was I? The florescent light above me was familiar, and not in a good way. My heart raced, confusion and fear moving through me. I needed to run, flee…didn't I?

"Nate?" Was he okay? What was going on?

My teeth clenched, and I hissed as a throbbing pain in my shoulder zinged into a sharp one. I blinked, my eyes straining to adjust and focus. Tiny caresses to the back of my head drew my attention and fuzzy mind.

I turned my head and found Nathan's blue eyes staring at me. He was a mess.

"Hi." His swollen and split lip twitched up into a smile. Added to that, there were bruises on his face, and it was also puffy.

The anxiety running rampant through me began to calm—he was all right. "Hi." There was a twinge in my jaw as I tried to stretch it out.

"How do you feel?"

I frowned, still trying to remember how I landed in the fashionable blue hospital gown I was sporting. "I hurt. What's going on?"

He pursed his lips. "Do you remember what happened? You've been out for almost twelve hours…I've been freaking out that you weren't coming back to me."

My shoulder hurt. It hurt a lot. "We made it out? How?"

His lips moved into a thin line, and I gathered he didn't like my response. "Well, I have some news."

I froze, unable to read from his expression if it was good or bad. "What?"

"For once in a very long time, it has a happy edge to it." His thumb stroked the back of my hand. "Vincent Marconi is dead…I'm finally free."

My eyes popped open wide. "Free? As in, he's gone for good?"

He smiled and let out a relieved sigh. "Yes, gone. Never to return."

"How?" I was still reeling.

"Noah. He shot him…just in time." His jaw clenched and tears welled in his eyes. "Fuck, baby, for a split second I thought I'd lost you. I owe him everything."

Noah? There was a vague memory of him standing in front of me, worried and knuckles white as he held a gun, but most of it was a blur after Vincent put the gun to my head.

"What happened after that? I mean, he's dead, but what about the rest of them?"

He blew out a breath and tightened his grip. "Vincent was the one with the vendetta, and he was the leader. Between him being dead and the legal actions against his organization, I'm the least of their worries. The fighting over who becomes the new head will ensue and become the focus."

I wasn't sure I believed him or his bravado. It seemed sincere, the relief evident in his body language, and he wasn't lying or putting on a front. My gaze moved around the room, and I noticed a cop standing outside the door. "Then why do we have an armed guard?"

"Noah did it just in case, but I'm not worried. One of Marconi's guys got into a shoot-out and lost, and the other two are in custody."

"Was it the one that followed us? Mack?"

He nodded. "Yes. He was Vincent's favorite. They also caught Vincent's son, Giovani, in a third car. Both had warrants out for their arrest and are in custody. Which is another reason I know we're free."

"Really?" Could it be true?

"You passed out from shock before that all went down. Paramedics came. It was a mess." He let out a

286

chuckle. "You missed all the bullshit of explaining what happened."

"I'll still have to."

"Yeah."

We were silent for a moment, simple comforting touches and light kisses.

"I'm tired of seeing you in a hospital bed." Nathan's voice was hoarse and he sighed.

"I'm tired of waking up in them."

His lip twitched, and he placed a kiss on my hand. "I only want to come back here when you're having my babies."

I smiled. It hurt, but not as much as the pain from wanting to be in his arms. "How about we start now?"

He let out a scratchy laugh. "God, baby." He leaned over and kissed my forehead.

"Get me out of here. I just want to be with you— only you." I kissed my way down his jaw. I didn't know if it was the meds or the situation, but I needed him.

His eyes lit up, and he hugged me, but very gently. "We have to wait until they release you." The thick emotions in his voice seeped through, and he sounded on the edge of tears.

I wanted to squeeze him hard to my chest, but my arm was weak.

"I want to go home. Now." I released him and looked into his eyes. "I want to be snuggled in bed with you, safe and warm."

He stroked my cheek and gave me an empathetic look. "Me too. I want that so much."

"Then let's go." I tried to sit up, but he placed a hand on my chest, stopping me.

"Not just yet. The doctor wants to keep you for the day."

I let out a whine and shook my head, not liking his response. My bed filled with my office god was calling me, and I wanted the hell out. "Why? I'm fine."

He cupped his hand under my chin, lifting my head up to look in his eyes. "I know you think you are, but my Honeybear is not the expert on this. They just want to make sure they know the extent of your injuries. We were tossed around in the car, then chased down and beaten. Your body's not meant to be pounded that way."

I smiled. "And you would know all about what kind of pounding my body can take."

"Stop it." He smirked and shook his head. "Rain check until we get you out of here."

"It'll be enough for now. A cock a few feet away from me and a man that loves and wants me, even when I look like shit."

He laughed. "Doesn't matter what you look like, because you're mine and I'll fuck you whenever I want to."

I sighed, closed my eyes, and muttered, "I wish it was now."

Nathan's lips formed a hard line and his fingers flexed. All I wanted was to be surrounded by him. We both needed it, were desperate for it. My skin itched to touch his, to be reminded he was real and we were all right.

The door opened, and in walked a woman in scrubs. As the door closed, I caught a glimpse of a man in uniform standing guard.

"Good to see you awake, Delilah. I'm Annie. How are you feeling?"

I snorted. "That's a loaded question."

She nodded and gave me a small smile. "I bet." She logged onto a computer and recorded some stuff from the machines I was hooked up to. "I'll let the doctor know you're awake and get you some food. I'm sure you must be hungry."

"Thank you."

The food came, and Nathan spent the next hour trying to spoon-feed me unappealing hospital food along with the worst lime Jell-O I'd ever eaten in my life. How could they screw up such an easy thing?

"I need out of here now, because if I gag on this shit and throw up, they'll find it as another reason to keep me here." I couldn't express my loathing of hospitals in words. Three times in one year was way too many.

He groaned. "Just humor me." He tried to give me one last scoop, but I smashed my lips together and refused to take any more of that crap.

A knock on the door interrupted Nathan's next attempt. We both turned to see a young man standing at the door. "Hi there. I'm Dr. Yeung. How are you feeling, Mrs. Thorne?"

"I'm ready to leave." My arm hurt, but I didn't care. I was going to make a good show of being the very essence of health to get myself out.

"Your wound has been treated, and we couldn't find anything else wrong while you were out, other than some cuts and bruising. Does your head hurt?"

"A little." I ignored the throbbing at my temples. "It's good."

He pulled out his little pen light, lifted the top of my left eyelid and peered inside. He did the same to the other side, and I sat there, holding my breath, waiting. A quick check of my pulse and heartbeat on the many machines that monitored me was next, and he seemed pleased with their results.

"Is she good?" Nathan asked, his voice hopeful.

The doctor slipped the pen back into his jacket pocket. "The bullet shot clean through and didn't hit any bones or vital areas. You'll need lots of rest, and once the wound starts healing, physical therapy. Other than that, everything looks good. I would like to keep you for another day for observation. You were out for a long time. There'll be some bruising and swelling that will go down in a few days." He headed toward the door and gave us a smile. "I'll check back in on you later, so relax for now. You're safe."

He left, and I sighed in relief, as did Nathan. Though I hated that I had to continue being in the hospital, it didn't bother me so much, because Nathan was there with me and he was all that mattered.

⇒•••◐◑●•••⇐

The next day, the ride home was surreal. I was stocked full of pain meds, and my arm was in a sling. I still couldn't believe all that happened. Everything that crashed down on us, we beat through.

"We made it," I whispered to myself for what had to be the tenth time. It was still strange to be alive when I thought I was about to die. Now, nothing and no one stood in our way.

Nathan stroked my hair. "Yes, we did. Now relax."

I rolled my eyes. "It'll probably be days or weeks before that happens." I wiggled in my seat to try and stretch my muscles out, and got a twinge. "There's so much tension in my back."

"From all the anxiety. We can go home, have a nice relaxing bath, and decompress."

"I can't get my wound wet yet."

"True. Speaking of—how are you feeling?"

"The meds are helping with the pain." I flexed the fingers on my left hand. The sling held my arm close to my chest, gauze wrapped all around my shoulder. A dull pain thumped through my shoulder, but I didn't mind—it reminded me I was alive.

Nathan's right hand rested on my thigh, and I gripped onto his pinky and ring finger. The angle was a little odd, but I reveled in the connection.

Stepping into our home was strange. Memories of all the turmoil, fear, and anger flooded me.

"Our sanctuary doesn't feel the same."

He chuckled. "Everything's changing with each passing minute, Honeybear. The present is different than when we left two days ago."

"There's a calm, almost like the turbulence was never here."

We clasped hands as we walked into the living room and stared at everything with fresh, new eyes. It was an almost foreign environment. All the fixtures were the same, but the atmosphere was different.

We let go of each other and wandered in opposite directions.

My chest ached as I breathed it all in.

A few moments later, Nathan stepped up behind me and kissed the top of my head. "Come on." He linked his fingers with mine once again and led me to the couch. We sat down, and I leaned my head on his shoulder. Neither of us knew what to do.

Minutes passed, and we sat there immersed in our new reality. No more looking over our shoulders, no more demons in the shadows, and no more need for masks. We'd both been running for so long that we didn't know how to take a breath, how to stop.

"So what's the next step? What do we do now?" I leaned into him.

"What would you like to do?"

"Well, after this week, I'm officially out of personal time. That's about as far as I've gotten." I sighed.

He turned to look at me, staring. "What are you saying?"

"That since I met you, I've blown through almost three months of built up personal time."

"Hmm, I see." He cupped my face, his thumb caressing my cheek. "And if you could do it all again?"

"While being in a car accident and gun fight wasn't fun, I wouldn't change meeting you for anything in the universe." I pressed my lips to his, but he didn't deepen it like I thought he would.

He stared into my eyes, a mischievous glint in his. "What if giving me up would stop an alien invasion that would decimate all life on the planet?"

I shook my head. "You're mine."

About K.I. Lynn

K.I. Lynn spent her life in the arts, everything from music to painting and ceramics, then to writing. Characters have always run around in her head, acting out their stories, but it wasn't until later in life she would put them to pen. It would turn out to be the one thing she was really passionate about.

Since she began posting stories online, she's garnered acclaim for her diverse stories and hard hitting writing style. Two stories and characters are never the same, her brain moving through different ideas faster than she can write them down as it also plots its quest for world domination...or cheese. Whichever is easier to obtain... Usually it's cheese.

Visit my website www.KILynnAuthor.com
Follow me on Twitter @KI_Lynn_

CPSIA information can be obtained at www.ICGtesting.com
Printed in the USA
LVOW04s1658261214

420463LV00004B/23/P

"You'd kill everyone on the planet just to keep me?"

"They'd just have to take me with you, because I'm never letting go."

"Me either."

His lips met mine, and he lowered me down onto the couch. I adjusted my legs and he settled between them, caging my body in his arms to keep his weight off. I winced a little in pain, but it subsided. It felt so good to have him close that I didn't care about the discomfort of my injuries.

"I can't find words to tell you how much I love you, how happy I am that you're alive." He shivered beneath me, his eyes closing as his jaw flexed. "Seconds. If Noah…" He opened his eyes, and tears filled them. "I died the moment I heard a gunshot. Everything in me shattered."

I ran my free hand against his face, soothing strokes to reassure him I was there. "I'm here. We're both okay. We're finally free to live." My breath caught, and so did my mind. Not because I was free, but because Nathan finally was. After all these years—we were both free from the monsters that hunted us.

"To live, to love, to be happy." He flashed a brilliant smile at me, and all I could do was swoon. "In fact, I was thinking…maybe it's time we thought about buying a place of our own. I don't need a hideaway anymore, I need a *home*. A place for you and me and our family."

My hand trailed down his neck, touching and soaking in his body heat, his essence. "The same thought crossed my mind."

"A house with a yard, maybe even a pool. Kids running around, family stopping by. Can you see it?"

I nodded and fought back a tear as I pictured it all. "It was a dream I once had."

"We can make it a reality. There's nothing and no one stopping us." His lips ghosted mine.

"The hardest part will be getting pregnant."

"Maybe. We've had a lot of stress over the last few months, and stress can hinder conception."

I bit my lip. "Guess we'll have to keep having lots of sex."

"No objections here. Fuck you all the time *and* knock you up? All around winner." He licked his lips and winked at me. His fingers flexed against my hips as he pushed his cock against my pussy.

Our lips met, and everything began to slip away as I melted against him. All the fear, anxiety, self-hatred, and negativity seemed to wash away from us both.

"Talk dirty to me?" I whispered into his ear.

He slammed his lips to mine, then pulled back, breathless. "Always."

The End